Run For Your Life!

By

Linda Laughlin

Run For Your Life!

ISBN-10: 1517256755

ISBN-13: 978-1517256753

This is a work of fiction. Names, characters, businesses, places, events and incidents are either the products of the author's imagination or used in a fictitious manner. In addition, the author has used names that are familiar to her for certain characters in this book. No resemblance to actual persons, living or dead, or actual events is intended.

ACKNOWLEDGEMENTS

Some might think of writing as a solitary endeavor, but not so with this first book. I had the idea for 'Run for Your Life!' in the back of my mind for several years. I made one try at putting it on paper and was having trouble with dialogue, so I turned to my cousin, who is also a writer, for help. Thank you, Laurna Joyce for all your assistance in giving voice to my characters.

Friends are one of God's greatest blessings. We have friends who have been there forever as well as newer friends. My friend Rita is a forever friend who has been there through the ups and the downs life has thrown my way. We've shared a lot of things, but what I will always cherish most is the laughter. (She also contributed certain items for my book cover.)

Tammi is a new friend. She arrived in my life from California and helped by sharing stories about life in San Diego. I haven't yet had the privilege of visiting the city except through Tammi's eyes.

Although I've not experienced what it is like to deal with alcohol and drug addiction firsthand, my friends Steven and Tammi let me know what it's like to cope with this problem. They have both walked that road and came out as winners. I am so proud of them both! They gave me the idea for Aline's character in the story.

Last, but certainly not least, thank you to my wonderful daughter, Mechelle. Shelly helped me with all things publishing and also filled my editorial needs. I appreciate your help and encouragement.

There are a multitude of others who have helped with their thoughts and have encouraged me along the way. Thank you one and all!

I have always thought of books as treasures. I wish you time and space to curl up and enjoy all the treasures in your life.
Happy Reading!!!

CHAPTER ONE

Carrie walked across the marble floor of the downtown office complex, her shoes making a tapping sound. She had been crying and her eyes were red and swollen. Jeff had to work, so she had gone to a friend's party alone. In the middle of a conversation, 'that woman' had said that Jeff was married. Carrie had been stunned, it couldn't be true! He spent all his free time with her and they went everywhere together. Carrie had been with him when he dined with the Governor, and Jeff always introduced her as his fiancée. She looked down at the beautiful solitaire engagement ring on her left hand as she stepped into the elevator and pushed the button for the top floor. Jeff would be there; he told her he had to work late. He would explain everything.

On the top floor, in the executive offices of Randall Construction, Jefferson Randall sat facing a man who was tied to a chair. Jeff's associates were gathered around him. The man had been badly beaten and was bloody and bruised.

"One last time," Jeff Randall shouted, "where is my money?"

The bound man could barely speak, "I promise you, Mr. Randall, I don't know anything about your money."

Jeff took a semi-automatic weapon from his desk drawer, aimed and pulled the trigger. A small red circle appeared in the center of the bound man's forehead. Instantly, the man's body slumped in the chair. A horrific shriek echoed through the room, drawing the men's attention to Carrie Adams standing in the doorway. Turning, she ran from the room. As she reached the hallway, she heard Jeff barking orders to his men.

"Leave the bitch alone; I know where to find her. Get this mess cleaned up, she may be stupid enough to call the police."

As Carrie ran out of the executive suite and down the hallway, a hundred things race through her shocked mind. She had never heard that gruff tone before or seen the cold look in Jeff's dark eyes. The echo of his demeaning voice rang in her ears.

I shouldn't have come unannounced: how could I have been so dumb? Jeff just shot a man! You're making excuses for a cold blooded killer! That's certainly not the man I fell in love with.

Can a person disappear off the face of the earth? Carrie asked herself. *That's exactly what I'm going to have to do, or die trying.*

Terrified, Carrie realized, *I have to get out of here!* She raced toward the elevator. Thankfully, it was still on the top floor. Stepping inside, she punched the button for the first floor. The fashionable three inch sandals she wore were not the best shoes for running, so she kicked them into the corner as the elevator descended. When did it get so slow? "Thank God," she said as she raced out the door and across the lobby.

In less than a minute, Carrie was unlocking the door to the convertible Jeff had bought for her. *He has never referred to me as a bitch before; could this really be Jeff? Concentrate Carrie, you don't have time to think about this now. Jeff said they had to clean up the mess, which should give me a half hour's head start. I've got to get out of Nashville. Everyone here thinks Jeff is an honest, upstanding citizen. No one would believe what he did to that man upstairs.*

Panicked, Carrie tried to make a plan. In her mind she kept seeing that man, slumped in the chair. *I can't go home to Texas; I can't get my parents involved. Who knows what Jeff might do to them? I'll need money, but I can get that from any bank branch. I fell for everything he said, I won't make that mistake twice.*

Carrie arrived at her apartment and rushed inside; *I'll give myself 15 minutes.* Grabbing her biggest suitcase she deposited it on the bed. She dumped in underclothes, then snatched a handful of slacks and tops from their hangers in the closet and put them inside. She went to the bathroom and gathered her comb, brush, makeup and toothbrush. Then it suddenly occurred to her, *I'm barefoot.*

Back to the closet, she slipped on a pair of comfortable shoes and snatched up her tennis shoes. The next stop was the desk in the corner of her bedroom where she kept her laptop and checkbook. Out of time, she turned to leave, then remembered that she had a passport and grabbed that. The only sound in the room was the rasp of the zipper and her heavy breathing as she closed the suitcase and then ran out the door. Back in her car, Carrie drove toward the interstate.

"Where to," kept rolling around in Carrie's head. *You're in Nashville, Tennessee and Jeff owns everything here, maybe even the police. What about Memphis, with an international airport? I'll get out of the country as quick as I can. Can Jeff trace me?*

* * *

After Jeff saw to it that there was no incriminating evidence left in his office, he headed to Carrie's apartment. He hoped the little fool hadn't done anything stupid, like call the police. He could always make up a story, but he hoped he wouldn't have to. Jeff pulled into a parking space, got out and went upstairs. He quietly let himself into the small apartment. A quick look around was all it took for him to realize that the apartment was empty. Jeff loved Carrie as much as he was capable of loving another person, and she had been a lot of fun. He quickly decided that when it came to his survival or hers however, it was his every time. Jefferson Randall hadn't built an empire by being soft, and he wasn't turning soft now. Carrie had left him, she'd run! Jeff knew that with her small town upbringing, she wasn't going to see what was at stake. *I have an empire to protect,* he thought, before making a quick decision. *Carrie has to be eliminated, it's the only way. She's beautiful, but I can't afford a loose end. Now all I have to do is find her!* He returned to his office and called Carl, his second-in-command.

"The bitch has run," Jeff told Carl when he answered the phone. "I want you to send some men to her parent's house in Texas. Don't make direct contact; just let me know if she turns up. I want you to find her. Now!"

Carl decided not to ask questions. You didn't question Jeff when he was angry. "Yes, boss, I'll get on it right away."

* * *

Carrie hit I-40, going west toward Memphis. She couldn't risk getting a ticket so she set the cruise control. Everything flashed through her mind at hyper speed. She kept wondering where she'd gone wrong. This was the second time she had picked the wrong man. At the University of Texas, she had been a cheerleader and had dated the football captain. They were the perfect couple and were sure Russ would be drafted into the NFL. That was before she found Russ having sex with that little slut. Carrie had made up her mind; she would never let her guard down again. Her next relationship would be on her terms.

After graduating from the university, Carrie had moved to Nashville. She'd vowed that next time she would find a man, not some boy looking to score. She wanted someone who would love her, marry her, and give her a home and children. That's what she dreamed of, the whole 'happily ever after'.

Jeff was everything she thought she wanted; he was very rich, powerful, and extremely handsome. The night they were introduced by a friend, he had looked at her like he'd won the lottery. *All this time I thought he catered to me, I was never in control. He was the puppet master and I played right into his hand. How did I not see that?*

I've got to stay focused, I can't think of Jeff. What should I do when I get to Memphis? Carrie tried to make a plan, wondering what the best way would be to throw them off her trail. *Should I buy a ticket to Mexico? I could use my credit card, but would Jeff be able to trace it? The charge will show up on my statement. He'll probably go through my mail for any clue. By that time I might be well hidden and maybe he'd never find me. I should get a plane ticket and get out of the country. The farther I go, the less likely he'll be able to trace me. I hate to run up my credit card when there's no way I can pay the charges.*

Being dishonest went against her grain; Carrie

wasn't brought up that way. Jeff had teased her about her small-town morals. 'A person is only as good as their word,' is what her father always said. This was different though, this was her life.

Suddenly, as if seeing a sign from heaven, Carrie spotted a lighted billboard. Reba McIntire's face smiled down at her and Carrie recalled an old friend, Jessica Smith. Jess's mother was a dark haired Reba, and Jess had often said she wished her mother had Reba's sense of humor. It might have helped when the duo got into trouble. The two girls had grown up in rural Texas and were always together, until the company Mr. Smith worked for transferred him to another state. Carrie hadn't seen Jess since junior high, but they were once as close as sisters.

Carrie's thoughts went back to her conversations with Jeff. I don't think I've ever told Jeff about Jessica. We were friends a long time ago. If I remember correctly, Jess married some guy from Oklahoma. He owns a ranch in some wide spot in the road; was it Cowlington? Who am I kidding, it didn't sound like there was much of a road. It was a small community in the middle of nowhere, that's just the sort of place I need to go. Carrie opened her purse and found her cell phone. She wondered, *can this phone be traced? One call and I'll run over it with the car and throw it into the Mississippi River.* She tried to remember who Jess had married. *What was his name?* "Information, can you get me the number for a Robert Banks in Cowlington, Oklahoma?"

Carrie dialed the number the operator gave her and let it ring. A man answered.

"Is this Bob?" she asked, "is Jess there?"

"Sure," he answered, and Carrie heard him yell for

Jess.

In just a minute a female voice answered, "Hello."

"Jess, this is Carrie Adams, from junior high. I'm in such big trouble!"

Bless Jess's kind heart, without missing a beat she warmly answered, "How can I help?"

"I can't explain over the phone. Please don't ask any questions. Can you come get me? I'll be waiting in Memphis, in Handy Park. Don't tell anyone where you're going. Don't mention my name, and can you come immediately? I know this is completely out of left field and I probably sound like a crazy person. I promise to tell you everything when you get here; please say you'll come."

Without a second's hesitation, Jess answered, "Of course, I'll be there as soon as I can. Whatever it is, we'll make it right!"

Hearing her answer, a desperate Carrie got all choked up. She managed to hold back the emotions rolling through her body. She wouldn't let herself give in to the terror, and she wouldn't cry over the phone. "Thanks Jess. See you soon," she answered.

Carrie disconnected the phone and noticed her hands trembling. She was relieved to know that Jess was willing to help. It had been so many years since they had talked. *I wasn't sure I could depend upon her. Thank God for friends!* It felt good; now she had a plan.

Knowing that she had Jess's support calmed Carrie. *I can't depend on the two people that should be helping me; calling my parents isn't an option. I'm lucky Jess cared enough to come running to Memphis. Jess didn't even hesitate!* Carrie's throat swelled, her emotions high, and she started to cry. Instantly, tears streamed down her cheeks and her eyes blurred. Seeing to drive was hard, especially with the cars going seventy miles an hour. She pulled over to the side of the road and let the tears fall. It seemed to help, and her spirits lifted. She thought about the people she loved and cared about most. Carrie heard her father's voice in the back of her mind. In that deep Texas drawl he would say, 'Buck up girl' and then his favorite saying came to mind; 'When the going gets tough, the tough get tougher'. Her course was set and it was time to move forward.

Carrie wiped her tear-stained face. Seeing a gap in the traffic, she opened the car door. After getting out, she placed the phone under the left front tire, got back inside and drove forward. She then retrieved the crushed phone from behind the car. *If it's possible to track a phone, now there's no phone to track. I'll still throw it into the mighty Mississippi when I get to Memphis,* she vowed as she pulled back onto the interstate.

It was a dark night and close to midnight when Carrie parked in the long-term parking at the Memphis International Airport. She got her suitcase from the back of the car. *How long before Jeff will find my car?* She wondered.

Carrie went inside and up to the counter. The ticket agent was a young girl working the late shift. Carrie told her, "I need a ticket to Mexico City."

Carrie saw curiosity on the young girl's face. *I need a story, a reason for my sudden trip,* she thought. "My grandmother died last week and left me some money," Carrie explained. "We used to talk about going to Mexico to see the Teotihuacan Pyramids outside of Mexico City. I'm going to honor her memory."

The young ticket agent smiled as if she had dreamed of visiting a faraway place. "I'm told Mexico City is beautiful this time of year. Your plane leaves at 10:45 a.m., you'll enjoy the sites. If you'd like, there's a shuttle bus outside that will take you to the Peabody Hotel," the agent said.

"Thanks!" Carrie replied, before taking her ticket and walking away. She went into the bathroom, took her manicure scissors out of her purse and cut off all of her beautiful long hair. *Jess isn't going to make it before sunup and I need a place to hide out for a few hours. The hotel sounds like a good idea.* She opened her suitcase to look for a hooded sweatshirt and found it in the corner of her suitcase. Carrie put the sweatshirt on and pulled the hood over her head. *I'm glad it isn't summer.* The suitcase wheels made a clacking sound as she left the bathroom and walked toward the shuttle area.

Watching Carrie approach, the shuttle bus driver said, "Good evening Miss, Peabody Hotel?"

"Please," she told the driver.

He was quick to take her bag and load it in the baggage compartment. Carrie climbed aboard and saw that several people had already boarded. The driver returned, got behind the wheel, and closed the door. They pulled away from the curb as he made an announcement. "We will be at the hotel in approximately 20 minutes. The Peabody Hotel is a landmark in downtown Memphis. There is a large fountain in the lobby, where everyone enjoys seeing the North American Mallard Ducks swim.

Carrie stared out the window, into the night. The driver continued his speech about the wonders of the Peabody, but she didn't hear him. So much had happened and she just needed a few minutes to unwind. She was safe, at least for the moment. Suddenly she caught something the driver said about Elvis and her attention returned to his commentary.

Memphis is the city of kings! Elvis made his home in Memphis, and BB King was a Memphis regular. W.C. Handy, who was considered one the fathers of the Blues, lived a good portion of his life in Memphis. There is a park named for him not far from the Peabody. He wrote a song, "The Memphis Blues", honoring our fair city in the 1900s. You see, a lot of famous people have enjoyed our wonderful city." A few minutes later the shuttle bus driver announced, "We're here!" They had pulled up in front of the hotel, and the driver climbed out to unload his passengers' luggage.

Carrie retrieved her bag and went inside the hotel. Walking up to the counter, she suddenly realized, *the desk clerk will need my ID. I don't have any way to pay except with my credit card, and that leaves a paper trail. I can't take the chance.* She turned and darted back out the double doors.

Luckily, the shuttle bus driver was talking with someone and had his back to her. Not wanting to be seen, Carrie slipped behind the bus. Standing by the rear bumper, she saw a bar across the street. *No one should notice me there.*

Carrie made her way across the street and went inside the front door of the dimly lit bar. She stood in the doorway for a moment, letting her eyes adjust to the gloom. Seeing clearer now, she spotted an empty table in the back, next to the pool table. No one would notice if she killed some time here. She went over, parked her suitcase, and sat down. The waitress came to see if she wanted something, and she ordered a draft beer.

Carrie picked a pool stick before noticing the girl about her age. She'd been playing pool, but her companion had deserted her. She strolled up, carrying her pool stick. “I won the last game, so I still have the table. Would you like to play me?”

“Sure, that’s better than just shooting the balls around,” Carrie replied.

The girl was quick to comment. “The locals certainly don’t want to play with me anymore. They don’t like that I take their money.”

“I haven’t played pool in a long time, but I used to be pretty good,” Carrie said. Seeing the waitress approach, Carrie paid for her beer and took a sip from the foam topped mug. As the cool liquid went down her dry throat, she added, “I didn’t know how thirsty I was!”

“By the way, my name is Jennifer Anderson, but you can call me Jen for short,” the girl announced with a smile.

“I’m Carrie! How did you know I wasn’t a local?”

“I’m in here a lot and this is the first time I’ve seen you. I’m a people watcher; nothing else to do around here. Believe me, for a town with such a big reputation, life here is a bummer. Tourists who have a lot of money are entertained with Beale Street and the Jazz. If you're an art or history buff, there’s the Pink Palace. For the kids, there's the Children’s Museum and Overton Park Zoo. Do you know what that bar in the Peabody charges for a draft? Seven bucks, that’s what. God knows I can’t afford that lifestyle. I’d be broke before I got a buzz on.”

What a twit, Carrie thought. Her quarters released

the balls with a loud, thundering noise and she began to fill the rack. She built it tight and then stepped aside for another sip of her beer. *I'll bet she has the saddest tale in whole world.* Carrie smiled and said, "Tell me about yourself, Jen."

Jen stepped up to the table, rested the pool stick across her bridged hand and hit the cue ball hard. Balls clacked against one another, then scattered and rolled across the green velvet with two solids sinking into one of the pockets. When the others came to a rest, she shot again and continued to sink one ball after the other. It was as if she wasn't even paying any attention to the game while her mouth was moving ninety miles an hour. "Nothing to tell, I can't afford to go anywhere, other than work and here. I hate this town. If it was up to me, I'd be gone tomorrow. That is, if I had a ride, which I don't, so here I am, taking up space."

What Jen was saying intrigued Carrie, who was studying the young woman. *Jen has long hair, the same color and style, I had before I cut it. Her eyes are light like mine. Her figure and height are the same; I'd say we look a lot alike. I wonder if I could convince her to trade identities. Wouldn't that be a hoot! Using her name I could disappear, and she'd lead anyone on my trail to Mexico City. If they caught up with her, they'd know it wasn't me the minute she opened her mouth. I think we're enough alike that Jeff's associates could spend weeks tracking her down. I'm sure it won't sit well when they discover she's not the one they want.*

"Eight ball in the far left corner," Jen announced and sank it into the pocket. She'd run the table without Carrie even getting a shot. *She's a pool shark all right,* b*ut I don't mind,* Carrie thought. She went over to put in more quarters for another game.

They played three games, with Jen running the table each time. Carrie laughed and asked, "Are you ever going to give me a chance to shoot?"

"I wondered how long it would take you to ask. Rack em up," Jen remarked with a chuckle. "Tell you what; I'll buy the next beer and then cut you some slack, if you'll tell me where you got the funky haircut.

"Don't you like my new haircut?" Carrie asked as she struck a model pose.

"Like I said, it's sort of, funky," Jen replied with a laugh.

"It's a cross between punk rock and a summer cut. I'm told it's the latest fashion from New York City," Carrie said, rising to her feet.

"That wasn't very nice of me," Jen admitted.

"That's okay," Carrie answered. *Under that gruff act she puts on, she is really kind of nice.*

Carrie looked up at Jen, who was standing at the head of the table giving her pool stick an extra dab of chalk, and asked, "What would you do if you had a free ticket to Mexico City? Would you go on vacation, or stay here and work?"

"If anyone gave me a free ticket to anywhere, I'd be gone."

"Forget the game. Step over here and let's talk," Carrie beckoned. They sat down together and Carrie leaned into the table toward Jen "I've got a ticket to Mexico City that my boyfriend gave to me. He's supposed to meet me later in the week. I've wanted to end the relationship, but when I try to talk to him he doesn't listen. I've tried everything I know not to hurt him. I could say, 'Go away jerk and don't come back,' but I really don't want to do that, and at the same time I don't want to go on this vacation. Don't you see? We look enough alike to be sisters. You could pass for me!"

Jen's eyes widened with excitement. "You mean you'd let me go in your place? How much would it cost?" Jen asked.

"Not a red cent," replied Carrie. "You'd have to pretend to be me in order to use the ticket. I've got my passport, ID, and ticket right here. We look enough alike to pull it off, even though there's a little difference in weight. If anyone asks, you have had the flu. I hate the idea of going so badly that I'll even throw in my credit card. With my limit, it has a thousand dollars left. I'm assuming you could have a wonderful time on a thousand, couldn't you?"

"I should say I could, and I will," Jen quickly replied. "What about the boyfriend? He'll know I am not you. How does he figure in?"

"You probably won't even see him. If you do, he'll realize it isn't me and leave you alone. He is a jerk, but he wouldn't hurt you," Carrie said as she handed everything over except her driver's license. "I'll need to keep this long enough to go to the bank when it opens," she explained. "I need to cash a check. You go by your apartment, pack, and meet me outside my bank at about 9:15 in the morning. That should give you time to get to the airport."

"What are you going to do till the bank opens?" Jen asked. Without allowing Carrie to answer, Jen continued, "Look, why don't you come home with me? I'll pack and we can take a cab to the bank. I'll wait while you take care of business, then you can give me the license."

"Sounds like a plan," replied Carrie.

"Alright, forget the beer and the game. The bar is getting ready to close anyway. Come on, let's get the hell out of here," Jen said.

Carrie grabbed her suitcase. The two women made their way out the door and down the sidewalk toward an older apartment building.

Inside, the apartment was small and there wasn't much furniture. Carrie didn't like to think someone had to live like this. *Maybe after this trip, Jen will see that life doesn't have to be this way. If she would quit feeling sorry for herself, maybe she could concentrate on getting a better education. She had plenty of determination when it came to playing pool. Oh well, that's not my problem, and I certainly have enough of my own.* She helped Jen pack, anything to keep her mind off what was happening.

The bank had just opened when Carrie walked up to the teller window. The older woman gave Carrie a curious look when she handed her a check for $6,580. "Do you want this all in cash?" The teller questioned as she looked at Carrie's identification. "That's a lot of money to be carrying around."

Quick to answer, Carrie explained, "I got a promotion and I've been transferred from Nashville to Memphis. I just bought a new condo and I'm going to buy furniture. I found a resale shop with some really nice things, some look like antiques. I'm hoping to make a better deal with cash. Don't worry, I'll be careful. This is all the money I have left!"

"If you're going to be living in Memphis, you'll need to transfer your account to a local branch. We can help you with that now," the teller said.

"I don't have my new address with me, but I'll do that in a day or two," Carrie told her.

The teller counted out her money, wished Carrie a good day, and said, "Have a good time shopping."

"Thanks, I will."

Carrie smiled as she walked out the door. *I'm getting good at these stories. Who would think I'd make such a good liar?*

Carrie was in the bank and out again in approximately ten minutes. The cab driver retrieved her suitcase from the trunk as Carrie reached through the window and gave her license to the new Carrie.

Starry eyed over her good fortune, Jen told her, "I don't know what to say except, thank you! Are we going to meet in a few weeks and go back to being us?"

"To be honest," Carrie explained, "I don't plan to stay in Memphis. When you get back, you can get a new license and just shred my stuff. I'll be getting a license in a new state. It's been a pleasure meeting you, Carrie," she said, calling Jen by her own name.

"It's been the thrill of my life meeting you, Jen!" Jennifer laughingly said, already into the part.

"Remember, you must hurry. Your flight leaves at 10:45. Have fun!" Carrie told the girl.

The new 'Jennifer Anderson' smiled and waved to the departing taxi thinking, *Jess is probably already at the park. I hadn't thought about the bank when I was talking to her. Please, don't let her give up and leave!*

CHAPTER TWO

The new 'Jennifer' gave one last look at the departing taxi. She had to get moving, Jessica should be waiting. She rolled her suitcase toward Handy Park, and as she passed through the park entrance she spotted Jessica sitting on a bench. *God bless her, she looks the same,* she thought. *Everything will be all right now!*

Jess got excited when she saw Carrie walking toward her. She jumped up and ran to meet her, not stopping until she had pulled her into a big hug. "Carrie, I was beginning to worry about you."

"Sorry, I had an errand and I forgot to warn you about it," Carrie said as she stepped away. "By the way, my name is Jennifer Anderson. I'm pleased to meet you," she said and she extended her hand, as if meeting for the first time. "Just call me Jen for short."

Surprised by Carries action, Jess drew her eyebrows together. She was puzzled at first, but then she quickly realized, *she's in bad trouble and has changed her name!* Playing along with her act, Jess replied, "Nice to make your acquaintance."

"Let's get in the car. I want to make a stop at the river and then we can blow this town. I'll explain everything while we drive. By the way Jess, have I told you how much I love and appreciate you being there for me?"

"No, but you're my BFF and that goes without saying," Jess answered.

Jess drove down the street toward the river. She saw the sign for the Tennessee Information Center and the Memphis Visitors Center, and it looked like those might be close to the water. Five minutes later, Jess found a frontage road with access to the river.

She stopped the car along the water's edge and Jen got out, taking something from her purse. She threw it as hard as she could, and it landed in the fast moving current of the Mississippi river.

When Jen got back in the car, Jess asked, "What was that all about?"

"That was what was left of my cell phone, after I flattened it with the car tire."

Jess was curious, "Where's your car?"

"I left it at the Memphis airport. Maybe I'm being paranoid, but that was my last tie to Nashville and the biggest mistake of my life. Now let's get on the road. You drive and I'll talk."

Jess turned the car around and made her way back to the on-ramp for I-40. Going across the Mississippi River bridge, the only sound heard was the hum of the car tires and the frequent whoosh from a passing vehicle. Jess couldn't help but notice that her friend hadn't said a word since leaving the river. *Maybe I should break the ice,* Jess thought.

"I sure am glad that the sunshine is behind us. Coming into Memphis this morning, the sun's bright glare almost blinded me."

"That must have been rough," Jen finally responded.

"OK, I'm listening. You said you would tell me everything," Jess reminded her.

"Alright, I'm just trying to think of where I should start. It's all so unbelievable!" Jen said in a shocked voice.

"Tell me whatever pops in your mind first," Jess said, hoping that when Jen got started everything would make sense.

"Jeff is a lot older than I am. He's not the type of man I thought I would ever go for. He has a rugged look about him, like the cowboys in the old western movies. Add to that the deep rumbling voice and the charisma, he just drew me in. He treated me so good and bought me anything I wanted, nice jewelry, that car. I attended a lot of business gatherings with him and he bought me clothes for every party. He really spoiled me. I was really impressed when we dined with the Mayor, and we even had dinner at the Governor's Mansion once. I couldn't afford to dress for a formal dinner party, so he took me to a designer dress shop. I'd never seen such beautiful clothes. I was his fiancée and he wanted me with him. I didn't see anything wrong with letting him buy me clothes. I didn't want him to be ashamed of me."

Glancing over at Jen, Jess saw her smile as she recalled it all.

"I felt like a princess wearing those dresses and the lace lingerie to go with them. That was the first time he bought me diamonds; a pair of beautiful stud earrings. Growing up in Texas we weren't poor, but I never had designer clothes like those. We'd been dating for five months when he gave me an engagement ring. Jess, we got along so well; we looked at everything the same way. In my mind he was perfect, and when he proposed, I could hardly wait to say yes. We spent a lot of time together and I was so happy! As time passed, I began to hear rumors that he was a married man. Last night, a woman mentioned his wife. I caught it and asked if she meant his ex-wife. She immediately back-tracked and said, "I'm sorry, Carrie, I shouldn't have mentioned her." I was so upset that I went to confront Jeff at his office.

I knew he was working late. I was so sure he would explain everything, that it was all a big mistake."

Listening with interest, Jess couldn't help but notice that Jen gave a long pause. "Go on, Carrie. Oh, I mean Jen."

Suddenly the whole story came tumbling out, the horrible thing she had witnessed and why she had run.

Totally shocked, Jess said, "How could something like that happen? You see these things in the movies, but not in real life!" Shaken and trying to keep control of the car, Jess realized that this was not an ordinary argument. Carrie was in a lot of trouble and the situation sounded dangerous.

"You see, Jeff's so powerful," Carrie continued. He knows all these people, and I was afraid to go to the police." She explained about the deal she had made with the twit, and then admitted, "I just want to disappear and go where he'll never find me."

"I can understand why. A murder and you're the only witness. If he could kill a man so easily, he could just as well kill you." Something suddenly occurred to Jess. "Could he be involved with the mob? He doesn't sound like an ordinary businessman. You hear of people who have a legitimate business and deal drugs on the side. If he has connections to a drug cartel, they have people living all over this country." All kinds of things ran though Jess's mind after hearing Jen's story. "You're going to need money to get away!"

"I haven't paid my rent yet and I was saving up to buy Jeff a diamond ring for next Christmas. I pulled six thousand out of the bank this morning before I met you at Handy Park. That's the unexpected errand I had to run."

"That sounds like a lot of money but it won't last very long, especially if you're on the run," Jess advised her. "Why don't you stretch out and try to relax. You look like you're wound tight and I don't blame you. It's a long drive, but I'll get you home where it's safe," Jess said. She needed some time to digest all she had learned.

"Jess, I already feel better just knowing we're together," Jen said, feeling safer now that they were on the road. "One thing I can be thankful for, I never told Jeff anything about you or Bob. He has no idea that you exist."

"Well, that's in our favor. Do you think he'll send his henchmen to find you; is he really that powerful? There's no telling what kind of connections he has." The moment Jessica said it, fear flashed all the way to the tip of her toes as another thought suddenly occurred to her. "Jen do you think he would hurt your parents?"

"I'd like to say no! The truth is, he had me fooled and I'm still trying to deal with that fact. He's not a gentleman, that's for certain. If he sent someone to talk to my parents, they might get suspicious and call the police. Jeff wouldn't want that. He may send someone to watch the house; I don't think he'll want to draw attention to himself though. I don't keep in touch like I should, so I pray that my parents don't find out I'm missing."

Staying awake and driving on adrenalin, Jess mashed down on the gas pedal. Now more than ever, she was anxious to get home to Bob. She couldn't help but be worried but she tried to comfort her best friend. "Do like I said and get some rest."

"Are you kidding? There's no way I could sleep." Jen was more relaxed, but sleep was another story.

"Whatever. You know, I kind of like this new name of yours. It suits you!" Jess hoped to distract her friend.

"That's good, because 'Carrie' is lying with her phone at the bottom of the Big Muddy," Jen joked.

"I thought she was on her way to Mexico City." Jess hoped trading identification would help her friend to lose herself.

"Yeah, well, she's not in this car, that's for sure," Jen answered.

"Seriously," Jess told her. "If you're going to change your name, maybe you should try changing your appearance as well. I mean, to me you still look like Carrie."

"Jen sat up straight, looked over at Jess, and told her. "You're right! Do you think I should buy different style clothes? I could try being more like that little twit I'm impersonating."

"You could do that, but it is hard to do a personality change. No one would ever call you a twit. What I was thinking is, maybe cut and shape your hair. You could try a different color, which would make a drastic change. It would give you an entirely different look. Right now, they're looking for a blonde."

"That's a great idea, Jess." Call her vain, but Jen hated the thought of coloring her hair. Being a natural blonde had always been a source of pride for her.

"I'll take you to my hair salon tomorrow," Jess said. "Saturday's their busiest day. Since I've been going there for years though, I think they'll do me a favor and work you in without an appointment."

Mexico City

The new Carrie Adams' plane had left Memphis International Airport and landed in Mexico City on time. Carrie was excited. *How did I get so lucky? All I have to do is pretend to be Carrie and have a good time.* She unbuckled her seat belt and went inside the airport terminal, stopping a minute to look at the framed posters advertising hotels. The crew passed her, heading for Customs. "Excuse me, can you recommend a nice hotel?" she asked.

The First Officer grinned at her and lagged behind the others. "My name is Gary Summers. He pointed behind her to a picture showing a downtown hotel. That's where the crew is staying. If you're by yourself, I would be honored to show you around. We have a day's layover. When you get your luggage and go through Customs, you can take the hotel shuttle."

"That sounds great, Gary. I'm Carrie." She couldn't believe her luck, a handsome guy was helping her and she hadn't even cleared customs yet. "I'll see you soon."

United States

Hours went by before they reached Sallisaw, Oklahoma. Turning south off I-40, they took Highway 59 and headed for Cowlington. The newly built four lane highway passed farm after farm. Fresh-cut grass lay drying before being bailed into hay. Off in a distance they saw cattle grazing in a pasture.

Crossing the Arkansas River for the second time, Jess told her, "This is Kerr Lock and Dam. We turn off in a few more miles; we're almost home."

"Good, I'm ready to stretch my legs." Jen couldn't wait to get out of the car.

By 4 p.m. they were turning onto the dirt and gravel driveway that lead to Bob and Jessica's home. The car left a billowing cloud of dust in its wake. Up ahead, tall, leafy oak trees surrounded a white, two-story farm house.

"Jess, this is a beautiful place," Jen said.

"Thanks, we like it," Jess replied as she parked the car facing a white picket fence and turned off the key. "I feel numb after that long drive. I'll leave the car here. Bob can put it in the garage later. You know, I'm not used to being up all night," she added, relieved at being home again.

"I'm sorry that I brought my troubles to you; I had nowhere to turn." Jen hated disrupting Jess's life.

"Don't worry about that." Jess didn't mean to make Jen feel bad. She was tired and she wasn't being tactful. "Like I said before, we'll make everything right."

Hearing the car pull up, Bob came out onto the porch. He had a welcoming smile on his face. He was glad Jess made the trip alright, although he hadn't expected her until tomorrow. She was home safe, and that was what was important.

Getting out of the car, Jen reached for her suitcase and rolled it along toward the house. She followed Jess through the gate and up onto the front porch, where Bob gave his wife a warm welcoming smile and kiss. When Jess introduced her good friend to him as Jen, both his brows lifted. *What is going on here? I've heard a lot about Carrie but nothing about anyone named Jen,* he thought. He couldn't help but wonder what was going on. A little standoffish, he said, "It's nice to meet you, Jen."

"You too, Bob, and thank you for your hospitality," Jen said. "I'm sorry to barge in on you and Jess."

"I wasn't expecting you until tomorrow," Bob told the women. "I've got iced tea made. Would you ladies like a glass?"

"That sounds perfect," Jess replied and looked over her shoulder at Jen. "Come on in so we can sit down and relax. We are tired; we decided not to stay over and drove straight home."

Like stepping back into another period, western furniture filled the large living room. It reflected the outside style of the house, except for the 40 inch flat-screen TV over the fireplace. The room had twelve foot ceilings with wide windows that were eight feet tall. There was a breeze blowing through the windows, and it rippled the long, sheer curtains. Jess reached over and turned off the TV and a panel automatically dropped down over the television screen. As the panel lowered Jen recognized what looked like an original Remington oil painting. Jen wondered, *could this be real? If not, it's a very good copy.* She let go of her suitcase and let it rest at the end of the sofa. "That's a beautiful painting and I want a closer look at it, when my eyes aren't crossed from lack of sleep."

Realizing that both women were worn out, Bob

said, "Let's go out to the kitchen. You can sit down and I'll fix our tea." He went to the cabinet to get three glasses and filled them with ice, then pulled a large pitcher of tea from the refrigerator and put it all on the table.

"Jessica I love your home, especially this kitchen," Jen praised as she pulled out a chair and sat down at the table.

"Thanks, we've put a lot of work into the house since Bob's grandparents died. This was their home originally, and they'd let it get a little rundown. The dining room is nice, but we love this big farm style kitchen."

Pouring the iced tea, Bob claimed his place at the head of the table. "Now, what the heck is going on?" he asked rather sharply.

Running on adrenalin, both women were exhausted. Jessica looked across the table at him, took a long drink of her iced tea and said, "Let me unwind for a minute and then we'll discuss it." She and Bob didn't keep secrets from one another and she knew he was confused.

Before long, the pitcher of tea was empty and they were telling Bob everything. They talked about what Jen wanted to do and how she planned to lose herself.

"This is a bad situation, Jess," Bob said with a look of concern on his face.

"I know it is! This is her life we're talking about. If Jeff's killed once, he could easily do it again," Jess replied.

"Uncle Ed called, just before you got home. He said he's leaving for California in a couple of days. Maybe Jen can hitch a ride with him."

"That's not a bad idea," Jess said. Turning to Jen, she explained. "Bob's Uncle Ed is a truck driver; he makes long hauls all over the country. He drives a big 18 wheeler and it has a sleeper with all the comforts of home, including a refrigerator,"

"I'd like to go to California," Jen replied. "It might be easier getting lost out there in some large city where no one knows their next door neighbor."

"I'll call him back and ask if he'd mind a ride-along," Bob said.

"Please, please don't tell him anything about the trouble I'm in. What he doesn't know won't hurt him," Jen pleaded.

"I suppose you're right," Bob said. He hated to keep Ed in the dark.

"I don't want to take any chances or put anybody in harm's way. Just tell him that I have friends in California, very little money, and I need a ride," Jen suggested.

"I guess that would be good enough," Bob replied. Looking over at Jess he told her, "Tom Henderson bought that horse I was thinking of selling. He paid cash and since you were out of town, I didn't go to the bank. Do you need the money for anything?"

Jess knew the look that Bob gave her. She'd seen it many times before. Her husband looked hard, but inside he was a marshmallow. "Jen needs it more than we do."

"No," Jen was quick to chime in. "You need your money. I'll be fine."

"On the run, you're going to need all the money you can scrape together. If you won't just take it, then consider it a loan. You can pay us back when you get on your feet," Bob said.

Jen was reluctant, but knew he was right. "You don't know me. Why would you help me?"

"I know my Jessica, and you're her friend," he told her. "That's all I need to know."

"I appreciate your help, more than you realize. Can you believe I was so gullible?" Jen remarked.

"It's the day and age that we live in, Carrie, I mean Jen. There are lots of deceitful people out there. You can't blame yourself for falling in love. A nice suit and important friends made him look respectable. I'd venture to guess he's more than likely mixed up with the mob or a drug cartel. They'll make charitable contributions in order to launder their ill-gained money, and it makes them look good in the process. This Jeff could be a drug dealer, hit man, or even the head of a mob family for all we know. You're on the right track, pretending to get out of the country and then going someplace unexpected. That's smart," he said.

"I was upset and scared out of my wits. I'm surprised I even thought of it. This is the most terrified I've been in my life. I just want to start over, someplace where no one knows who I am or where I come from," she said.

"Well, that's settled; I want to get cleaned up before dinner. Do you want a shower, or how about a nice hot bath, Jen?" Jessica asked.

"You mean with lots of bubbles, like we used to take when we were kids?" Jen remembered them as children, laughing and sharing a tub full of bubbles. They had such fun.

"I have lavender bubble bath in the guest bathroom. Will that do?" Jess asked with a smile. "I personally prefer a quick shower. I'm afraid I might fall asleep in the tub and drown."

"You know I love lavender. I can already feel myself being pampered. God, I've never been so tired before," Jen replied. "I think I can stay awake; a nice hot soak sounds too good to resist."

Bob laughed and said, "I'll leave you girls to your bubbles and shower while I go call Uncle Ed and set things up. Then I need to go feed the horses. I invited Ed to supper when I thought I'd be eating alone. If you ladies aren't too tired, this will give Jen a chance to meet him. That way, she won't be leaving out with a total stranger."

"Will it really be that simple with your Uncle Ed?" Jen asked.

"I think it will. After all, I am his favorite nephew, and I rarely ask anything of him. He'll go along with our plan," Bob answered. "He gets lonely on the road and will enjoy the company."

"I want to thank you both," Jen replied before leaving the kitchen.

After Jess showered and put on clean clothes, she left the master bedroom and walked down the hall. She knocked on the guest bedroom door and when there was no answer, she realized Jen was still soaking in her bubbles. She opened the door and walked across the bedroom. At the bathroom door, she knocked again and called out, "I'm going downstairs to start dinner. You don't really want to eat Bob's cooking, and I don't want to see the mess he makes in my kitchen! Come on down when you're dressed."

"Okay," Jen yelled from the tub.

Later that evening, after tending to the animals, Bob came in the back door. As he entered the kitchen he smiled and said, "Something sure smells good in here. I'd planned on cooking, but you know I'm not very good at it."

Jess looked up at the sound of his voice and returned his smile. "What time will your Uncle Ed be here?"

"I figure around 6:30."

"It's a good thing I made something simple. It's almost that time now," Jess pointed out.

"I'll run upstairs and take a quick shower." Bob gave her a kiss. "I know making the return trip without a stop wore you out, but I'm glad you're home. I wouldn't like you staying in Memphis under the circumstances."

He was halfway up the stairs when Jess called out. "Bob, call down the hallway and ask Jen to come set the table. She should be dressed by now."

"Okay, be back in a flash," Bob called back.

A few minutes later, Jen walked into the kitchen. She looked better, although she still had dark circles under her eyes. "I hear you need some help."

"Yes ma'am, Uncle Ed should be here anytime now. The plates and glasses are in that cabinet and the silverware is in that drawer," Jess instructed.

"What's he like, Jess?"

"You remember my dad, don't you?" Jess's dad had built them a tree house. It hadn't mattered to him that they were little girls, and they had loved it.

"Uncle Ed reminds me of Dad. He's getting older, lost most of his hair and has a spare tire around the middle. He's a big talker and is always telling stories, most of them hilarious," Jess answered.

"It's important that he's easy to talk to." Jen

couldn't imagine going across the country with no one saying a word.

"He's really sort of funny. He'll keep you laughing. He's got a lot of stories that he likes to tell. I've told him before that he should have been a comic instead of a trucker. He just laughs and says that being out on the road is in his blood. He's a good man or I wouldn't let you go off with him," Jess assured her.

"Good." Jen had finished setting the table.

"You'll be in good hands, and you'll enjoy the trip." Jess laughed.

"He's that entertaining?" Jen asked.

"I would say so." Jess said, and then paused to listen. "That sounds like his pickup now."

Just then they heard Bob's thundering footsteps coming down the stairs. As he approached the front door, he called out, "Come on in!"

Making his way across the front porch, his Uncle Ed said, "I thought Jess was going to be out of town?"

"She's already back," he answered. "They decided not to spend the night in Memphis."

Ed chuckled, "I haven't had a good homemade meal since the last time you invited me. Not only is that girl you married pretty, she can cook too."

"Jess and Jen should have it on the table by now so let's go ahead and eat."

Coming into the kitchen, Bob introduced his uncle to Jen. The four sat down around the table and dropped their heads in prayer. As the prayer ended, Ed spoke up, "Pass me them biscuits, girl. Jess makes the best biscuits in the country."

Everyone gave a hearty laugh and Jess handed him the plate. The conversation that emerged around the table reminded Jen of being at home with her parents. *I miss them*, she thought. *I hope they're alright. I'm ashamed I haven't kept in closer contact. When my life was so full, it was easy to forget to call them. Please God, keep them safe!*

Uncle Ed's voice interrupted Jen's train of thought. "So Jen, I hear you have friends out in California and need a ride. It's not the fastest way to travel, but I'd be happy to have the company. Want to do a ride-along with me?"

"I'd like that, it sounds like fun. I've always wanted to see some of the country. I love the mountains, and I bet I'll see some before we get to California. I've never been west of Texas." Jen was excited; things seemed to be working out.

Sopping up his last bite of gravy with his biscuit, Ed replied, "I don't mind at all, I'll enjoy your company. Having you along will make for a nicer trip."

"Thanks, I sincerely appreciate the invitation. When should I be ready to go?" Jen asked.

"I have some things I need to do tomorrow. I was planning to leave the next day before the cock crows," he chuckled.

"That means we'll have to be up by at least 4 a.m.; he'll be on the road by 5," Bob explained.

"Do all truck drivers start that early?" Jen asked, somewhat surprised.

"No, but he does," Jess laughed.

"I'll be there with bells on," Jen assured him.

"Well, I hate to eat and run but you know what my schedule's like," the older man reminded them as he slid back his chair and stood. "Thanks Jess! As always, that was a mighty fine supper!"

"I'll walk you out," Bob told him and the two men left the kitchen. They went out the front door and made their way to the yard gate. "I'm glad you can help Jen out, for Jess' sake," Bob said, expressing his gratitude.

"That's not a problem. She seems like a sweet little gal."

"They've been friends since kindergarten. They got separated after junior high school. Jess feels close to her, like a sister. That's why it's so important to help her," Bob explained.

"Alright then, I'm just glad I could help. You know I like to get an early start, just give me a chance to get the truck warmed up."

Bob chuckled, "I think we surprised Jen about you leaving out so early. I don't believe she expected that."

"That's what makes life fun! I'll teach her a lot of new things. See you day after tomorrow," Uncle Ed waved, then got in his pickup truck and drove off.

Bob walked back inside to the living room, then flopped down on the couch and grabbed up the remote control. He surfed though the channels for a moment before finding a program to watch until bedtime.

"Dishes are done," Jess announced as she and Jen joined Bob in the living room. Jess sat down on the sofa next to him and Jen sat in the matching chair. "I don't know about anyone else, but I'm pretty tired!" Jess added.

Jen yawned and said, "Me too. The food was delicious, Jess. I was so hungry; now all I can think about is sleep."

"You girls can go on up to bed. I'll lock up and be

up in a bit," Bob told them.

Jen looked at Jess's droopy eyes. "That's all the persuasion I need, how about you? Let's go to bed, Jess."

Jess leaned in to give her husband a kiss. "I'm right behind you, Jen."

They got up late the next morning and had breakfast. Bob was already out of the house, working with some young horses.

"We have one day to spend together, so let's make the most of it and get your hair done," Jess said.

"I'd really like that. Taking the manicure scissors to it didn't work all that well. I really made a mess. All I was thinking about was the need to change my appearance. What do you think about me becoming a redhead?" Jen asked.

"I've never liked redheads." Jess stood back and looked at Jen. "Black might make your complexion look washed out, but I think a soft sable brown would bring out your eyes."

"You like brown because that's your hair color," Jen teased.

"I'm still leaning toward brunette. Let's drive to Sallisaw and see if we can get you in without an appointment," Jess said.

They spent the time it took driving to Sallisaw to discuss old times. When they arrived at Jess' regular beauty salon, they found that all four ladies had clients in their chairs. "We were hoping one of you might have an opening," Jess told them. "My friend got this idea that she could cut her own hair. You can see it didn't turn out too well."

Dolly was just finishing the lady in her chair. "You

come on over here, darlin. My next appointment just canceled." Dolly sat Jen in the chair. "Oh my, you have made a mess of things. We can put in some layers and give you an Elizabeth Taylor look."

"Oh Dolly," one of the other hairdressers laughed. "These two are so young; they don't know who Elizabeth Taylor is."

"Well, how about I give you lots of layers and curve it around your face like this," Dolly said combing Jen's hair toward her face. "It'll be real cute."

"Since there isn't much hair to work with, I'm going to leave it in your hands," Jen laughed. "I was thinking I might like to be a redhead."

"I don't think I'd go red, but maybe a soft sable brown. If you're set on red, I could put in some highlights." Dolly was still combing Jen's hair. "I think it would be stunning that color." Dolly pointed to a picture on the far wall.

Jen liked it. *A chestnut brown with some soft, blond highlights,* i*t would change my looks without making me looked washed out,* Jen thought. *I may be running, but I can still look good.* Jen turned to Jess, "What do you think?"

Jess studied her face. "Dolly's right, it'll be a beautiful color."

"Okay Dolly, turn me into Elizabeth Taylor," Jen laughingly told her.

Dolly colored, cut and shaped Jen's hair. "When you wash your hair, towel it almost dry, fluff it up with your fingers, and let it finish drying. It should just fall into place. Wash and wear, how much easier can it be?"

Admiring her new look, Jen commented. "Thanks Dolly, I love it," Jen paid for her new color and cut and they went back to the car.

"Let's make one more stop," Jen suggested. "Where could I get a money belt? I don't want to keep all this money in my purse."

"Good thinking!" Jess was trying to think of a place but she had never seen a money belt. "You know, the pawn shop has a lot of different things. They've got purses with a compartment for ladies to keep their guns in. Maybe they have money belts."

Two hours later they were back in the car going toward home.

"I love the hair; that color really brings out the color of your eyes." Jess had never seen Jen look more beautiful. "I bet Elizabeth Taylor never looked so good."

Both women dissolved into laughter.

Arriving home, Bob heard their laughter before he saw them. When he saw Jen's new look he couldn't help himself, he gave a low wolf whistle. "What happened to the woman with the bad haircut?" He looked at his wife who was still laughing.

"We traded her for Elizabeth Taylor, whoever that is," Jess told him.

"That's easy," Bob told them. "She was a big movie star, who was married about a dozen times. You remember, Jess. She was in that old horse movie, 'National Velvet'. My mother loved that movie."

Bob went out to take care of the stock and the two women headed for the kitchen. It was time to make dinner. "I'm going to remember this day, forever." Jen said, suddenly feeling sad. "Tomorrow I'll be gone."

"Two friends spending the day together is about as

perfect as it gets," Jess said. "I don't want to think about tomorrow."

When Bob got back, things were not as festive. The reality of Jen's leaving had changed the atmosphere in the kitchen. They all had dinner and Bob decided to retire early. He could watch a little television in the bedroom and let the two women have their last night to themselves.

Jen and Jess talked for a while, but knowing that they needed to be up early, it wasn't long before they went to bed. Life was changing; all they could do was move forward and pray for the best.

CHAPTER THREE

Bob, Jess and Jen woke up early; it was 4 a.m. and still dark outside. They got dressed, then went down to the kitchen and fixed breakfast. It was after they had eaten and were having a second cup of coffee that they heard the big truck. They walked out the front door and waited on the porch. Jen was surprised by the sight. She had never paid much attention to big trucks until that moment when she saw all the lights. In the predawn darkness she could see the outline of the semi, lit up like a Christmas tree. Approaching the farm house, Ed pulled on past the porch.

"His truck is gorgeous," Jen said.

"Yeah, he bought that new truck after my aunt died. He started spending more time on the road about that point. The truth be told, I think he missed her and the house didn't seem the same without her. He upgraded the sleeper and then added the chrome on the fenders and wheels. The last thing he added was all the extra running lights. Looks sharp don't it?" Bob asked, clearly thrilled with the results.

Ed drove down toward the barn. Bob had loading chutes for shipping cattle and horses, and there was room to circle the tractor trailer around. The truck turned and eased up towards the front porch of the farm house. They heard the sound of the air brakes as he came to a stop, then Ed swung down and came through the front yard gate. He was used to rising early, and to him the trio looked to be half awake. He found that amusing and called out. "I see two ladies who don't look like they have their eyes open," and laughed.

"It's not funny, you ole coot, so don't you laugh! Not everyone wakes up bright eyed and bushy-tailed like you!" Jess yelled, teasing Ed, but at the same time sounding very serious.

Bob agreed that they did look like a rag tag bunch. He got up early, but not this early. Ed had always been one to rise before dawn. He would tell anyone who would listen that it was the best time of the day. There weren't many that would agree with him. Bob chuckled to himself. *It's too early in the morning for me, but I wouldn't dare say anything.* He took the large suitcase down the porch steps for Jen and Ed helped him put it inside the sleeper.

"I sense that the girls need a minute to say their goodbyes." Bob told his uncle, and he was right. He knew his wife all too well.

Jess got all choked up. "Jen, I've just found you again. I'm worried about you, and I'm certainly not ready to let you go half way across the country."

"I feel the same, but you know I have to leave. It's best for everyone concerned. Besides, I'd die before I let anyone hurt you or yours. Tell you what, every now and then I'll send you a postcard that says, 'Wish you were here, love, Cousin Gertrude'. Then you'll know that all is well." Jen told her before giving Jess a long, last look. "Bye, BFF," she said and hugged her one last time.

"Come on, girl, we're burning daylight!" Ed called out.

Jen went to the big truck and Ed showed her where to put her feet in order to climb up into it. Then Ed walked around, got into the driver's seat and gave a short blast of the air horn. "Don't want Bob's horses to break out of the stock pens," he told Jen with a chuckle.

Jen rolled down the window. "Thank you," she yelled as she waved goodbye.

Ed put the truck into gear and let off on the clutch. "We are California bound!" he laughed as he shifted a second and then a third time, pulling away from the farm house.

Before long they hit the highway going north, toward the interstate. Leveled out and rolling, Ed asked her, "Well how do you like riding in a big truck?"

"We're so tall; it's great looking down on all the cars."

"You know, I wasn't born yesterday, Jen," Ed told her. "I know there's something more to this than meets the eye. I'll not ask any questions. I just want you to know girl, if you ever want to talk, I have a good ear. I know I run off at the mouth some, but anything you tell me is between us."

She had asked Bob not to tell him anything, was what popped into Jen's mind. She looked over at Ed and wondered, *how much does he know?* Then she quickly decided, *I think he is just guessing. I don't think Bob would tell him, not after hearing what Jeff is capable of.*

"I appreciate the offer, but I just want to get to California and start a new life." Jen hoped Ed would drop the subject. "I have friends who will give me a place to stay and help me find a job."

"What kind of job are you hoping to find?" he inquired.

"I don't really know."

"At your age? Why wouldn't you know?" Ed asked. "You should have some idea about what you want to do with your life."

"I guess because I'm ready for a change, but I haven't decided what kind of change," Jen answered.

"You might want to try truck driving," Ed suggested with a laugh. "There are more women on the road every day."

"I'm not sure I'd like driving one of these big rigs." Jen couldn't imagine driving for a living, mile after mile, it must be boring.

Coming up on the Vian exit, Jen noticed the rolling hills. The rising sun was behind them, but it spread light across the western horizon, bringing out the green of the leaves on the trees. They went across the Arkansas River Bridge and Jen commented, "This is my third time to go across this river."

"The river cuts a path through Colorado, Kansas, Oklahoma, and Arkansas before reaching the Mississippi down below Pine Bluff," Ed told her. "This is the last time you'll see it; we'll be traveling almost due west. Not too long ago, a big barge hit a support on this bridge and caused part of it to collapse. It was real tragic, all those cars going off in the water. Drivers couldn't stop in time and piled one vehicle on top of another. A lot of people were hurt and some died. It was a sad day."

Passing the Muskogee Turnpike exit to Tulsa, Ed told her, "From here on out, it's mostly flat land."

Hours passed as Ed barreled down I-40. His conversation was never boring and he kept Jen entertained. Reaching Oklahoma City, Ed was starting to get hungry. This was always his favorite stop and was where he hooked up with all the other chicken haulers. He pulled a refrigerated trailer and hauled frozen chicken from Springdale, Arkansas. Pulling over at a truck stop, Ed parked his rig. The first thing he noticed was that the parking lot was full which probably meant the restaurant was crowded. *I wonder how long it's going to take us to get served.* He thought. *Oh, well, might as well go find out.*

"Are you ready to eat?" Ed asked. He enjoyed talking to Jen; it made the time pass faster.

"I'm starving; I can't eat much when I get up so early." Jen also needed to stretch her legs.

"That's one thing about being on the road; you eat when you're hungry," Ed told her. "Most truck stops are open 24/7, and if they don't have a restaurant, they at least have a cold case. You can always find something to tide you over."

They went inside and the place was full, all the tables taken. Ed saw that his friends had a booth along the wall however. He took Jen over and made introductions. "This is Tommy Toes, Bee Catcher, Bronc Buster, and Jake Break. That's not their real names, but the ones they use over the radio."

"What do you mean?" Jen asked.

"They're our CB handles, darlin," Tommy Toes answered.

"Come on and sit down," Bronc Buster invited.

"We do need to order a couple of plates of food before we pull out," Ed said.

"Bee Catcher, get over on the other side," Tommy Toes told him.

Bee Catcher got up and Jen slid in next to Tommy Toes. As she did, Bee Catcher asked Ed, "What's with an ole coot like you running with this cute young thing?"

"Get your mind out of the gutter," Ed said. "This

is my niece."

During their meal Jen got better acquainted. The problem was that these men were more curious about her than Ed. She heard a little of the conversion between Ed and Bee Catcher, and sensed that Ed was being a gentleman and trying to protect her reputation. She kept her cool and stuck to the simple story about her childhood. Everything went well and then Ed said, "Alright boys, it's time to go."

Bee Catcher hung back at the cash register, talking to a cute little waitress. He waved them on out, "Go ahead guys, I'll catch up."

Each went toward their individual trucks except for Tommy Toes. He was a little guy about the same height as Jen, and he walked in their direction. "What did he mean about catching up?" Jen asked.

"Have you heard the song 'Convoy'?" Tommy Toes asked with a grin.

"I sort of recall a movie by that name. It had Kris..." Jen paused, trying to remember his last name. "That man had the most beautiful blue eyes, why?"

Tommy Toes reached his arm around her shoulders and hugged her in a casual non-threaten way. "Cause we got us a con--voy!" he said in a tone like the song, quivering his voice and stretching the word out to make it funny.

"Oh, I see," Jen giggled. She liked this group. Who knew she would find men like these? She had inherited an Uncle Ed and a bunch of truck driver buddies. *How strange and wonderful life can be*, she told herself.

They all loaded up and pulled out. They were CB hounds, and the chatter over the radio was heavy. Jen was having the time of her life learning how to talk on the radio. One would say something she didn't understand and Ed would translate for her.

"This is great fun! Can everyone hear us?" Jen asked.

Ed laughed, "Sure can, or at least everyone on this channel. Don't say anything X rated!"

They were close to Amarillo, Texas and it was time for a break. All five trucks pulled into the truck stop and parked side by side in a line. By that time they had gotten to know Jen, and they were all trying to out talk each other. The banter continued while they ordered, ate and paid out.

Taking notice of another pretty girl, Bee Catcher stopped at the pump counter. "I'll catch up to you."

They all laughed and left him to his new conquest. Apparently, like a sailor with a girl in every port, Bee Catcher had a girl at every truck stop.

Reaching Ed's truck, they climbed aboard and left out.

Coming up on Tucumcari, New Mexico, the men were gabbing over the radio. Someone, not in their group, made a comment about keeping women in their place. "Just keep them pregnant and barefooted," they said. It was demeaning and Jen got angry. Suddenly, her silence was noticeable.

Later they were gathered around another restaurant table and Tommy Toes asked, "What caused you to get so quiet all of a sudden?"

"Married truckers leave their wives alone for weeks at a time to take care of the home and kids, then you make light of what those women do." Jen was angry all over again. "Their job is important; they're responsible for the next generation. Hearing that man belittle his wife pissed me off. He should be ashamed."

Everyone laughed and Bronc Rider replied, "Don't blame us for the asshole. We agree with you. Let that be a lesson to all of us. Don't piss Jen off!"

"It's time we get back on the road, boys," Ed instructed. They all rose, left their coffee money on the table and headed out.

Climbing back into the truck, Ed gave Jen a long look. "You look tuckered out. Why don't you crawl in the back and get some sleep. We'll have plenty of time to talk later."

"I am really tired," she said. She hadn't noticed before, but the sleeper was tall like walking into a big closet. She went through the open doorway and saw the bunk beds, with her suitcase parked on the floor. She looked around at the refrigerator and sink framing the beds on one side. The other side had a mini clothes closet and some drawers. She couldn't believe it, all the comforts of home, and it was surprisingly roomy. Jen heard Ed tell her, "Climb under the covers on the bottom bunk and stretch out."

"Alright," she answered back, and shut the curtains between them.

Hours went by as the miles piled up. Ed thought to himself, *Jen should be waking up about now.* When they pull into Albuquerque, New Mexico to fuel up, everything remained quiet in the sleeper. Out on the road again, they were headed for the Arizona state line.

As two more hours went by, Ed started to get worried. Coming into Gallup, New Mexico, Jake Brake called out on the radio, "I need a pit stop."

"I'm ready for a hot shower," Ed said.

"That's unanimous," Tommy Toes came back.

All five trucks pulled into the next truck stop. Just as Ed started to open his truck door, he heard Jen's voice. "Are we there?"

"Not yet. This place has showers inside if you want one." Ed was feeling pretty grungy. "I'd like a shave, shower, and clean clothes myself."

"Me too! Are the showers private or open like the gyms at school?" Jen popped her head out from between the curtains and asked.

"The men's are open, I don't know about the ladies," Ed laughed. "If they're open, no one looks anyway. You'll do fine, grab a change of clothes and come on. After we clean up, we'll go check out the café and see how long a line they have. You had quite a nap and I'll bet you're hungry."

"I am ready to eat, just give me just a minute," she answered before turning back and getting some clothes from her suitcase.

They all hit the showers before heading to the restaurant. A good hot meal was just what they needed. Food in the truck stops was always plentiful and usually tasted good.

An hour later, the guys climbed into their trucks; they had loads to deliver. As Jen got into Ed's truck, her daddy's saying came to her again. "When the going gets tough, the tough get tougher!" Jen didn't realize she had said it aloud until Ed gave a bark of laughter.

"I like that saying, girl. Now let's get this load on down the road."

Nashville, Tennessee

Carl Higgins had been with Jeff for years and he would do anything, no questions asked. Jeff trusted him as much as he trusted anyone. Carl had his men observe the Adams home for days but saw nothing out of the ordinary. Calling Jeff in Nashville, Carl made his report.

"Carrie probably didn't go home, but stay a few more days to be sure," Jeff told him.

The next day Jeff got a phone call, "Mr. Randall, this is the Memphis airport security. I'm contacting you about your car. It's still in long term parking, but I wanted to let you know that someone backed into it. I'm really sorry, sir. It's pretty bad; the back fender has a large dent. You may want to get it fixed before the driver gets back from their trip."

Jeff smiled at his luck. "I'll send someone to pick it up," he told security. "Thank you for letting me know what happened."

After he hung up, Jeff called a contact to discover which flight Carrie had taken. A minute later, he had his answer. "You know I shouldn't be doing this. She went to Mexico City, Mexico," the man on the other end of the line reported.

Soon, Jeff had someone in the Mexican city looking for Carrie. It wouldn't be hard to locate her, or even to arrange for an accident.

Several days later in Mexico City, a car came out of nowhere, striking a young woman crossing the street. The car stopped and a man got out. He went to the body and checked for a pulse, verifying that the young woman was dead. The man then picked up her purse and got back inside his car. Blocks away, he stopped, took the identification out of the purse and made a call to Nashville, Tennessee.

"The woman is dead. There is a driver's license, passport, and credit cards all in the name of Carrie Adams. Have the money wired to my account and I will have them forwarded to you. It is a pleasure doing business with you." After hanging up, the man slipped the car back into gear and drove down the street as if nothing had happened.

A patrol car was cruising the city streets when they came upon a mangled body. It looked like a hit and run. It was a woman, but she had no identification. The officer looked around before calling in the accident.

The officer's sergeant arrived just as the ambulance pulled up. No one had seen anything, and there was no identification on the body, the officers reported. She looked like a tourist, he added.

"Somewhere, someone will make a missing persons report. That's how we will find out who she is. Then we can connect the dots," the sergeant said, and they sent her body to the morgue.

Three days later, in Nashville, Jeff received a letter that contained Carrie's passport, driver's license, and credit card. He had thought highly of Carrie, and he liked the picture they had made as the golden couple. His friends had envied him, it was a shame she had a conscience. He put everything back inside the envelope and put it inside his office safe. *Problem solved*! He thought.

CHAPTER FOUR

Their convoy pulled into a large truck stop in Flagstaff, Arizona and the trucks all moved to the back of an enormous parking lot.

"The federal government regulates the hours we can drive." Ed said as he climbed out of the driver's seat. "I'm going to climb into that top bunk and get some shut eye. Do you think you can sleep after the nap you took?"

"I've missed so much sleep over the last few days, I do believe I can." Jen told him, and claimed the lower bunk she had used earlier. Ed fell asleep immediately and the cab filled with his snoring. Jen smiled as she listened to the sound. It was reassuring, and it wasn't long before she was asleep.

The next thing Jen knew, Ed was shaking her awake. "Let's get something to eat, girl. We have to get back on the road."

Back on I-40 going west, everything seemed to be going smoothly until Ed saw a flashing light on the dash. "What the heck?" he said. He got on the radio, talking with his buddies and trying to figure out what the light could mean. No one seemed to have an answer.

Ed was worried. "If this has anything to do with the refrigeration, I could lose my load. I don't even want to think about all those chickens in the back thawing out."

"We're only a few miles from New Ludlow. You could pull over there; they have a tire and repair shop, come back," Tommy Toes radioed.

Bee Catcher cut in, "That's only for tires."

"Trucks buy diesel in Ludlow all the time. They've

got to have some kind of mechanic," Bronco Buster replied.

"Maybe you should try making it on into Barstow," Tommy Toes said. They all knew a bigger place was sure to have a mechanic.

"I'd rather not take the chance. If nothing else, surely someone will know who to call. At the very least, I want to find out what it could be and where I need to go to get it fixed. You go on. I'll catch up sooner or later," Ed told the guys.

Ed pulled off the interstate at New Ludlow. He saw a gas station and a Dairy Freeze. He turned to the south side looking for the repair shop. Another gas station, a café and a motel were lined up next to a trailer court. The tire and repair shop was in the same driveway as the Ludlow Café. He pulled the big truck in and parked, set the air breaks and got out.

Climbing down from the truck, Jen asked, "What are we doing here?"

Ed explained about the light and then asked, "Are you hungry?"

"Not a whole lot, why?"

"I saw a Dairy Freeze when we first pulled off I-40. Why don't you take a walk and check it out? Maybe find a way to pass some time," Ed told her. "I've got a feeling we're going to be here a while."

Jen made her way back under I-40 and found the Dairy Freeze on the north side. As she walked up, she saw a lady at the sliding window. The lady opened the glass and said, "My name is Rosa. May I take your order please?"

"I want chocolate malt." Jen replied. When Rosa brought her the drink, she paid for it and then began walking back. The air was still and hot. *Being in this heat will melt my malt,* she thought and took a sip.

In the meantime, Ed had discovered a teenager in the back of the garage breaking down a tire. He walked up and explained his problem.

"No, we don't have a mechanic around here. We've just got the bare necessities now days. I'm sure you probably know that everyone moved away from the old town of Ludlow, it's a ghost town now. We rebuilt here next to Interstate 40 in 1970. Primarily we're just a tire station, but you might be in luck because my uncle's inside. He's a diesel mechanic and retired a few months ago from that big truck stop in Barstow. He's not taking to retirement real well, and if anyone knows what your trouble is, it'll be him. He'll probably like having a mystery to solve."

"That's great. Let's go have a talk with him," Ed told the kid.

Jen looked around at the scenery; the mountains and hills seemed to surround the flat lands of desert bush and shrubs. She made her way back to the repair shop but didn't bother to stop and talk with Ed. He said it would be a while, so she continued on southeast, past the repair shop. *I'll go sightseeing. I guess you could call it that, although there isn't much to see except for desert,* she decided.

Jen passed a couple of older buildings and a few blocks farther and she saw a cemetery with makeshift crosses scattered amongst more permanent headstones. *God, how old is this?* She wondered. The most desirable thing was the Ironwood tree in the middle that created a shade. She went up to it and sat down. *Being in the shade is a little cooler, if 105 degrees is a little cooler than 110 degrees*, she giggled. She took another sip of her now melting malt. Her body temperature seemed to be lower sitting in the shade, and she was more relaxed leaning against the tree trunk. *Well, I made it to California, now where do I go from here? I need a more detailed objective. I like being around Ed. He's funny and protective, and the guys are nice. They really want me to be a part of their convoy.* She smiled as she thought about the first time they had met. Tommy Toes' funny imitation of C.W. McCall and their antics had certainly made her laugh. She then looked out at the vast openness of the desert. The light blue shades of the mountains looked far away; it was a gorgeous sight. She had never thought about the desert being so beautiful before.

This place is close to Death Valley; I saw the sign. This desert has no water and without water no one can survive. Survival, that's what I should be concerned about. I need to decide what I'm going to do with my life. Ed wants me to try truck driving. If I was continually on the road, would Jeff be able to find me?

I can't stay with Ed. I can't take the chance that he'd get hurt because of me. Dear God, how could things have gone so wrong? One minute I believe that I'm the luckiest girl in the whole world, and the next I'm running for my life.

It was then that Jen looked over at the headstone closest to her and read the date. *That girl, Leah Marie Scott, was born on the same day I was,* she thought. Then, an idea popped into her head. *I need another name change, and this grave gives me an idea. She died at a young age, I could become her. I could take down this information, go to the state capitol, and get her birth certificate. With a birth certificate I could get a driver's license or a state-issued ID. I'm also going to need a Social Security card. Most people get those when they're children, so all I'd have to do is re-apply for hers.*

Trying to decide what to do, Jen looked around. Next to the girl's headstone was a double marker with the same last name. From what she could tell by the dates and names, these may have been the girl's parents. *There is no one to know if I borrow their daughter's name. If I remember my geography, the capital of California is Sacramento, I could get a new identify there!* Jen got excited. She liked this idea and jotted down the information on the headstones before leaving the cemetery.

Jen made her way back to the Dairy Freeze to get another chocolate malt. *This is in Ed's best interest, not to mention mine, but how will I convince him that we need to go our separate ways? It isn't like he's not expecting it. We told him that I have friends out here. I just need to come up with another story. I'll borrow Ed's map and see where I need to go.*

Jen confirmed with Rosa that Sacramento was indeed the capital. Sipping on her fresh chocolate malt, she made her way back to Ed's truck.

Ed was still with the mechanic, but Jen knew where his map was located. She borrowed it and made a plan. She knew that Ed would take I-5 on up to San Jose; she had heard the guys talking about it. *I've gotten to know Ed and he won't let me just walk away. He'll feel responsible and want to know that I'm alright. I'll tell him my friends live in Stockton. It's close enough that he can let me out in Livermore and I could take a bus from there. He'll go for that, he's got to.*

Ed came out of the garage and looked around for Jen. He found her sitting in the shade of the building. "Well girl," he called to her, "I think we found the problem. That was a lot of fuss for a little fuse. Let's get going, I need to drop these birds."

Jen climbed in the truck and Ed got them back on

the interstate.

"What were you looking for on the map?" Ed asked.

Jen decided to try her story. "I was thinking that I'm going to miss you and the guys, but Livermore would be a good place to catch a bus into Stockton. That's where my friends live, out near the college. A college town is a good place to build a new life, and I've been thinking that I might decide to go back to school."

"I kind of thought you might like to keep on trucking. We make a good team you know, and we seem to hit it off real good. I could teach you to drive. A team can run more hours and make more money. And that way, you could see Jess now and then," Ed encouraged.

"Ed, I really like you and I think of you as my adopted uncle. Going cross-country has been an adventure. Someday, we'll reconnect and have fun reliving the last few days, but it's not what I want to do every day," Jen explained.

"Alright, girl. Let's see if we can find out where the bus station is in Livermore. I'm going to miss you, that's for darn sure."

Ed got quiet for the first time since Jen has known him. Now that the guys were so far ahead and were no longer in radio range, Jen had no one to talk with. She sat and listened to the other drivers chat. "How long will it take us to catch up with the guys?" Jen asked.

"Depends on whether they're still in Barstow. If they're still on schedule, they'll be getting ready to pull out. If you want to run with them, we won't get a break," Ed answered.

"Doesn't matter, you're the one driving. I was just wondering how far ahead they are." Jen really liked running with the guys but she didn't want Ed tiring himself out by trying to catch up.

Ed made no comment. Jen realized that the atmosphere inside the cab had changed. It was as if he'd gone back to being a lone driver. Without the guys to talk with, this trip would seem lonesome. It would be like being out in the desert, cut off from the world. *That's the reason for the convoy, she reasoned. It keeps the group together and sane. I wonder how many people living out here are driven mad. You could lose your mind, living in an endless sea of sand and not a single soul to talk to.*

Jen didn't say any more to Ed. She could tell that he was sort of upset. The last thing she wanted to do was hurt him. *I have to do this. He doesn't realize that it's for his own good*, she thought. *This is the only decision I can make. I'm happy enough riding with Ed, but since I mentioned taking a bus, he's been very distant. I don't mind though, since it gives me time to think.*

After days on the road, Jen looked down and noticed her clothes. *My pants are dirty, my blouse is all wrinkly, and I feel all sticky and sweaty from my time in the desert heat. I wish I could take another long, bubble bath,* she thought. That reminded her of the one she had at Jess and Bob's farm house. *I wonder what Jess is doing right now? She's probably kicked back on her sofa with her feet up and watching a soap opera while I'm confined to this bumpy seat. I can't believe I thought it was fun in the beginning. Boy, am I ready to get out of this rig.*

Watching the changing scenery out the window, she wondered about the pioneers. All those tough men and women who traveled across this vast country by wagon train, making their way to the west coast. We have one thing in common; we're both looking for a new life. *Gosh, I don't know how they made that long trip. Look how long it took us to get from Sallisaw to Needles. In a wagon, those folks might have made it to Henryetta in the same amount of time. That's if the weather stayed good and no angry Indians slowed them down. I'm glad I'm not living in that era, although it might be easier to disappear.*

It was quiet since no one was talking on the radio. Jen's mind wandered to Nashville and Jeff. She had a flashback of him kissing her; he was a great kisser. She recalled the intimate times they had shared and their first date. Jeff knew how much she liked music and he bought them tickets for a dinner cruise on the Showboat General Jackson. They had served dinner and there was a stage show. The singers were great, but they had the most fun watching a ventriloquist. He had live dogs and some sort of a device that made it look like their mouths were opening and closing. She remembered them trying to figure out how it worked. They had laughed and it had been so much fun. That was the night it had all begun for them, and her life had seemed so perfect. She had no clue how it would all end. *He took me places like that because we wouldn't be likely to run into his wife.* The bitterness of his betrayal came rushing back. She couldn't help but miss him. *I loved him so much and still do, I guess. He really had me fooled. It's almost like he was two different people. I only knew the nice Jeff, until that night. I have no choice but to forget him. He's bad, a killer, and running is my only way out.*

Jen saw a roadside tavern off in the distance. *I remember my Uncle Richard talking about a friend of his named Joe Wilson. He retired from the Navy and opened a bar in San Diego. Maybe that would be a good place for me to go. A Navy town, you wouldn't think they would let the mob operate there, with the government being so involved. I would think the Navy would keep a tight lid on it. Jeff managed to get around the regular police, but the military police would be harder to bribe. San Diego is a real possibility. I've heard the weather is nice and the temperature is mild most of the year. I might miss the changing seasons, but I wouldn't miss the 100 degree summers.*

Thoughts about Jeff made Jen think of the real Jennifer. *As Carrie, she's probably having a great time and here I am stuck in the cab of an 18 wheeler with a crabby old man. When I get to Stockton, the first thing I should do is find the library and look at the obituaries. I need to try to learn how Leah and her parents died. Too bad I can't do that in Barstow. It's closer, so they would probably have more information about the folks who lived in Ludlow. Leah Marie Scott has a nice ring to it. I like it, it sounds classy, and it reminds me of Lisa Marie Presley. I always liked her name, but I think I like Leah better.*

Passing a rise on the left of the interstate, the city of Barstow spread over the landscape up ahead. Ed still wasn't talking and neither was Jen. It wasn't long before they pulled into the truck stop. It was a large place and Jen noticed big rigs parked everywhere. *We'll never find them among all those other trucks,* she thought. About that time a familiar voice was heard over the radio. Tommy Toes' drawl filled the cab. "About time you came draggin in."

Like he had an extra hand, Ed grabbed the mic, "It was only a bad fuse. Can you believe all that trouble just for one little fuse?"

"Sounds like you lucked out," Broncobuster

chimed in.

"Waited on us, did you?" Ed questioned. He knew that waiting on him could be a risk. If they had a problem down the road they might not get their loads in on time.

"We had little else to do. Besides, you have our girl with you," Bee Catcher said.

"I knew you couldn't be waiting for me," Ed chuckled and parked his rig. *The guys are going to miss Jen as much as I will,* he thought.

Like flipping on a switch, Ed's good attitude suddenly returned. He was cheerful again and looked happy, as if all those miles with him giving Jen the silent treatment had never happened. He grinned at Jen and said, "Let's go freshen up."

Jen was glad his good mood had returned. "I'm ready," she replied and grabbed some clothes. "After my walk in the desert heat I definitely need a shower."

When they climbed down out of the cab they found all four of the guys standing around the truck, wearing grins from ear to ear. Tommy Toes reached out and steadied Jen, helping her until her feet were planted firmly onto the pavement. He winked and said, "We took a vote. We all missed hearing your voice."

"So you're all going to be late getting your load in, just because of me," Jen scolded.

"No, we'll make up the time when we hit I-5," Jake Brake noted.

Just then, Ed came around the front of the truck, "You boys had coffee yet?"

"Been waitin' on you, Ed," Bronco Buster answered.

The group of six made their way across the parking lot and inside. "First things first, I need a quick shower and clean clothes," Jen said. "I was out in the desert heat and I feel all sweaty."

"Me too, we'll meet up in the restaurant," Ed told them.

Joining everyone at the table after getting clean, Jen suddenly felt a little sad. She ordered coffee and then told them her plans. "You guys are the best, and I'm never going to forget you. It's like I inherited four hard driving trucker brothers, and I love you all."

Everything was normal again after they left Barstow. The closer they came to Livermore, the quieter the radio got. Jen started to realize that these men had all gotten far too attached to her. *It's unbelievable that we could form a bond so quickly, but Ed's the glue holding them all together. It's like he's Papa Bear and they're his sons. They're all strong, intelligent men, but they look to him for reassurance. Families aren't always formed by blood. Sometimes, they're forged together by love and respect. That's what formed the bond between these men. With every mile, their bond gets stronger.*

Bee Catcher's voice came over the radio to alert them. "Ed, when you get to Livermore, we'd be much better off to call a cab. It's really hard to maneuver around that bus station. The streets are always full of parked cars on both sides. I know, because I used to date a little gal who worked downtown. I didn't know I had a choice the first time I went to see her so I braved the drive. My trailer almost hit three cars before I got there. After that I got smart, parked my truck and took a cab,"

"That's probably a good idea," Ed answered, and then asked, "Are you boys gonna wait till I get back?"

"Hell no, we're going with you. You can't kick our little sparrow out of the nest without us," Tommy Toes said.

"Give me that mic, Ed," Jen said and snatched it out of his hand. "Look you guys, I appreciate the thought, but I'm not a little bird. I'm a grown woman who's capable of taking a cab to the bus station. Stop the daddy act, pull over and call for a cab to come pick me up. It's going to be hard enough to say our goodbyes at the truck stop. If you fools aren't careful, you're going to have me crying like a baby," Jen snapped.

No one said a word, not even Ed.

After a long pause, Tommy Toes broke the silence; "Hey guys, remember, don't piss Jen off."

Suddenly everyone laughed, "All right, have it your own way," Bee Catcher said

They went into the restaurant and everyone was all too aware that this would be their last meal together. They tried to keep the banter going, but no one's heart was in it. All too quickly, it was time to say goodbye.

Jen climbed into the back of the taxi cab and told the driver to take her to the bus station. She leaned out of the window and waved farewell to the five 'teddy bears' watching her drive out of their lives.

The taxi dropped Jen off at the bus station, and as luck would have it, a bus to Sacramento was scheduled to leave within the hour. Since no one was there to see her, Jen bought a ticket to the state capitol. She checked out the station while she waited and remembered her promise to Jess. In a little corner, Jen found some postcards. She bought a card, some snacks, and a bottle of water for the bus ride.

Sitting down on a bench, Jen wrote the simple message to Jess. "Wish you were here, love, Cousin Gertrude." *I won't mail it until I get to Sacramento. I prefer to send it from a larger city.* She thought of all the wonderful people who had helped her during the worst time of her life. God had blessed her with such special friends. She was feeling just a little sorry for herself, and the tears began to fall. Ed would probably tell her, "Shake it off, girl. It's time to get moving."

They announced that the bus to Sacramento was ready to board. Jen wiped her tears and walked toward the exit. The next part of her adventure was about to begin. *When the going gets tough, the tough get tougher*, she thought, recalling her dad. *I love him so much.* She could almost feel him walking beside her as she boarded the bus.

CHAPTER FIVE

Jen stepped off the bus in Sacramento, California at 8 o'clock in the morning. *Dear God in Heaven, did we stop at every little town between here and Livermore?* She asked herself. She got her suitcase and went over to the information desk in the large bus terminal. When it was her turn, Jen smiled at the lady behind the counter. "I have some business in town that will take a day, and then I'm heading south to San Diego. I need to know the bus schedule."

"A lot of these buses stop all along the way, but we have an express that goes straight to Los Angeles. The express leaves at 9 a.m. and 4 p.m. and it's around a six hour trip. We have customers who like to see all the little towns, though I don't happen to be one of them," explained the agent. "If it works into your schedule, the express would save you some time."

"That definitely sounds best," Jen told the lady. "Is there a rental locker large enough to hold my suitcase?"

The agent directed Jen around the corner to the locker area.

"One more thing," Jen asked, "where is a good place to get breakfast?"

"The cook here at the bus station café makes a really good omelet," the agent answered. "I should go home and make my own, but I can't resist Lou's omelets."

Jen put her suitcase into a locker and the key in her purse. Then she walked into the café and spotted an empty table for two. She couldn't help but think about the guys and the fun times they had around a restaurant table. *Don't start down that road,* she told herself. The waitress brought her a cup of coffee and left her with a menu. After deciding on a Denver omelet, Jen asked the waitress, "Do you know where the California Department of Public Health is located?"

"I'm not sure, but the State Capitol is about six blocks north," the waitress explained.

"What about the nearest library?" Jen asked.

"Oh, that's easy. It's just across the street."

Twenty minutes later, Jen was walking across the street to the library. Once inside, she looked to the left and saw the information desk. After explaining that she wanted to check on an obituary, Jen was shown upstairs to the second floor. Ten minutes later she had found the obituary of Leah's father. Another twenty minutes and she had found the mother's obituary. She printed both obituaries and paid for the copies.

Jen got on the Internet and looked up the address of the Department of Public Health. She also checked to see what was required to get a birth certificate. *Proof of identity, which I don't have*, she thought. *What can I do?* She looked up the tax records for the city of Ludlow. I*'ve gotten good at lying so what's one more story? This time I could go to prison if I'm caught.* Jen didn't have a choice; she had to become this girl. It was a matter of life and death. The thought put her on alert again and she felt the fear race though her system. Looking through tax rolls, she found a record for someone who had been paying taxes for over 30 years. Jen copied down the name and address of a Ms. Opal

Winslow and then went up to the librarian. "May I borrow a sheet of paper?" she asked.

"Sure," the attendant said and gave her a piece of plain typing paper. Jen sat down at a corner table trying to decide what to write. She had noticed older people's hands sometimes shook and their writing had a spidery look. With what she hoped was a shaky hand, she wrote.

To whom it may concern:

My name is Opal Alice Winslow and I have lived in Ludlow, California for over 40 years. I have known Leah Marie Scott since the day she was born. Her folks were Mr. and Mrs. Henry L. Scott. Leah's mother and father are dead, God Bless their souls, and Leah has never driven a car so she doesn't have any identification. Her birth certificate has gone missing and she needs a new one. I swear that I know Leah Marie Scott is her true name.

Jen signed it, Opal Alice Winslow. After reading it she added an address below the name.

Jen took the letter and her copies of the obituaries and left the library. She walked the six blocks to the building that housed the Department of Public Health. *Here goes nothing,* she thought to herself and entered the building. She found the right office and, after saying a prayer, opened the door.

A young lady looked up as she entered. Smiling, she inquired, "May I help you?"

This is it; Jen thought and told her, "I need to get a copy of my birth certificate."

"Just fill out this form and I will need proof of identification," She looked bored, like this is the last place she wanted to be.

Jen went ahead and filled out the form, then returned to the counter with her copies. "I'm sorry. I don't have an ID. All I have is this letter from a neighbor lady. You see, my mother died and left daddy with six small children. I was the oldest, and though I was only twelve, I was real grown up. I helped raise my brothers and sister so I never had a real job. I never learned to drive either. Now my daddy's gone and I can't find my birth certificate anywhere. Please, can you help me?"

"Let me see what you have." The lady behind the counter took the papers and read the letter. "You did know this should have been notarized?" The clerk couldn't help but notice the stress on Jen's face or the pleading look in her eyes. "I'm not really supposed to do this, but let's look and see if you're in the system. If I don't have to do an extended search, maybe I can make an exception."

Jen let out a quick sigh of relief and watched the young lady type in the information. Suddenly the printer was spitting out a paper. Could this be her birth certificate? The clerk took the copy and put the California seal on the paper. She paused, as though having second thoughts. "Maybe I should wait for my supervisor to return. As I explained to you, I'm really not supposed to do this without identification. I could get into all kinds of trouble, maybe lose my job."

Jen noticed the woman's name tag. "Look Emma, I don't want to get you into trouble, and I certainly don't want you to lose your job. The problem is, I can't get an ID without my birth certificate, and I can't get my birth certificate without an ID. Please! I came all the way to Sacramento on the bus. I've got to get back to Ludlow. I still take care of my brothers and sister. Please, don't make me go all the way back home to get Miss Opal's letter notarized."

Emma's heart reached out to the young woman. *How much trouble can the* lack *of a notary seal cause? Leah Scott looks like her life has been full of difficulty and it's time she had a break. If my supervisor questions me, I saw her driver's license.* She took the information and stapled it to the form for Leah Marie Scott's birth certificate. Jen couldn't believe it when Emma handed her the document.

Trying to act calm, the new Leah Marie Scott expressed her gratitude and quickly walked out the door before Emma could change her mind.

Stepping out into the sunshine with her new identity in hand, Jen couldn't help but be happy. *An ID poses no problem now that I have a birth certificate. Next stop is the Department of Motor Vehicles. I go in, they take my photo, and within a few minutes I'm officially Leah Marie Scott.*

A few doors down and Leah was asking how she could get a copy of her Social Security card. "I must have had one when I was little," Leah said, and stuck with her story, "My parents are dead and I can't find my card."

Another counter and another woman. "Fill out the information on this application." Again, they asked the same old questions, plus a new one. "Have you never had a job?" the woman inquired.

Leah again explained how she had stayed home and helped her father with her siblings. "I never had time to work a real job, or do anything else for that matter. I'm grateful that I managed to graduate from high school. I got my education while the other children were in school."

"Yes, here it is." After a few minutes the woman had a social security card for Leah. "Is that all I can help you with?" the woman asked. She looked busy and was not really paying much attention.

"Yes ma'am," Leah answered and then walked out the door. In her purse she carried all the identification she would need to start a new life.

Making her way outside the building, Leah saw a small park. She went to a bench and sat down. Her heart was pounding. *Talk about being scared, I wasn't sure I could pull that off. Please God, don't let all of these lies be for nothing. I don't know if I can go through this again,* Leah prayed. Looking down at her watch, she decided that she would be able to make the express bus that left at 4 o'clock, and was surprised that she'd gotten everything done so quickly.

Leah walked back inside the bus station and again went to the ticket counter. "Can I get a ticket to San Diego?" She asked. "I want the express bus, if that's possible."

The agent smiled and checked the time. "I should be able to get you on the express; it's leaving in a few minutes. It's non-stop to L.A. but there's not an express bus to San Diego tonight. If you want to ride express, you will have to stay over in Los Angeles.

"Can I connect to San Diego tonight on the regular bus? What time would I get there?" Leah asked.

"You can get a late bus out tonight and it takes about four hours. That will put you in San Diego around midnight," the agent told her.

Leah quickly decided, *I don't want to find a motel in Los Angeles. San Diego may be just as bad, but it's my last stop*. "Give me a ticket to San Diego tonight," she told the agent.

The agent issued her ticket. "They will be boarding any minute now," she explained.

Leah retrieved her suitcase from the locker then darted to the sales area. *I haven't had time for anything to eat since this morning.* She grabbed two bottles of water, some peanut butter crackers, and a couple of candy bars. *Not exactly nutritious but it's the best I can do.* The call for the express bus came over the loud speakers, and Leah paid for her purchases before sprinting for the bus. She gave her suitcase to the bus driver to load in the luggage compartment and found a window seat. *I do love to watch out the window*, she thought, as people kept boarding.

The bus was filling up fast. A couple of young girls walked down the aisle. They were laughing and talking like they had known each other forever. *Was I ever that young?* Leah thought. They were both beautiful, one tall and dark-haired and the second a petite blonde. The blonde sat down next to Leah and the other girl took a seat across the aisle.

"Hi, I'm Christie," the blonde said, introducing herself as she sat down, "And this is my friend Kathy."

They're like two playful puppies. "Hi, my name is Leah."

"Isn't this exciting?" Kathy chimed in, "We're on our way to Hollywood."

"Not Hollywood exactly," Christie explained. "We're going to Los Angeles."

"What are you going to do in Los Angeles?" Leah asked.

One question was all the girls needed. Christie launched into their story. "We've lived all our lives in Lincoln, California. We just graduated from high school, and have been saving our money, since our junior year." She made it sound like that was a very long time. "My mom has a sister who lives in Los Angeles and she's supposed to take care of us, like we need that." She rolled her eyes in typical teenage fashion.

"She has six kids to take care of so that shouldn't last long," Kathy inserted into the story.

Christie continued. "We plan to find an apartment, although we can't afford all that much at first. Kathy is going to be a model and I'm going to be an actress." She stated it like it was a fact, not something they were dreaming of.

Kathy spoke up. "Christie is great. She was in a play at the Off Broad Street Theater back home. They do comedies, and Christie's a natural. Everyone said she reminded them of Goldie Hawn. We weren't sure who that was until we looked it up on the Internet. She was on something called 'Laugh in'," Kathy told Leah.

"Anyway, one of us is sure to find work and she will help the other one." Christie continued her story. "When we're both working, we will find a nice house near the ocean."

Only the young can be so optimistic. Leah thought. *These two are so naïve. Should I try to warn them? No, I wouldn't have listened to anyone trying to rain on my parade, so I should just keep my mouth shut. Dear God in Heaven, please watch over them,* she prayed.

The miles rolled by with the girls chattering about their plans. Christie described the play she was in, and she had the whole back of the bus caught up in her tale. Everyone laughed as she told about a mishap when a young man forgot his lines. *She really is funny; maybe she will be a star. Do they still discover people in Hollywood?*

The bus finally rolled into Los Angeles and Leah checked her ticket to see when her connecting bus left for San Diego. Then she asked the driver to make sure that her suitcase would be transferred to the San Diego bus. Seeing a mailbox outside the terminal, she remembered the post card to Jess and dropped it inside. She still had a little time, so she decided to get a hamburger. As she went toward the terminal restaurant, she noticed a rather haggard looking lady collecting Christie and Kathy. *That must be the aunt with all the kids. The girls were right; this lady won't have the energy to keep up with her six kids and those two lively girls.*

Leah was just finishing her dinner when the bus for San Diego was called. She boarded, and again found a seat next to a window. It was night and there wouldn't be much to see, but she could lean her head against the window and take a nap. She rode through the night and the seat next to her remained empty. It was a welcome break after that six hour ride with the chattering teens. The roar of the bus engine reminded her of Ed's big rig. *I wonder where he is?*

Leah was jarred awake by the bus driver announcing their arrival in San Diego, and got stiffly to her feet. Outside, she collected her suitcase and tried to decide what to do. She had just sat down on a bench when an older, nicely dressed woman joined her.

"You just came in on the bus, didn't you?" the

woman inquired. “I was sitting a little further back.”

“Yes,” Leah answered. “I'm new to the area, as you may have already guessed, and I need a place to stay.”

“I'm going home and there is a motel near my neighborhood. It's not fancy, but I think it would be an acceptable place for a lady to stay,” she said. “I know that is important when you are traveling alone. Would you like to share a taxi?”

“Thank you for the information, and I would love to share a cab.” Leah took her suitcase and followed the woman out to the taxi area. “How long have you lived in the San Diego area?”

“Most of my life,” the woman told her. “I have been to visit my youngest son and his family. They would have brought me home, if I had waited for the weekend. To be honest, the children were making me nervous. I’m not used to having the young ones around anymore. So, I just happened to remember a doctor’s appointment and came home.” She laughed at herself. “I should be ashamed, they really are good children.”

A few minutes later they were pulling in to the motel. It was older, but looked quite safe. Leah was thankful not to have to spend the night on a bus station bench. She paid her share of the fare, got out of the cab and waved to the woman. “Thank you for sharing the cab.”

Inside, Leah asked if they had a vacancy. When the clerk gave her a choice between a king and two queen beds, she heaved a sigh of relief. “I want the cheapest room you have,” she told the clerk.

“They are both the same,” he explained. “How long will you be staying?”

"I'm not sure. I don't have a definite plan, can we leave it open?" Leah asked.

"It's the middle of the week and a little slow. You're checking in after midnight, so if you will book for three days, I won't charge you for tonight."

"Let me check the room and if it's clean, then you've got a deal," Leah replied and extended her hand for the key.

"Lady, you strike a hard bargain," the clerk said as he handed her a key.

The room was nothing fancy but it was spotless. Leah left her suitcase and went back to check in. *This should be a good place to rest and decide what I want to do.* After filling out the information card, she told the clerk, "I've been on the road a couple of days. Could you let the maids know that I won't need them to clean the room in the morning? I'd appreciate it if they'd just allow me to sleep."

"I will mark it on the work schedule. Put your 'do not disturb' sign on the door, just in case. Goodnight," the clerk told her.

Leah stumbled to the room. She felt dirty and couldn't stand to sleep without a quick shower. She set the water temperature and stepped into the tub, then grabbed the bar of soap and began to scrub her tired body. Shutting off the water, she dried off and pulled her nightgown over her head. She was numb, her feet were swollen, and she ached all over. She dragged herself to the bed, and by the time her head hit the pillow, she was asleep.

It was afternoon when Leah finally woke up, and it felt like a swamp had taken up residence in her mouth. She climbed out of bed and into the shower again. Half an hour later she had showered, shampooed her hair and brushed her teeth, and she felt almost human again. She dressed in black slacks, a loose white shirt, and tennis shoes before heading out the door.

When she went outside, the sun seemed brighter and it almost blinded her. *I'm going to need a good pair of sunglasses; they don't call it Sunny California for nothing. It should be fun exploring the coastal area*, she thought to herself.

Leah made her way to the front desk, and after asking for directions she walked down the street to a little mom-and-pop restaurant. It was supposed to serve the best spaghetti in town.

It was a cute little place with red-and-white checked tablecloths. A waitress came up, giving her a menu. "Welcome to Little Italy," she said, smiling. "What can I get you to drink?"

Leah decided to splurge and ordered the house wine, with spaghetti and meat balls. The French bread was crunchy with lots of garlic, just the way she liked it. *It's a wonder what a good meal will do for a girl,* Leah thought. She paid the ticket and went back out into the perfect day.

I think I am going to like San Diego, Leah told herself. *It's a big town but it has a welcoming feeling. The weather is warm without being hot, and there's a breeze blowing in from the ocean.*

Back at the motel, Leah chatted with the woman behind the desk. "I came here because I'm trying to find a man."

"Who isn't, sweetie?" the woman answered with a knowing wink.

"Okay," Leah laughed. "Let me put it another way.

I'm trying to locate this man named Joe Wilson. I think he owns a bar and grill here in San Diego. Any ideas on how I can find him?'

"With everybody on Facebook, let's see what we can find." The clerk put the information into the motel's computer. "Simple as pie. Ocean Front Bar and Grill with Joe Wilson listed as the owner. I'll write down the location for you." She found a pad and handed Leah a piece of paper with an address on it.

Leah couldn't believe it was that quick. *Boy, am I out of touch. Throw away my cell phone and I forget everything I ever knew.* She tucked the paper with the address into her purse. "Thank you," she told the clerk. "Would it be possible to call me a taxi?"

"Sure thing, sweetie," the woman said. She called it in and then told Leah. "Oh, by the way, if Joe Wilson doesn't work out, let me know. I may not be as picky," She said with a laugh.

Leah couldn't believe her. *Is she that hard up for a man that she would take one without setting eyes on him? Welcome to California!* Leah laughed as she stepped into the taxi.

Texas

While shopping for groceries, Alice Adams saw Jessica Smith's mother at the supermarket. She was concerned about Carrie. It had been too long since she had checked in. Alice had called everyone she could think of, including that man Carrie had been dating. She didn't think Carrie and Jessica had kept in touch, but she got Jessica's phone number. Jessica's parents had moved away while the girls were in junior high, and they had moved back to Texas just last year. Alice was ready to try anything, and maybe Jessica had heard from Carrie. When Alice got home, she put her groceries up and dialed the number she had gotten from Mrs. Smith.

Surprised by Mrs. Adams' call, Jess didn't dare discuss Carrie over the telephone. She denied hearing from Carrie, all the while feeling guilty for lying. In an instant she made a decision. "We're coming to Texas for a visit next week. Could I stop by and see you?"

"I would love that," Mrs. Adams replied. *Jess knows something,* she thought to herself. *Why doesn't she just tell me? I have to be calm and wait, but this is going to be the longest week in history. Please God, let her know what happened to my Carrie.*

Jess hung up and explained to Bob. "I know we weren't planning to drive to Texas, but Carrie's mother deserves to know what happened. Maybe I'm being paranoid, but I don't think I should tell her what I know over the phone."

"After what Carrie told us, I agree. It is pretty hard to wrap your mind around what happened in Nashville. I think you did the right thing," Bob told her. "When would you like to leave?"

Two days later Jess was in Texas, but she wasn't looking forward to talking to Mrs. Adams. How much should she tell her? In the end she decided to hold nothing back.

Mrs. Adams listened to the whole story. As Jess talked, she grew more agitated. "Carrie's a smart girl. I'm surprised that she's gotten herself into this mess. At least she had the good sense to call you for help. What bothers me most is why she didn't come to us."

"Carrie knew Jeff would stop at nothing to find her. She thought this would be the first place he'd look. Have you heard from him?"

"I called him last week and asked if he knew where Carrie was. I told him we hadn't heard from her and were worried. He said they had argued and he hadn't seen her in more than a month. We haven't had any phone calls or visitors asking about Carrie. I'll tell you this though, I had a feeling awhile back that we were being watched. Now it makes perfect sense."

"It was probably his men. Carrie was right not to get you involved. She never told Jeff about me and that's why she came to us. I know it'll be hard, but try not to worry. I know she'll be alright as long as she's with Ed. The only thing we can do is let her disappear and pray Jeff doesn't find her." Jess had been doing a lot of praying since Carrie left.

"There's no way I can let her father know all of this. He'd go berserk and confront Jeff. I'll have to decide how much I can tell him," Mrs. Adams confided to Jess. "I'll have to tell him something. He's about ready to call out the National Guard."

"Say a prayer. For now that's all we can do," Jess told her, and then added, "Whatever happens, do not contact Jeff. That's the worst thing you could do. I really must get back to my parents."

"Of course, and I'm so happy you came to see me." Mrs. Adams showed Jess to the door. "Thank you for all you did for Carrie. I'll still worry, but at least I know why I haven't heard from her. Please, call me if you hear anything, and thank you again, Jess."

CHAPTER SIX

It was a short cab ride, and before long Leah was walking into the Ocean Front Bar and Grill. She was finally going to meet the man her Uncle Richard had talked so much about. It was the middle of the afternoon and things were a little slow. She saw a large, muscular man standing behind the bar polishing glasses. He looked up and asked, "May I help you?"

"Just wanted to check things out," Leah smiled. "I knew someone who was in the Navy. He used to tell stories about San Diego and a favorite bar and grill. I'm not sure this is the one, but it looks the way he described it." *Leah, you are getting to be quite the storyteller.* She smiled at the man. "I'm looking to make a fresh start and I wanted to check out the town."

"You don't look old enough to need a fresh start," the man told her. "My name is Joe," he added and held out a big hand for her to shake.

"I'm Leah and it's a pleasure to meet you." Leah looked around. The bar had a lot of glass, and the wood paneling had a warm glow to the finish. The long mirror hanging behind the bar reflected the light from the chandeliers. It may have been a bar, but it had a nice relaxed atmosphere. There was a separate dining room for those who wanted a quiet place to eat and visit with friends.

"So Leah, if you don't mind my asking, why do you need a fresh start?" Joe gave her a look, like he saw a lot more than the average person.

"Well, I lost my dad and I wanted to try someplace new." *Keep it simple*, Leah told herself. *The real Leah's father did die not long ago.*

"Well, I can understand that," Joe said. About that

time the phone rang and he answered it. The conversation lasted for a few minutes and then he slammed the phone down. "Damn!" he said, and then apologized to Leah. "Pardon my language."

"What's going on?" Leah couldn't help but ask.

"There is some kind of virus going around, and that was the second girl to call in. How is a guy supposed to operate a business with everyone getting sick?" Joe complained.

"Look, as I told you, I'm new in town. I've never worked a bar, but I'm reasonably intelligent and I'm here. I would be happy to help out," Leah offered.

"I'm not a real trusting guy. I'm the type who usually does a background check on all my new employees," Joe realized he was in a pinch and this girl was offering him a way out. He was usually a pretty good judge of character and he studied her for a moment. "I hope you're not going to make me regret that I trusted you?"

Leah looked him straight in the eye. "Joe, I promise you. I'm not a thief, and I really need the work. I'll do a good job and won't let you down."

Joe paused again; if she didn't work out, he wouldn't have to keep her. "It's not as if I have a lot of choices. I don't mean to sound so gruff; I really do appreciate the offer. We keep clean aprons and order books at the end of the bar."

About that time, a blonde woman came rushing in. "Ann and Aline called in sick," Joe told her. "This is Leah and we're going to give her a try. She's never worked in a bar, so I need you to show her the ropes."

Barbara motioned for Leah to follow her,

"Welcome, come on back and I'll try to give you a few tips before this place starts to get busy. It's a week night, so it shouldn't be too bad. With just the two of us we'll have plenty to do though. Grab an apron and an order book."

"Who are Ann and Aline?" Leah asked.

"Ann works the day shift. Aline usually works nights with me. Ted is the regular bartender, and our cook's name is Frank. Most of us have worked here so long we're like one big family. We keep the cash register behind the bar. We take the tab and the bartender rings it up. Joe expects a lot, but he's a great boss.

Barb shows her what she needed to do, and then Leah worked non-stop until after 11 o'clock. "If this isn't very busy, I don't know if I'll survive a busy night," she told Barbara with a laugh.

"It's hard at first, but believe it or not you do get used to it." Barbara pointed to her feet. "If Joe keeps you on, you might want to get some shoes with better support. These are the best I have found." She stuck out her foot to show off her shoes. "Comfortable shoes are a good investment. Take it from someone who has waited tables all her life. If you take care of your customers, they tip well. This is a nice place, most nights we make good money."

Joe got Leah's attention and waved her over to the bar. Ted, his regular bartender, must have been off since he had worked the bar all night.

"How did it go?" Joe asked her with a knowing grin. *She's a hard worker, but her feet must be killing her. It's hard running around on this concrete floor.*

"Do you think I might have a coke? I think I about walked my feet off," Leah said as she slid onto an empty bar stool.

"Barbara can handle it until closing. You did well for your first night." Joe passed her a coke. "If you want a job, you're hired. I will need for you to fill out some forms and get your address and Social Security information, but you can do that tomorrow. Dress code is black pants and white shirts. I don't mind tennis shoes if they are black or white, but no wild colors. If you think that you can handle the job, I'm hiring."

"I would love to work here. I'll manage the busy nights; Barbara tells me it gets easier. Thank you for giving me a chance. I don't have an address as of yet, I just got into town and I'm staying at the Super 8 Motel. If it's alright, I'll give you my address after I find an apartment." Leah was exhausted but happy to have a job.

Joe was thinking it over as Leah reached into her apron pocket where she had stashed her tips and found a couple of dollar bills. "Here, let me pay for my coke."

"You work here, so sodas and coffee are on the house," Joe volunteered. "You look bushed. Do you want me to call a cab for you?"

"That would be great." Leah looked down at her swollen feet.

Joe gave her another of his knowing looks. "I don't know what it is about you. You make me forget the rules I've always relied on," he said, thinking that it sounded like she was down on her luck. "I have an apartment upstairs. It's small, a little run down and has been vacant for quite some time. You can see it tomorrow if you want. If you think it will work out, then I'll rent to you. I'll even throw in some paint if you want to fix it up. You won't have the expense of getting back and forth to work, and it will give you a chance to get your feet under you. Your shift starts at 4 o'clock. Come in a little early and we'll take care of the paperwork, then I'll show you the apartment."

"That works for me. I'm paid up for two more nights at the motel. If I like the apartment, I can move right in," Leah told Joe. She was about ready to drop in her tracks.

"I hope I'm not going to live to regret this, girl," Joe said. "Go on and get out of here. See you tomorrow."

Leah slid off the bar stool and collected her purse from under the counter. She put her tips in an inside pocket, took off her apron, and then went back to Joe. "I promise, I'll do my best to make sure you never regret giving me this chance. This means more to me than you realize. Thanks again, Joe."

Joe nodded at her as he saw the cab lights pulling up outside and told her, "Your ride is here."

Leah called goodbye, gave a wave to Barbara and then walked out the door.

On the ride back to the motel, Leah thought about the night. *If I take this apartment I won't need a car.* She remembered the beautiful convertible she had abandoned in Memphis. *It was in Jeff's name; I hope he's found it by now.* She was tired but she had a pocket full of tips. *With my salary and tips, I should do alright. If that apartment isn't a real dump, I'll take it. I don't need much. I can save, in case I have to run again. That's a terrible thought. My feet are swollen from all the traveling I've done in the past week. After working tonight they really hurt. I don't know if I could run again; it might be simpler to let Jeff shoot me.*

The cab pulled in at the motel. Leah paid the driver, got out, and went to her room. She carefully locked the door and fell onto the bed.

The next morning, Leah got up around 8 a.m. She had never been one to sleep in. She took a shower and dressed in another pair of black slacks and a white top. *Since this is to be my work uniform, I need to buy some more clothes. Maybe I can find a nice resale shop. I am going to take Barbara's suggestion and find some better shoes.*

Leah checked out the lobby; they served a free breakfast. She ate, called for another cab and headed back to the bar. As she walked in she noticed a woman behind the bar. She smiled and held out her hand. "I'm Leah, is Joe around?"

"My name is Maggie. You must be the new girl; it's nice to meet you. I'm glad Joe hired you; the help is getting a little sparse around here. Joe is in his office, it's through there," she told her, pointing to a door. "Welcome!" she added.

"It is nice to meet you, Maggie," Leah said. She found the small office, knocked, and entered when she heard Joe call out to her.

"I didn't know what time you would make it. Fill out these forms so you can get paid, and then we'll go check out the apartment."

"Good morning to you too," Leah said, making note that he hadn't offered a greeting.

So she's a smart ass, Joe thought and gave her another one of his puzzled looks. *She is so familiar, she's got to be related to someone I know*. "Sorry, good morning! Here are the forms. I wasn't expecting you in quite so early."

"I'm used to getting up fairly early. I almost never

sleep in, and I couldn't wait to see the apartment." Leah saw Joe's serious expression, sat down and began filling out the forms. "I know you told me not to expect much, but I'm excited just the same."

Joe shook his head, a smile playing on his lips. "You're a real eager beaver," he teased. "I hope you're not disappointed with the job or the apartment."

"I just like to know where I stand, even though it was hard standing on my feet, no pun intended," Leah laughed, "I enjoyed working here. As to the apartment, I don't need much. If I stay upstairs then I won't need to worry about a car. I like that idea, no payment, and no insurance."

"Come on then," Joe said and led her out a back door to a staircase. "It's well lit," Joe explained as he pointed to the lights and security cameras covering the parking lot. "This is where the employees park. It's safe; I haven't had any problems." As Joe climbed the stairs, he pointed out two double-wide windows across the back. "There are windows across the back as well as the front. It gives the apartment a lot of natural light."

Inside the door was a short hallway. "The apartment is here on the right," he said. "I have a laundry room on my side and I use the rest for storage. The restaurant kitchen isn't as large as I would like, so I use the extra space up here."

They entered the apartment. It was a long, narrow room with a galley-style kitchen across one end. It was painted a hideous color, almost mustard yellow.

"You did say something about new paint, right?" Leah asked, wondering who picked out the color.

"Yes, it is pretty ugly, isn't it?" Joe said, "Other

than the color, what do you think?"

"I'm assuming there's a bathroom. Let me go check it out." Leah walked down the hallway. She saw that the bathroom was small, with a pedestal sink and claw-foot tub. It was old, but the finish on the fixtures was in good shape and there was also a shower over the tub. As a whole, there wasn't anything that some paint and elbow grease wouldn't fix. Beyond the bath she found a small bedroom, but what instantly claimed her attention were the two large windows opposite the bed. *That will make this room all light and airy. I can just see it with potted plants on the wide window sills,* she thought. Looking down at the floors, she could tell they were once a nice hardwood. Currently, they were pretty beat up and needed refinishing in the worst way.

Leah came back down the hall, ready to discuss terms. In the living area she got a surprise when she looked out the two large windows. She hadn't noticed before, but beyond the building at the edge of the employee parking lot she could see the ocean. There was a ship on the horizon. It looked small and far away. She instantly fell in love; she had never lived close to the ocean, and it was hard not to seem excited. She tried to keep her cool. "Joe, if you'll let me paint, then that will make everything look clean and fresh. I don't know what to do about the floors but I'll figure something out. Someday, will you put washer and dryer connections in for me? For now I just want some wall paint and enamel. I hope you'll let me paint the kitchen cabinets, along with the table and chairs to match. All the leather sofa and chair need are a good cleaning."

"Are you sure you're not biting off more than you can chew, girl?" Joe asked. "To be honest, I didn't remember the apartment being in such bad shape."

"You aren't going to change your mind, are you?" Leah couldn't bear to lose the apartment.

"No." Joe shook his head. "If you want it, I won't go back on my word."

"Good, it's a decent size and I definitely want it. With a couple of gallons of paint I can make this place look nice, and I love the windows."

Joe liked Leah's attitude. "Alright girl, let's go buy some paint. About the washer and dryer, I have a set in the storage area. I wash the bar towels and table linens up here. You're welcome to use that."

"That's wonderful, I'll keep everything done up for you. It's the least I can do since you're allowing me to use the washer and dryer. "

Joe liked that she had offered to help. "I need to check the hot water tank to make sure it's still working. Since I didn't realize this place was going to take so much work, I'll see if I can find someone to help you. I have a friend who does remodeling. I'll ask him what he thinks about the floors."

Leah was thrilled. "Thanks Joe." He looked like a big teddy bear; he even growled on occasion, but she liked him. On impulse, she gave Joe a big hug. Things were looking up.

"Can I go with you to the hardware store?" Leah knew she would love to pick out the paint.

"Sure, you're the one who's going to be living here," Joe told her. "You need to be the one to pick out the paint colors. You don't want me doing it after seeing the color of this living room. Maybe the paint changed color, because I don't believe even I would pick out something this ugly."

"I should get some cleaning supplies. Do we have time before I go to work?" Leah was so excited that she didn't want to wait another minute.

"I already have that stuff. Get what you need from the bar. It's in a storage closet near my office. We should be able to go to the store before your shift starts," Joe told her.

"Great! I can't believe it, my first day in town and I have a home." Leah was so excited she almost danced out of the apartment and down the stairs.

"We should have you ready to move in by next week," Joe said.

"No way," Leah told him. "I'll be out of that motel tomorrow. It's too expensive."

"You can't move in that soon," Joe explained. "The place is a mess."

"Nothing a mop, soap, and water won't fix. With that and a little elbow grease, that apartment will shine. Come on, Joe, I'll clean the bathroom and air out the bed. That's all I have at the motel. If I stay here, I won't be spending all that time running back and forth in a cab. It'll be fine." Leah looked at him, begging him to understand.

"Come on, then. If you're going to move in, we need to get cracking."

Getting into Joe's car, Leah looked up at the apartment. *It doesn't look like much now, but it will be great. When I'm finished it will look fresh, and with those windows cleaned it'll be like a whole different place. Joe may be a grouch but he has a good heart. He's giving me a chance at a new life.*

On the way to the hardware store, Leah knew they didn't have a lot of time. *I'll look for a seashells border to go around the kitchen cabinets. When I get a chance to go to the beach, I can collect some real seashells. White walls will make the living area look larger. I want blue paint for the bedroom and bath. I'll need pillows and towels, maybe in a print. I can see plants in the windows. The window sills are wide, and they'll be a perfect place to set flowers, or maybe herbs.*

Once they arrived at the hardware store, Joe was surprised that Leah picked out everything she wanted in just one pass. The entire trip didn't take over 30 minutes. Once back at the apartment, they carried the paint and supplies up the stairs.

Setting the paint cans down in a corner, Joe stood looking around and thought, *I really didn't know it was this bad.* He looked over and saw that Leah was wearing a wide smile. She was so excited, and Joe shook his head in wonder. He asked himself, *"Women, are they all nesters?"*

Leah looked at Joe. "As soon as my shift is over, I'm coming back up here to sweep and get it ready to mop in the morning."

"There's no need to rush. Besides, you'll feel different after working all night," Joe said. He couldn't get over how willing she was to fix things up. He wouldn't let anyone live in such a mess, and he felt responsible. *It's my apartment and she'll be paying me rent.*

Leah didn't want to go back to the motel but she had paid for another night. She was up early the next morning and checked out of the motel before heading for her new home. She could hardly wait. She grabbed cleaning supplies and scrubbed down the bathroom. Next, she aired out the bed. She was just starting on the kitchen when Barbara popped in.

"Joe says you're moving in! I have a pillow, some

sheets, and an extra coffee pot I can lend you." Barbara told her. "You can use them until you get a chance to go get some of your own. Boy, this place is a mess."

"Wait until I get done with it. It's going to be beautiful," Leah assured her.

Barbara helped her make the bed, and then it was time for them to get to work. They made it through their shift, and after saying good night Leah climbed the stairs for her first night in her own apartment.

Leah woke up, anxious to get started. Her legs didn't want to cooperate however. Muscles aching and feet swollen, she staggered into the kitchen and made a pot of coffee. Carrying her first cup back to the bed, she fluffed up the pillow and climbed back in. She sat there sipping coffee and waiting for the caffeine to kick in.

Finding herself more alert now that her cup was empty, Leah put on her old sweats and went to work. She scrubbed down the kitchen cabinets, then went over and opened up the first can of paint, stirring it until it was well mixed. Filling up her roller with paint, she began painting the wall, starting at the front door.

Leah had barely started when she heard a knock. Opening the door she found Ted standing there. "Good morning." He sounded so chipper.

"What are you doing here?" Leah asked, sounding a little grouchy. The last thing she needed was someone taking up her precious time.

"Not just me. Barbara's on her way up. Joe sent us to help you paint," Ted answered. "Looks like someone didn't get much sleep."

"I did stay up later than I should. You don't have

to do this just because Joe sent you. I'm capable of fixing up this place on my own," Leah explained, not wanting to impose on anyone.

"Well, you don't know Joe; what he says goes. We're here to work, and work we will," Ted told her. He winked, letting her know he wasn't mad.

"Joe is persistent, that's for sure. It might take me longer by myself, but I can do this." Leah was wondering what to do.

"May I come in?" Ted asked. "Or are we going to stand here all day arguing?"

"Oh, sorry Ted," Leah gave in and moved out of the doorway. "There's another roller over there, help yourself."

Ted rolled up his sleeves, picked up an extra roller and began stroking paint onto the next wall.

About that time Barbara peeked in the door. She had her arms full and she looked at Ted. "Why did you run off? I needed help carrying all this stuff up the stairs."

"What stuff?" Leah asked. She watched as Barb laid sack after sack down on the snack bar.

"It's wallpaper border. It's some my husband and I had left over when we redecorated our place. You may not want it, but it's here just in case. I hate that I can only help out one day. My mother is good to watch my daughters while I'm at work, but I hate to ask her for extra time."

"Thanks for bringing the border. I'll look it over later. Today's fine; I wasn't expecting anyone to help at all. I'm sure you have busy lives," Leah said.

"Do you have an extra roller?" Barbara asked.

"Yes ma'am, right there by your sacks," Leah answered. "No wonder Joe insisted I have extra rollers. He planned to recruit volunteers." Within minutes they were all three painting away. Leah noticed how fast they both were and was glad that Joe sent them. She couldn't help but ask about Joe, and even though Ted was reluctant to discuss him, Barbara wasn't.

Barb freely told Leah, "Joe's a really nice guy. He's the best boss I've ever had. He has trust issues though. I assume you've noticed."

"You can't miss it, but I really like him! What's Maggie's story?" Leah couldn't help but be curious.

"She's like the bar downstairs; she's always been here. Maggie was best friends with Joe's wife, Mary. She died of leukemia a few years ago. I think Frank is the one who introduced the two of them. They married kind of late in life. I guess that's why they never had kids. Frank and Joe have been friends since their Navy days. When Joe first opened up, he brought Frank in as cook. Mary and Maggie both waited tables. Mary got sick so she had to quit, and Maggie wanted to slow down so Joe put her to tending bar. Days are slower and that suits her. Joe's had a rough go of it. I don't know what I would do if I lost my husband."

"Alright, you two, that's enough gossip for today. I'm finished with my wall and it's almost time for our shifts to start." Ted started cleaning paint off his roller.

Barbara looked down at her watch, "You're right, Ted. We'd better get this paint cleaned up and get down to the bar. Leah, I brought my clothes with me. If you don't mind, I'd like to shower in your bathroom."

"That's fine with me, Barb, we'll take turns. You know, it seems like we just got started and it's already time to quit. I appreciate your help. The living area's done." Leah thought that getting to know Ted and Barb was a bonus.

The next day Ted was back, helping Joe check out the hot water tank. It was in good shape, but then they found out that refrigerator wasn't cooling, "I'll make arrangements for a new one." Joe told them.

After Joe left, Ted and Leah finished painting the hallway and bathroom. Later, as Leah started down the stairs, ready for her shift, she met Louie and Lois. The cook and waitress from the morning shift had already put in a day's work. They had to be tired, and Leah was of the opinion that it wasn't fair for Joe to draft them.

"We thought we would paint the cabinets," Louie offered. "Joe said something about doing the table and chairs in the same enamel. Do you want us to do them while we're at it?"

"That would be great, but aren't the two of you tired after working all morning?" Leah asked.

"We had a slow morning and we want to help." Louie told her.

"It will be fun," Lois added.

"Your idea of fun is a little strange," Leah told them with a laugh. "Thank you both for your help, it means a lot."

At the end of Leah's shift she was pleasantly surprised. The painting was almost done. I'll start on my bedroom tomorrow, she thought.

The next morning, Leah began painting early and she had her bedroom finished before noon. I'll have enough time to go shopping tomorrow. I want to buy towels, sheets and a blanket. I need to return the things Barb loaned me, she might need them.

On the fourth day Leah got up around eleven. With the painting done, she visited a neighborhood resale shop. In the window were some dishes with a pale blue design. She also found a beautiful bedspread and some throw pillows. Leah brought the dishes home, washed them, and put them on the freshly painted shelves in the kitchen. The bedspread was still in the plastic cover; it looked new, and was perfect on her bed. The apartment was really coming together. It's amazing what you can find in resale shops. I guess the Navy families get rid of things so they don't have to move them.

When Leah went in to work, Joe told her, "I've set it up with my friend. He's going to refinish the floors. It will take a day to sand, a day to varnish, and two days for the varnish to dry. I don't like putting you out, but you'll need to stay at the motel until it's finished." Remembering she might be short of money, he added "I'll foot the bill."

Leah responded, "You don't have to do that, Joe."

"It's my apartment," Joe said. "You're paying rent so you shouldn't have to pay for a motel."

By the end of the week, Joe knew the varnish should be dry so he decided to go check. Using his spare key, he let himself into the apartment. Opening the door, he was surprised. Leah was right; cleaning and a coat of paint worked wonders. The floor gleamed in the sun coming from the windows and they looked new again. I'm glad that girl landed here. The customers really like her and she's a good worker. I like having her around, he told himself. Closing the door behind him, he walked away with a feeling of pride.

CHAPTER SEVEN

Leah was sitting in a wing-backed chair she had rescued from a secondhand store. The print was a bit faded, but it was perfect sitting by the living room windows overlooking the bay. She had been in her apartment for almost a week. Ted was turning into a good friend. He helped a lot when she was working on the apartment, and he always seemed to turn up when she needed a strong back to help her lift something. She thought he had a boyfriend. Maybe that should shock her since she had never known anyone who was gay, but he was a nice guy and that was all that counted. She looked at her watch; it was time to go to work.

Leah walked into the back door of the bar just as Frank was taking a large pan of fish out of the oven. "Something smells great," she said as she walked through the kitchen.

"I'm trying something different," Frank explained. "Come taste it and tell me what you think."

Leah walked over and accepted the plate Frank offered to her. "This is wonderful," she said after tasting the fish filet. "You aren't going to stick it between two pieces of bread, are you?" She teased.

Leah had gotten to know the staff and was starting to feel at home. She went into the bar area and collected a clean apron and her order book. As usual, Joe was sitting at the end of the bar drinking a cup of coffee. A nice looking man was setting next to him.

"Leah, I want you to meet one of San Diego's finest," Joe called to her. "Leah Scott, this is a friend of mine, Steve Burke."

Leah watched as the tall, muscular man got up from the bar stool. He had dark hair, but what struck her first were his blue eyes. They were the color of the ocean. He also had an easy smile. "Leah, it's a pleasure to meet you," he said in a deep, soft-spoken voice. He looked at her with those compelling blue eyes and it was as if he saw all the way to her soul.

"It's nice to meet you," Leah said, still looking into his eyes. "You're a police officer?"

"Steve is a homicide detective with the San Diego Police Department," Joe explained to Leah. Joe turned to Steve. "Leah is the newest member of my staff and she's new to the San Diego area."

"Gentlemen, go back to your coffee. Does anyone need a refill?" Leah asked. She moved behind the bar to get the coffee pot. *Steve Burke is one fine looking man*, she thought. *Too bad I'm not in the market.* Russ and Jeff had taught her that men were more trouble than they were worth. If she ever let another one into her life, it would be far in the future. Not to mention, how many years before she could be sure Jeff would not come crawling out of the woodwork? Leah refilled the men's coffee cups and moved out onto the floor. It was time to get to work.

Things were a little slow, even though Wednesday was Karaoke night, there hadn't been a lot of customers stepping up to the mic. Everything was winding down, and it was Leah's turn to go home early. She dropped her apron in the clothes hamper and put her order pad under the counter. She had always liked to sing and had a pretty fair voice, so she stopped by the D.J.'s table and asked if he had the old Billy Joel song "Just the Way You Are". She stepped up to the mic and started the opening lines of the old ballad; "Don't go changing to try to please me; I never wanted you that way." As she ended the song with the line "I love you just the way you are," the room broke out in applause. She smiled, thanked the crowd, and started for the back door.

"It seems you are a lady of many talents," Joe said, as she passed him.

"It was fun. I hope it was okay, since it was at the end of my shift," Leah answered.

"The customers seemed to like it, and I know I did." Joe looked into her eyes. "What did you think of Steve?"

A suspicious thought crowded into Leah's mind. *Was Joe matchmaking? I might as well nip that in the bud,* she thought. "I go for older men," she told him with a smile. "I'm holding out for my boss. If I can't have him, I won't accept second best." She turned and started once more for the door.

"The boss is old enough to be your father, or maybe your grandfather. I have a feeling you are trying to tell me to mind my own business," Joe said as she opened the door.

"I love you Joe, but mind your own business," Leah laughed as she went out the door.

Under the glow of a full moon, she climbed the stairs to her apartment. She loved coming home to the clean smell. No matter how tired she was, she felt a sense of peace when she walked in the door. She went into the living room without turning on the lights, kicked off her shoes, and slid into her favorite chair. She looked out at the harbor lights in the distance. From that far away, the view looked like a soft painting, with the moonlight giving everything a soft glow.

Alone In the silence of the apartment, she could hear the faint echo of music from downstairs. The image of Steve Burke came to her mind. She thought back to her time with Jeff and remembered him bringing her a book on flowers. She had spent hours poring through it and dreamed of the flower garden she would plant when they got married. Being with him had been such a farce. *I'm not a good judge of men. I'm making friends, and I don't need some hot-looking Casanova screwing up all I've accomplished.* She walked into the bedroom, took off her work clothes, pulled on her gown, and crawled into bed. *I didn't realize how tired I was,* were her last thoughts before sleep claimed her.

Leah was awake and had just poured a glass of OJ when she heard a light tapping on the door. She belted her robe before opening the door. There stood Joe with a frown on his face. "I didn't knock very loud; I didn't want to wake you if you were still sleeping."

"What's up, my friend?" Leah turned and walked into the kitchen. "I haven't made coffee yet. I swear, I think you main-line the stuff. Do you want some orange juice?"

Joe climbed onto a bar stool. "No, I never drink the stuff unless it has vodka in it."

"Sorry, I don't have vodka. Come to think of it, I've never seen you drink anything but coffee." Leah stood across the bar from Joe, drinking her juice.

"This isn't something I get into very often. Why do I seem to find myself telling you things?" Joe shook his head, and continued. "A few years ago, after my wife died, I found myself getting a little too fond of the hard stuff. I wasn't an alcoholic, but I was staying drunk most of the time. Mary had just died and I told myself that it was to dull the pain, and there was a lot of pain. God, I loved that woman. She was my other half and I didn't know if I could go on without her. On a lot of days I didn't even know if I wanted to go on. One day I took a long, hard look at myself. I was drunk most of the time and the truth was, Mary would have been ashamed of what I had become, so I decided to cut out the booze. I have a beer once in a while, but that's about it. Leah, about what you said last night, you were joking, right?"

Leah laughed, knowing instantly he was referring to her parting comment. "Had you worried, did I? Of course I was joking! Look Joe, I like you a lot and I think we've become good friends. I just walked away from a very bad situation. It's not something I really want to talk about, but I realized that I make bad choices when it comes to relationships. I've decided to swear off men, at least romantically. Maybe in the next 10 or 20 years I'll have matured enough that I can trust my own judgment."

"That's a long time," Joe smiled. "I wanted to be sure we were alright. It seems we walked into a very rare friendship. It's like we've known each for a very long time." Joe shook his head. "I don't understand it, but I'm beginning to accept it."

"Let me slip into some sweats and I'll make us a pot of coffee and some breakfast." Leah turned toward the bedroom.

"I had another reason for coming up," Joe told her before she could walk out of the kitchen. "Besides, some of us have already had breakfast. Come sit with me a minute and then I will leave you to your coffee."

As Leah settled on the bar stool next to Joe, he started to talk. "You said something the other day about learning to tend bar, and I've noticed you seem have a head for business. I've got people who have been with me a lot longer then you. Good people, but they don't have your way with numbers. You're young, have you thought about your future? What do you want to do with your life?"

"I've been thinking about that," Leah told him. "I like the bar and I like working with numbers and people. I've thought about taking some on-line accounting courses. I don't think I'd like to go to school full time; I guess that leaves out brain surgery."

They both laughed.

"Would you consider taking on more responsibility at the bar?" Joe continued. "Ted and I will teach you to work the bar; there are times I need the extra help. Would you be interested in coming in a little early on Mondays and Thursdays? Ted is good at ordering the liquor but not that good with numbers. I'll tell him I want to train you for backup. You can learn to place orders and keep an eye on his arithmetic at the same time. If this works out, maybe you will want to take on more. I'm not getting any younger and I may need an assistant manager someday. I think you have a lot of potential. Do you want to give it a try?"

Tears gathered in Leah's eyes before she could brush them away. She leaned over and gave Joe a kiss on the cheek. "Thanks Joe, I would love to give it a try. Just promise me, no more matchmaking. Okay?"

"No more matchmaking, at least not for another 10 or 20 years," Joe said, with a laugh. He got up and walked to the door, and then paused, turning back to

Leah. "Oh, by the way, since this is Thursday, come on down when you can and we'll get you started. Ted will be placing the order for this weekend. No time like the present to see what you're getting into. Shake a leg, girl," he said, and with a wave was out the door.

Sometimes Joe said something that reminded Leah of Ed. She missed the ole coot. What was that line from the old television show? "I love it when a plan comes together." Time to get dressed and go downstairs; life was looking good.

Ted was behind the bar and Joe was sitting at his customary spot when Leah came down. Ted smiled and said, "I hear you're going to learn to keep bar? We're going to do inventory and see what we need for the weekend. Joe says he wants you to learn everything. I went to Bartending School, I'll see if I have any of my old books lying around. Otherwise, you will just have to learn from the master." Ted hooked his thumbs through imaginary suspenders.

Joe looked up and told Ted, "Check on a substitute for the whiskey you've been using to mix Manhattans. The distributor has raised the price. Let's see if we can change brands without changing the taste. I prefer not to have to raise the price we charge."

"Sure," Ted answered. He pulled out a preprinted inventory sheet and showed it to Leah. "This is what we keep in stock," he told her. "We'll see what is in our inventory and that will tell us what we need to order. Are you ready to go upstairs?"

"What do you mean Joe, about finding a different brand of whiskey?" Leah asked.

"Whiskey is just like corn or peaches. Several

companies make them and most pretty much taste the same. A brand you recognize probably costs more, while the next brand on the shelf may be cheaper. That's the reason I asked Ted to check. If we stick to the brand we're using, I am going to have to go up on the price," Joe explained.

"It sounds like there's more to bar tending than just getting someone a beer and mixing drinks," Leah commented.

"That there is," Joe told her. "As Ted told you, some people go to school. I learned by trial and error. You make too many mistakes and you learn the hard way; you lose money."

Leah and Ted finished their inventory and Ted showed Leah how to compare what they had in inventory to what they would need for the weekend. Then he took her upstairs to check the stock from the storage room. After that, they went back down the stairs and checked in with Joe.

"If I keep a record of Ted's inventory sheets, I can see a pattern. That gives me a good idea how much stock we need to keep," Joe said. "If we start running short, then I have Ted up the order. You can't make money if you don't have what the customers want, and I try to keep plenty in inventory." He wanted Leah to know what to look for. There was a fine balance between keeping the bar well stocked and having too much stock.

It occurred to Leah that she might need to go to school to learn accounting, but Joe was going to teach her to run a bar. Firsthand experience was the best teacher. "What's next?" Leah asked.

"Have Ted let you call in the order, and then get Frank to fix you something to eat. I know by how quickly you got down here that Miss Eager Beaver didn't take time to eat." Joe smiled. He seemed to smile more with Leah around.

Turning, Joe saw Steve enter the bar. "Are you taking an early dinner?"

"I caught a case and missed lunch," Steve said as he slid onto a bar stool. "How's the new girl working out?"

"She's doing great. Don't go looking in that direction, boy. The lady is a little gun shy," Joe answered.

"Anything worth having is worth waiting for. Besides, cops go slowly. Gives a lady time to know what she's signing on for. The police force and the Navy are hard on the ladies." Steve looked around. "Is she here?"

"Mary, God rest her soul, spent a lot of lonely months when I was deployed. The Navy wives had a support group, and cops' wives probably do the same thing. It's not easy knowing your man is in harm's way. When I bought this place I thought we would have all the time in the world, spend the rest of our lives growing old together. Now, I'm the one alone," Joe said.

They turned as Leah and Ted came back into the bar. Leah was carrying a plate and a glass of tea.

"Come join us," Joe told Leah. "Ted, I think Steve would like to see a menu."

"Whatever Leah is having, it certainly smells good. Maybe I could try that," Steve answered.

"This is a new item Frank's trying. He made grilled fish with rice pilaf. Here, take mine and I'll go get another one." Leah answered.

"No, you sit down and eat; you're going to be working and you need your energy." Steve pulled out a seat for Leah.

Joe motioned for Ted to take Steve's order. Leah would have preferred to eat her meal without Mr. Hunk to distract her. *Down girl,* she told her hormones. *You've sworn off men, remember?* Why couldn't she have met someone like Steve first? *Two bad relationships did not make a girl feel confidant.*

The group fell into an easy conversation. Joe asked, "Steve, are you still doing some volunteer work out at Seal Beach Wildlife Reserve?"

Steve was quick to tell them about the latest project he had helped with. He talked about the giant sea turtles that had almost been wiped out. "We don't have nesting sites this far north. I helped out at a nesting site in Florida once though. It's fun to guard those little fellows as they hatch out. They take off the instant they hatch and head straight for the ocean like they have some kind of homing device planted inside. We try to keep the birds away and give them a chance to reach the water's edge. I guess every little bit helps, since the population is growing."

Steve had captured Leah's attention. "Oh, that sounds like fun. What do you do here in California?" She asked.

"We catch them, tag them, and keep a file on weight and health. Next time I go out, I'll give you a call. Maybe you can go with me," Steve told her.

"That sounds nice, but I stay pretty busy." She stood, collected the dishes and turned toward the kitchen. "Thank you for asking."

When Leah was out of sight, Steve turned to Joe. "That is about the most polite brush off I have ever gotten."

"I told you," Joe said. "I don't know the details but she's definitely gun shy."

Steve paid for his lunch. "Tell Frank I really enjoyed the fish. It's time I went back to work."

Joe had a knowing look on his face when Leah returned to start her shift. "Not one word," she told him.

Joe smiled, "I think the lady protests too much. I won't say a word about how much a certain cop seems to like her."

Leah ignored him and started her shift. Joe could tell that she and Steve were attracted to one another. *If it's meant to be, it will work out. Steve needs someone like my Mary, and Leah just might be that someone. I promised no matchmaking, but that doesn't mean I can't give them a little push in the right direction. Watching those two is going to be fun*, Joe thought.

Days went by and Steve dropped in more often, then suddenly he was a regular. He was there for lunch almost daily and each time he asked Leah to do something special with him. Steve found at least a dozen things that he thought Leah might like to see or do, and Leah politely declined each and every suggestion. Joe couldn't help but be amused, and he added his two cents at every opportunity. He tried to help Steve, but Leah had gotten very good at politely declining Steve's invitations.

Joe didn't know it, but Leah couldn't shake the idea that maybe she should give Steve a chance. He was nice, and so very handsome. It was circling around in the back of her head like a merry-go-round. That merry-go-round kept turning and she jumped off, running away as if she didn't want to ride. In reality, she wanted it so bad she could taste it. *To live a normal life, have a man I could love and respect, maybe a couple of kids. It sounds wonderful but I'm afraid try. I thought I could be happy living alone, browsing the small shops around town and working. But it isn't enough. My life seems so empty. It's flattering to have a man like Steve show an interest in getting to know me.*

One night when things were slow, Leah took a quick break with Barbara. "Barb, what do you know about Steve?"

"He's a really sweet guy," Barbara answered. I've noticed he's coming around a lot more lately. I think he likes you. Are you interested?"

"Earlier today, Steve asked me to go out to the refuge center with him. This isn't the first time he's asked. I'm reluctant to accept though."

"If it was me and I wasn't married…" Barbara smiled. "Like my mama always said, I wouldn't let the screen door hit me in the ass! If I was single I would jump at the chance to go out with him. He's handsome, reliable, and takes his job seriously. I do know that you'll not find a better man. Look at you, you sit up in that apartment and read books. Life is passing you by and you need to do something about that."

"My last relationship ended when I discovered he was a louse," Leah explained. "I'm not a good judge of character. I can't afford to choose the wrong man again; the price you have to pay is too high. I've sworn off men."

"Big deal!" Barbara wasn't buying it. "You don't have to marry the guy; just go out and have a little fun. It's nice dating a man who appreciates a woman, and by the looks that man gives you, he definitely likes what he sees. That man I married is into whatever makes me happy, that's why I love him so much."

"The men I've dated were into what they could get." The look on Leah's face told Barbara how afraid she was.

"I don't think Steve is like the other men you've dated. I've never seen any signs that he's a user. No, I still say he's one of the good guys." Barbara gave Leah a bright smile.

"Think so, huh?" Leah wanted to believe her.

"I do, and I personally think you would be foolish not to take him up on his offer," Barbara encouraged.

"I'm thinking about it." Leah turned and checked the bar for customers. "We'd better get back to work or Joe will wonder what happened to us."

Later that night Leah found herself making a decision. *The next time Steve asks, I'm going to accept. It's time to get out of the rut I'm in.*

The next day, Leah was anxious to see Steve. She couldn't wait for the lunch crowd to come in and she found herself watching the door, but he didn't show. *Drat that man! Just when I made up my mind to play ball, he's a no show.*

The evening passed in slow motion. Most of the customers had left for the night, and it was time to start cleaning up and getting things ready for tomorrow. To her surprise, Steve came walking in the door just before closing. He didn't even look her way, just headed straight up to the bar and claimed the stool next to Joe.

Joe gave his normal greeting. It was easy to tell by

the expression on Steve's face that he had a lot on his mind. "What will you have?" Joe asked.

"I need a shot of whiskey," Steve said. "No, make that a double."

That told it all, Joe thought and poured him 3 ounces.

Steve gulped down the liquor and pushed the glass back to Joe.

Without saying a word Joe poured the second drink, then put the glass in front of Steve.

Steve took a sip before saying, "We had a particularly bad homicide today."

"That's rough," Joe responded, wondering what it was all about. He knew Steve couldn't tell him much, not as long as there was an ongoing investigation. "Want something to eat?" Joe asked.

"No, I grabbed a sandwich earlier. I just need to unwind. It's always hard, finding some kid dead who had her whole life ahead of her." Steve answered.

"How old was she?" Joe asked.

"A teenager; this is our second in the past three weeks." You could hear the sadness in Steve's voice.

"Got any leads?" Joe asked.

"Not a one. No DNA, no fingerprints, no nothing, just dead bodies." Steve looked like he had just about reached the end of his rope.

"That's tough. They give the case to you?" *They would be smart if they did*, Joe thought.

"No, so far it's been San Mateo County, at least until 10 o'clock this morning. Another girl was found, and we're assuming by the size of the entry wound that the same caliber gun was used. She was killed assassin style, with a single shot to the forehead. It sounds like these kids were running drugs. The way they were killed, it's the only thing that makes sense. They must have known too much and wanted out. It's not my case, but I'll be helping out." The tone of Steve's voice told the story.

"That's hard to take, finding a young girl like that." Joe couldn't imagine how Steve dealt with such tragedy.

"Fishermen spotted her. At first they thought it was a seal resting on the shoreline. When they got close enough, they realized it was a person and called it in. I've been there all day. I've never understood what it takes to make some sick bastard do such a thing." Steve finished his whiskey and pushed the glass away.

"Me neither. You need another one of those?" Joe asked. He hoped Steve would decline, and he did with a shake of his head.

Leah approached the two men. She sensed the tension in the air. "Anything wrong?" she inquired.

"Don't mind me," Steve answered. "Bad day; sometimes being a cop sucks."

"Sometimes life in general sucks," Leah answered. "Anything I can do to help?"

"No." Steve put some money down on the bar. "It's about closing time, I think I am going to head out. I'm beat."

"Steve, wait a minute. I know this is a bad time. On your next visit to the Reserve, could I go with you?" Leah hoped it wasn't too late to ask.

Steve smiled. "That would be great. It may be a few days, but I'll give you a call." He turned and pushed open the door, feeling good in spite of all that had happened. "Have a good night," he called out as he left.

In a world where everything seemed to be in the crapper, sometimes something good slipped in.

CHAPTER EIGHT

Leah looked over at Joe. "What's going on with Steve?"

Joe didn't want to scare Leah so he didn't go into detail. "It's his job. Hey, I thought you had sworn off men?" he chuckled lightheartedly.

"I knew you'd throw that back at me." Leah shrugged.

"I didn't mean it like that," Joe explained, "but I believe you've done the right thing. There's no law that says a girl can't change her mind."

"I've never seen green sea turtles before. That's the only reason I'm encouraging him." Leah smiled, took off her apron, and marched towards the back door. "See you tomorrow."

"Leah, I've never heard you lie to other people; don't start by lying to yourself," Joe cautioned.

She giggled and then closed the back door behind her.

Going up the outside stairs, Leah realized that she was usually worn out after her shift, but tonight that wasn't the case. Wearing a smile on her face, she thought, *I can't wait to go out to the Reserve. Steve is an interesting man and I hope we can be friends.* Leah had made some friends, but she was afraid to share too much, afraid she might give something away. She thought of Joe's parting remark. *If he knew all the things I've kept from him. I'd like to be able to offer Steve more than friendship. Maybe someday,* she told herself.

Entering the apartment, Leah changed into her nightgown and sat down in her favorite chair. She looked out the window at all the streetlights shining in the distance. *I feel like a teenager. You would think I'd never been on a date before. Barb's right, it's time I rejoin the land of the living and get on with my life. After all, that's why I created a new one. It's been a long time since I had any fun.* Leah got up, went to bed, and fell asleep thinking about Steve.

That next day at noon, Steve was a no show. Leah couldn't help wondering why, until she caught a glimpse of the newspaper lying on Joe's desk. The headline said it all; 'Teenage Girl Found Dead,' and she instantly thought, *Except for the age, that could have been me.* A shiver of fear went rushing through her body. *Are Jeff and his men still looking for me? Calm down, they're looking for Carrie. I've got a different name and I've covered my tracks. Jeff is halfway across the country. There's no way he can trace me.*

Coming back from the restroom, Joe saw Leah standing and staring at the newspaper. It didn't seem like three months since Leah had walked into the bar. He'd already read the newspaper story. "That girl lived in another county. Someone dumped her body in Steve's jurisdiction. There were two other girls before her and that's why he was so upset last night. Don't worry, he'll find whoever killed her. He's a good cop." Joe thought what he said should have taken that worried look off Leah's face but it didn't. *What the heck has happened to my girl that this would be so upsetting to her?* He sat back down in his desk chair thinking. *Someday she'll open up. We're getting closer every day.*

"I feel sorry for those girls' parents," Leah told Joe.

"Me too," Joe replied with sadness in his voice.

Leah picked up her clipboard. "I'd better get started. I have an order to call in."

She was terrified and hoping that it didn't show. Leaving Joe's office, she made her way upstairs. In the storage area across the hall from her apartment, she started counting bottles, hoping that the inventory would take her mind off her troubles. She was also having second thoughts about going out with Steve. *If I get involved with him, he might see too much. After all, he is a cop! He's trained to pick up on things. If Jeff finds me and Steve gets in the way, Jeff will kill him. If only I could tell Steve. Could he keep me safe and help me bring Jeff to justice? I've covered* my tracks *and my trail ended in Mexico City, unless… I never checked on Jennifer. I wonder if she's back in Memphis.*

Leah finished her inventory and went back to Joe's office. It was empty, and sitting on Joe's desk was his computer. He'd told her a million times that she could use it. She got online and found the number of the bar across from the Peabody Hotel in Memphis, Tennessee. One quick phone call; nobody would have a reason to trace it.

When a voice answered Leah asked, "Does Jennifer Anderson still come in there and play pool?"

"Nah," the man answered. "It was in all the papers. The chick took a vacation to Mexico and was killed by a hit-and-run driver. Who knew she could even afford a trip like that? I sure didn't."

"Thank you." Leah uttered the words and then quickly hung up the phone. *I should go to the library tomorrow and use their computer. I don't want Joe to catch me reading old newspaper clippings about Memphis. That man said it was in all the papers. Did Jeff have anything to do with that hit-and-run? If he had her killed, maybe the newspaper will shed some light on what happened.* Upset and wondering if she had put the girl in harm's way, Leah lowered her head. Dear God, if I caused her death please forgive me, she prayed.

Finding out Jennifer was dead hit Leah hard. This proved that life was fragile. *I'll go out to the Reserve with Steve. I'm not dead yet and I'm tired of acting like I am. I'm going to enjoy life while I have the chance. I'm not giving up that easy; I want to live and I will fight for that right.* Leah picked up the phone and placed the liquor order for the bar before leaving the office.

Without Leah knowing, Maggie had been watching through the glass window in Joe's office door. She saw the distraught look on Leah's face as she hung up the phone. Her instincts told her something wasn't right with that girl. Maggie had a tendency to mother all the girls, and Leah was no exception. Maybe it'd be different if she'd had a daughter instead of four boys. Maggie was no different from anyone else in Joe's bar; they'd all grown fond of Leah. Maggie had been Mary's best friend and she knew Mary and Joe's hopes and dreams. They had both wanted a family, but it just wasn't meant to be. She'd seen that Daddy look in Joe's eyes when he looked at Leah, and she had seen how happy Joe had been, happier than he had been in years. Maggie couldn't help worrying.

Before leaving that day, Maggie walked into the office to have a chat with Joe. She didn't waste time explaining that she was worried. Leah was usually so happy, but here lately she had a sad look on her face. Joe had noticed the look Leah wore when they had talked earlier, but Leah was a compassionate person. Maybe she was just reacting to that article in the newspaper. He was in denial and didn't want to believe anything bad.

"You must have read the paper this morning, well, so did Leah," Joe told Maggie. "It seemed to hit her pretty hard. We'll keep an eye on her. I hope this is a case of your mind working overtime."

"I hope you're right. That girl is becoming special to a lot of people around here. Frank's always been an ole grouch and she's got him wrapped around her little finger. One word from her and he's ready to change the menu just to please her," Maggie said to get her point across. "Oh, well, I'm tired and I'm going home."

"I've noticed Frank trying out new recipes. I've also noticed the new items are selling well. Try not to worry, Mother Maggie." Joe laughed, adding, "See you in the morning." Joe got up from his chair and followed Maggie out the office door. He went to his favorite bar stool and sat down. Watching Maggie go out the back door, he didn't want to believe she could be right. *Leah was just upset about the newspaper article. Who wouldn't be?* He quickly decided.

It's then that he saw Barb come bouncing through the front door. "You're never going to believe it, Joe," she called out to him.

"What am I not going to believe?"

"My sweet, adorable husband just made reservations for the two of us. We're going on a cruise to Mexico. He made a suggestion at work that's going to save the company some big money, and can you believe it? They gave him a bonus. He booked us for a seven-day cruise. We never had a honeymoon, and when vacation time rolls around we never go anywhere. Just think, my mother is taking care of the girls. I won't have to cook, make my bed, or do laundry for one whole week. I plan to swim and lay around the pool in the sun. It came at a perfect time since next week is my vacation." Barb was practically jumping for joy.

"That's great, Barb. I've got you covered. I spoke with Aline the other day and she would like to help out. Her health problems have improved, and she'd like to earn some extra money. She's offered to work anytime I need her, so I'm going to let her fill in for your vacation."

"Did she say why she quit so suddenly?" Barb asked.

"We didn't go into it. She was sick, remember?" Joe offered by way of explanation.

"Oh yeah, she was sick," Barb answered. She couldn't prove it, but she was thinking that what Aline had been was drunk. She didn't tell Joe, he was so strict with his employees. Barb was aware that if Joe knew what she suspected, well there was no way he would allow Aline back in the bar. *Joe's a smart man; he'll figure it out. If Aline is an alcoholic, she won't be able to cover it up for long. I don't care about that. I just need her to be here for my vacation,* Barb thought. *Does that make me a selfish person?*

"Do you take vacations every year?" Leah chimed in.

"We do, but normally I stay home taking care of the kids and my husband does upkeep on the house. We might visit the zoo or take the kids to the beach, but he and I have never gone away alone. Can you tell I'm excited?" Barb was on cloud nine.

"It shows," Leah replied and gave Barb a wide smile. "I am so happy for you."

Ted came in the door wearing a grin on his face. It

was then that Frank came out of the kitchen. "What's with him? Her vacation isn't what's made him look so happy." Frank liked the way the employees in this place cared for one another. They were family. When something good happened to one, the others cheered them on.

"Mind your own business," Joe barked. "You got things ready for dinner?"

"Now what do you think? I've always got things ready to serve. What's wrong with you, can't you take a joke anymore?" Frank reached up for a cup of coffee.

"Sorry. My minds on other things today," Joe answered.

"Well, get over it," Frank barked and laughed at him.

That's all it took to bring Joe out of his slump. He had a good crew; they watched out for one another.

The next day Leah got up early, dressed, and took a cab to the library. She searched for the newspaper article about Jennifer. It wasn't long until she found it.

Memphis Woman Vacationing In Mexico City Killed In Hit and Run Accident

Jennifer Anderson, age 25, was killed in a hit-and-run accident according to Mexican police. No identification was found at the site of the accident. The Mexico City Police Department was able to identify the body with help of fingerprints, and dental records. A resident of Memphis, Ms. Anderson was raised in the foster care system. No relatives have been found.

It was hard for Leah to believe that Jennifer was dead. She made her way home with a heavy heart. She didn't really know her, but she grieved for the young woman. *Was it my fault or just an accident?* Leah was afraid she knew the answer to that question. She couldn't help feeling guilty; she'd sent Jennifer to Mexico with her identification, knowing Jeff was hunting for her.

At home Leah couldn't forget the article and a sadness weighed heavy on her heart. *I may as well go downstairs and get something to eat,* she decided. The furthest thing from her mind was Steve. He came in right at noon and claimed a bar stool next to Joe. They talked a few minutes and then Steve motioned for Leah to join them.

Leah lifted her hand holding the coffee pot up in question, then grabbed a cup for Steve at his nod and went toward the bar. Walking up, she heard Steve say, "I've sprung you from your day of drudgery. I got a phone call and we've got less than a half hour to get out to the wildlife refuge. They've sighted green sea turtles feeding in the bay. Patty and Floyd are getting a group together to catch and tag them. Let's go, we're meeting them at the refuge."

"Joe, is this alright with you? I'm scheduled to work," Leah asked.

"Sure, go on and have a good time. It's looking like a slow day." Joe couldn't be more pleased. *Leah hasn't been herself. Maybe this will be just what she needs.*

"Change your clothes and wear some old tennis shoes. Hurry, I'll meet you out front," Steve said.

Leah's eyes were bright with excitement. "Okay," she replied and went out the back door.

It was a short drive to the refuge. In less than 10 minutes time they were pulling into the parking lot. Steve introduced Leah to Patty and Floyd who were an older couple. They all took off across the sand toward one of the boats. It was a cool, breezy day and they were soon skimming across the bay searching for the giant turtles. The group had brought transmitters and identification tags to attach to the turtles' shells. They would catch them by throwing a net over them as they foraged for food. Once in the boat, they would take them to shore to tag them.

"Green turtles have their natural enemies, sharks and killer whales, but the greatest threat comes from humans in the form of speeding boats and fishing nets," Steve explained. "In the past, we've had poachers who killed them for their meat and shells. Through the transmitters, we've been able to track them to the Mexican beaches where they breed."

They saw another boat which had managed to capture two smaller turtles in their net. The boat's occupants maneuvered the turtles on board and then headed for the shore. They would make a chart for each turtle with weight and size, then get blood and skin samples before tagging and releasing them.

"There's one swimming to the surface," Floyd alerted them and grabbed up the net while Steve took hold of the other end. Together the two men threw the net just as the turtle's nose came out of the water. The net spooked the turtle and it took a dive, but Floyd pulled the draw string closed. The turtle was trapped and they hauled it toward the boat.

"I think it's a female," Patty yelled watching her flippers fight the net.

The two women jumped into the fray. They were tripping over one another trying to get the turtle into the boat. Leah laughed, thinking that between the waves and the turtle splashing salt water, she was going to be soaked.

It took all four of them pulling hard to get the large female into their boat. Happy to have her on board, they all began laughing. It was then that Leah noticed that the turtle seemed to be going to sleep. "Is she okay?" Leah yelled to be heard over the sound of the boat motor.

"She's fine," Steve told her. "It's like a defense mechanism. When they're caught, the turtles just seem to shut down." The turtle's eyes closed as she lay in the bottom of the boat. Patty wetted a towel and laid it over the turtle's head to protect her from the sun. Floyd grabbed hold of the motor handle and headed to shore.

On land, they carefully lifted the turtle from the boat. She lay motionless while they measured her length, then put her in a Velcro sling and suspended her with a rope in order to get her weight. While Steve and Floyd steadied the creature, Patty expertly inserted a syringe into the upper side of the turtle's neck in order to get a blood sample. The last thing they did, after cleaning the algae off her shell, was to glue a transmitter near the shell ridge. Patty again poured water over her carapace before removing the wet towel, and then they gently nudged the female awake. The big turtle slowly made her way to the water's edge and slipped back into the bay.

They took these same steps, over and over again, all afternoon. By the time they finished, all four were soaking wet. It was getting late, and all the boats headed for the beach one last time.

They tied the boat to the pier next to the parking lot and made their way back toward their vehicles. "I had fun. Thank you for letting me help," Leah told Patty and Floyd.

"Get Steve to bring you back another time," Patty told her.

Reaching the car, Steve helped Leah into the passenger's seat, then went around and got in. Looking at her, he asked, "Would you like to get something to eat?"

"I would really like to, but I feel like I deserted Joe," Leah explained. "I think I should get back and finish out my shift. I'm glad you suggested I wear something old because I'm soaked. Could we go to dinner some other time?"

"Let me make sure I understand; you're willing to go out with me?" Steve smiled. Leah nodded and returned his smile as he admitted, "I was afraid you were going to make me wait forever. You haven't given me much encouragement."

"Let's just say that I had a change of heart. It's not you, Steve. I wasn't sure I wanted to date anyone. Sometimes relationships are painful and I recently walked away from a really awful one. Can't we try being friends and just see where it goes?" Leah smiled, adding, "For now, I really need to be getting back."

Steve started the car and drove back the way they came. He was attracted to Leah and this was the first encouragement he had gotten so he was feeling hopeful. Joe seemed to believe it would work out, and maybe it would.

As soon as they reached the bar, Leah asked Steve, "If you don't mind, pull around back? There's an employee's parking lot. My apartment is upstairs and I want to get a quick shower. You can go in the back way if you want to get something to eat. Let Joe know that I'll be down in about 15 minutes."

Steve was a wet mess but he wasn't ready for the night to end. He walked in the back door of the bar and found Joe in his usual place, at the end of the bar.

Looking up Joe inquired, "How did it go?"

"Great, she wants to have dinner some night," he answered while claiming a bar stool next to Joe.

Steve placed an order with Ted and then confided in Joe. "All this time I was afraid she would never go out with me. You said I needed to be patient, and it's finally paid off. Thanks for the advice; I might have given up otherwise."

"I know her better, that's all," Joe said. "You look like someone tried to drown you."

"Leah said to tell you she'll be down in 15 minutes, but I don't know a woman alive who can shower and change that quickly." Steve laughed.

The men looked up as Leah entered through the back door. It had been exactly 14 minutes. She was dressed in black slacks, a white shirt and clean tennis shoes. Her face lit up when she saw the two men sitting together.

Joe grinned at Steve, "She looks to be among the living, and I believe she's a minute early. Never under estimate our girl."

Steve laughed, "I wouldn't have believed it if I hadn't seen it for myself. That lady's full of surprises, and I look forward to learning them all."

Leah grabbed her apron and started taking orders.

Joe didn't say a word. *I should have realized Leah would come back when she was finished at the Reserve.* There was pink in her checks, and she had lost the sad look he had noticed before she left. *These two will be good for each other.* Joe thought.

A half hour later, Leah took a break and went back to get a sandwich. She slid onto the stool next to Steve and began to tell Joe about the turtle rescue with Steve adding comments occasionally.

An hour later, Steve left and the bar settled down for the night. It was closing time and Joe watched his crew lock up. Soon, the place was clean and everyone was out the door. Leah went upstairs to her apartment and her thoughts went back to Jennifer. There was no way of knowing if Jeff was responsible for Jen's death, but she couldn't get it out of her mind. *I guess it could have been an accident. Her identification wasn't found, Carrie's identification that is. Could someone have stolen her purse? They could have sent it to Jeff as proof of her death. Am I safe? I guess only time will tell.* Leah went to bed but her sleep was troubled, and in her dreams she saw Jennifer being hit by a car. She then saw Jeff laughing and that jolted her awake. When sleep claimed her again, the same dream woke her once more.

The next morning found Leah tired and depressed. It was like she had never gone to sleep. *I've got to put this out of my mind. I can't bring Jen back, and worrying about it is driving me crazy. It's in God's hands now.*

Leah had coffee and then made herself breakfast before putting a roast in the crock pot. She liked cooking for herself once in a while and her favorite was comfort food like her mother always made. *I need to find some way to get word to my parents. They must be out of their minds with worry. Maybe I could take a trip and get in touch with Jess, then she could contact my parents. It is hard to know what to do.* She got out the cleaning supplies in the hope that keeping her hands busy would stop her from thinking about Jennifer or Jeff. By the end of the afternoon she had a clean apartment, and it was almost time for her to go to work.

The rest of the week went by quickly. Leah stayed so busy that she didn't have time to think. Having Barb gone meant there was more work to be done. Maybe Aline was once good at her job, but she certainly wasn't pulling her weight this time. *I miss Barb! I'll be glad when she gets back*, Leah thought to herself.

Leah went downstairs early to have lunch with Steve. On days he couldn't get away, she brought her lunch back to her apartment instead. That Friday, she came in the back door and after calling a greeting to Frank, she went to find Joe. "Everything is in the dryer upstairs," she told Joe. "Anything else I need to catch up on?"

"I've been keeping an eye on Aline. She isn't used to the routine anymore and she falls behind a lot. It was nice of her to offer to fill in, but I don't think I'll use her again. I've been thinking, maybe I should hire a part-time person, someone who can help out on weekends and for vacations. Our business is picking up so we could use someone else," Joe told her. They saw Ted coming through the front door. He was never early, and the look on his face told Joe that something was up.

Ted got straight to the point. "We've got a problem. You know that expensive bourbon you keep on hand for certain customers? I used the last of it late last night and the backup bottle is gone. I was surprised because I remembered seeing it earlier in the week. I checked the Tuesday inventory and it was on the sheet. Now, I suppose Leah could have made a mistake but I don't think so. She has always been extra careful when she counts the stock. Joe, that bottle is gone. Something else unusual happened this week as well. Ole Jake asked me if we had started watering down our drinks. I didn't mention it because it seemed so ridiculous that I thought he must be joking. We serve good liquor and we don't short the drinks. I got busy and forgot all about it until last night. Something just doesn't add up."

Joe took a deep breath. "Why didn't you tell me this last night?"

"I had to be sure," Ted answered. "I didn't want to raise a fuss and then have the bottle show up."

"Damn, I guess I am getting old, because I didn't put two and two together. All the signs were there but I just didn't want to see them. Aline isn't pulling her weight and she hangs around behind the bar. I saw her behind the bar a night or two ago and thought she was helping you out." Joe got up and started toward his office. "I'll check the security cameras and see what I find. She was a former employee and I got sloppy. I'll be in my office if you need me."

After Joe left, Leah asked, "Do you think she's stealing liquor?"

"I was afraid she was drinking when she worked here before. I guess I should have told Joe. It's not a good idea to have an alcoholic working in a bar. I had no proof, and then she started calling in sick. When she handed in her resignation I didn't think any more about it. For a man who owns a bar, Joe has zero tolerance for drunks," Ted explained.

"Poor Joe, he would probably help her if it was just a drinking problem. He isn't going to forgive her for stealing." Leah didn't envy Joe having to deal with this sort of trouble.

An hour later, Joe came out of his office with a sad look on his face. "Aline took the bottle, and she's been helping herself to the open stock. She pulls the pourer out, takes out a glass, and replaces it with water. She's careful to only take a little from each bottle so it doesn't taste too watered down. Half my stock must be affected. It's Friday and I can't work through the weekend with watered down liquor. When Aline gets in, tell her I want to see her in my office. In the meantime, set aside all the unsealed bottles and open up new ones. Leah, help Ted when you have time. After I talk to Aline, I'll be out to work the bar. Ted, if you don't mind, could you help Leah cover the floor? We'll have to hope we have enough liquor in stock to make it through the weekend."

"Will do boss," Ted said. "Leah keeps us well stocked. If we don't end up with a ship load of thirsty sailors, we should be alright."

Joe headed back to his office while Ted and Leah got to work behind the bar.

"You know, we could sample the liquor, just to see how watered-down it tastes." Leah said, and then started to laugh. "Only a few swigs and I'd be falling down drunk. I don't think Joe would appreciate that."

Ted laughed at the picture that made. "Come on friend, let's get to work."

Ted and Leah were hard at work when Aline came in at 4 o'clock, and they sent her back to Joe's office. Fifteen minutes later, out she came. They could see she was furious as she stormed out of the bar.

"Poor Joe, I don't think that went well," Leah remarked to Ted.

Neither one said anything when Joe joined them. Finally, he broke the ice. "I fired her and she won't be back. She tried to deny it until I showed her the video."

"We pulled everything that wasn't sealed and replaced them with fresh bottles. The opened ones are under the sink," Ted told Joe. "We thought about sampling everything, but decided that you might not like finding us tipsy."

Joe laughed at the silly look on both of their faces. "No, finding the two of you drunk would have been the last straw. I don't think Frank and I could keep the place open by ourselves. We'll check the bottles out, one at a time. You picked a good place to put them, because they may need to go down the drain. After closing, if either of you want a drink feel free to sample."

Over the next few hours Ted and Leah worked their butts off. At closing time Joe, could tell how exhausted they both were.

"Thank you," Joe told them. "I couldn't have made it through the night without you."

"I can say this; I never realized how hard it was waiting tables. I've got to hand it to you, Leah. It is harder than it looks and I don't envy you the job," Ted remarked.

"Let's get the heck out of here. Come on Frank,"

Joe called out to his friend before telling Ted and Leah, "This is going to be a back breaking weekend so you had better get all the rest you can. I sure will be happy to have Barb back."

"That makes two of us," Ted said.

"Me too," Leah chimed in. "I thought you and Frank might stay late, sampling."

"I'm too tired to even sip," Joe complained. "After things settle down and we're back to normal, Frank and I can check out those bottles."

"Is someone talking about me?" Frank asked, as he entered from the kitchen.

"I'll fill you in later," Joe said.

"Don't bother, I overheard it all. Next week sounds good to me," Frank replied and then laughed. "It's your own damn fault, you know. You let that girl fool you. I had her pegged for an alcoholic; she didn't have me fooled for a minute."

"I'm out of here," Ted said.

"Let's all go," Joe replied. As everyone filed out, he thought, *I did not let Aline put one over on me. That old fart in the kitchen didn't realize she was drinking either.*

CHAPTER NINE

Monday morning found Joe sitting at the bar. He was exhausted and realized he needed to make some changes. As soon as the evening crew came in, he was going to call a meeting. Business had been growing, and because he had such good people they had made things work. Last week had shown him that he needed to add to his employees however. Now that he thought about it, he needed people on both shifts. The day shift was easier to cover in an emergency because they weren't as busy, but the lunch crowd had gotten a lot bigger over the last year. He alerted the morning crew, telling them they needed to stay a little later.

When Joe saw Barb come in he noticed that she was positively glowing. He wasn't sure, but he wondered if it was just the vacation, or had that cruise jump started her marriage? The trip may have been just what she needed.

After everyone gathered around the bar, Joe called for their attention. "I want to thank each of you for being exceptional at your jobs. We all work well as a unit, and this place usually runs like a fine car. Last week, with Barb on vacation, the car stalled however." Everyone laughed. "I had a wake-up call. If everyone is here then things run smoothly. But, there are times like this week, when someone needs to be off. I've decided that, with the increase in business, we need some part-time help. I would like to start by hiring someone for days. If you know of anyone who would like to work 10 a.m. till 2 p.m., please tell them to come see me. I realize it may be hard to find someone for 20 hours a week, especially when those hours fall in the middle of the day. Next, I want someone who is willing to work evenings and weekends. I need them Fridays and Saturdays, with at least one weeknight. They will need to be available from 4 p.m. till closing. It's going to take a little while to hire and train new people. I'm going to call the employment agency, but if you know someone you think would fit in let me know."

Joe motioned for Ted, Leah, and Barb to stay and told everyone else they could go. "When I had my wake up call, I realized that the three of you work every weekend and that needs to change. Just because I spend my life here doesn't mean you should. I'm going to alternate and give you Friday or Saturday off. When it's your Saturday, you will also get Sunday and that will give you the weekend. Thank you for all your hard work." As he spoke, customers started coming in. Knowing that the place was about to get busy, he concluded the meeting.

Later, when Barb took her break she sought Joe out.

"We're glad to have you back," Joe told her. "I don't have to ask if you enjoyed your vacation."

Barb laughed, "Boy, did I. I was sorry to hear about the trouble with Aline, but I kind of had a wakeup call too. I'm missing out on so much with my family by working so many hours."

"You're not going to quit me, are you?" Joe asked, hoping he wasn't about to lose Barb.

"I'll admit Joe, I was considering changing jobs. Jay and I hardly see each other, and since I work nights I don't spend much time with my girls. The four of us need some time together. My mother keeps the children from the time school lets out until Jay gets home, and that means we don't have to hire a babysitter. It seemed perfect at the time, but with me working nights he's with the girls more than I am. They're growing up and they need their mother more now. We did a lot of talking on the cruise and we came to the conclusion that money isn't everything. I love working here; we're like family. I'm glad about these new hours. Having some weekends off, maybe it will work out for me."

Joe was relieved. He could tell Barb didn't want to quit. She really needed to spend more time with Jay and her girls however. "I've been blind," Joe confided. "Give me some time; I don't want to lose you."

"I'll definitely give you some time," Barb laughed. "I might be able to do something else for you. My mother's having trouble making ends meet. Her retirement income doesn't stretch as far as it once did. I'll tell her about the day job and if you want an older woman..."

"It sounds like she would fit right in with the over-fifty staff." Joe laughed, "Tell her to come see me."

Things were picking up and Barb went back to work. Joe made his way back to his office. He had come close to losing Barb without even knowing it. Thankfully, that didn't happen. Sitting down at his desk, he made a call to the employment agency.

Later in the evening, it was time to start checking out that stock Ted and Leah pulled last Friday. Joe was standing at the sink with a bottle in each hand and was pouring shots when Steve entered the bar.

"You have a problem that you want to talk about?" Steve inquired, nodding toward the group of bottles sitting in front of Joe.

Joe laughed, "You might think so." About that time Frank joined them.

"Steve, are you a new member of Joe's booze tasting society?" Frank asked.

"Okay, what gives?" Steve was puzzled by what was happening.

Joe didn't really want to explain. "I had a former employee fill in last week and didn't give it another thought. Turns out, the reason she quit was that she had developed a taste for the hard stuff. She hasn't been able to hold down a job and she's broke. She knew how I felt about drinking, but I guess she thought she could hide it. The heck of it was, she did, until Ted noticed an expensive bottle of bourbon was missing. I took a look at the security cameras and saw her taking the bourbon. She had also been removing the spouts from the open bottles and pouring herself a drink before replacing it with water. Now, I have to figure out how much of my stock is watered down. There may be a better way, but I thought the easiest was to have a drink. I fired her and told her if I ever saw her in here again that I would press charges. I know it's the middle of the day, but do you want a drink? It's on the house."

Steve shook his head and laughed. "I don't think that's such a good idea since I'm on duty. This is my dinner break. Maybe you should think about making a complaint? Some of those bottles look expensive."

"Not unless she comes back in." Joe slid a shot glass toward Frank and lifted his own glass. "Aline wasn't always an alcoholic, and she gave me some good years as an employee. Maybe she'll get some help."

Frank took a sip out of his glass. "That one needs to go down the drain, it's mostly water. Next," he said, holding out his glass.

"This may take a while, unless all of them are water." Joe laughed and poured Frank another drink. Joe took a sip of his and emptied his glass in the sink before pouring the two bottles down the drain. The three men were all laughing like fools when Leah appeared.

"What's so funny, or are you all drunk?" She asked as she studied each man.

"Hell girl." Frank told her, "There would have to be some booze in those bottles for us to be drunk. Aline must know how to hold her liquor, to have fooled everyone."

They all had a good laugh before realizing how very sad the situation was.

When Leah recovered from her giggles, she told the men, "I didn't know her very well, but I feel sorry for her. It sounds like she was out of control. It must be hard having the need for whiskey ruling your life."

"That's the reason I didn't press charges," Joe explained. "There, but for the grace of God, go I."

No one said a word. They all knew that Joe had been a drinker at one time.

Leah went to get her apron while Joe sniffed one of the bottles. It smelled like booze so he poured Frank a drink and watched him raise the glass to his mouth.

"This one is good. She must have missed it," Frank said, "What say we leave the rest for another time?"

Steve placed his order for dinner with Ted, and Joe went to find Leah. "Why don't you take a break and keep Steve company? I plan to give you that weekend off just as quickly as I can arrange it. That might be something Steve would find interesting," Joe said with a grin on his face.

"You're doing it again, matchmaking," Leah replied, but she was still smiling.

"Maybe, but I don't think you mind anymore," Joe told her.

"I must be nuts," Leah said and then went back to the bar and Steve. She passed Frank going back to fix Steve a plate.

"You look like the cat that swallowed the canary," Frank told Joe.

"Not really. It's nice to see Leah and Steve together," Joe replied.

Leah got a soda and slid onto a bar stool next to Steve. Ever the gentleman, he stood when she walked up.

"Stop that," Leah said.

"But my mother taught me to do that when a lady joins me," Steve told her.

"I wouldn't want to contradict your mother," Leah laughed, "But here you're a customer, and not bound by your mother's rules."

By this time they were both laughing. "Sweetheart, I hate to tell you this, but if I know what's good for me I am always bound by my mother's rules. That is one tough lady. You kind of remind me of her," Steve said.

Blushing like a school girl, Leah ducked her head, wondering. *Why couldn't I have met Steve first?*

"Leah," Steve said, reaching over to lift her chin. "We're making progress; don't back away. When are we going out to dinner?"

"I'm off on Monday and Tuesday. Would either of those days work for you?"

"Tuesday would be perfect. Could I pick you up at 1 o'clock? We could spend a few hours at the zoo and then I want to take you to a little Italian restaurant," Steve suggested.

"That sounds good to me, I love Italian food," Leah told him, with a laugh. "There's nothing better than crusty bread with lots of butter and garlic. You have to eat some too though, so you won't know I smell like garlic."

"I love garlic bread." Steve liked that Leah made him laugh, and he was starting to realize that there wasn't much that he didn't like about her.

"Joe's hiring some new people. When he gets them trained I'll be getting a Saturday and Sunday off at least once or twice a month. There are some places I would like to see in Northern California. What's your favorite place?" Leah asked Steve.

"I love to hike in the mountains of Northern California. Do you like to hike?"

"I've never been hiking, but I love the mountains," Leah explained before laughing. "I guess if you can walk, you can hike!"

"That sounds right," Steve chuckled, "I've got to get out of here. You are too much fun to talk to and I'm running late."

Leah was looking forward to their date Tuesday, and it seemed to take forever to get there. Steve and Leah had seen one another, but they hadn't been alone. Tuesday at 1 o'clock Steve was knocking on Leah's door.

"Hi," she greeted Steve with a smile. She was wearing a simple, sleeveless dress in soft yellow with sandals. "I've been looking forward to this. Am I dressed alright?"

Steve had never seen her in anything but slacks. He definitely approved of the dress, and was pleased to note she had beautiful long legs. "You look wonderful," he told her. "Are your sandals comfortable? We are going to be doing a lot of walking."

"I remembered," Leah said. She picked up a light, short-sleeved jacket and her purse before they left the apartment. It was a mild, sunny, perfect California day.

When they arrived at the zoo, the first place Steve showed her was the big cat habitat. They were beautiful lying there in the sun.

"They're magnificent," Leah said. "I know they're dangerous, but they look like ordinary house cats."

"I like to watch them, all that muscle and controlled power." Steve was studying the big cats. "You're right though, they do look like cuddly kittens. It's hard to believe they could kill without a second's notice."

"Like someone else I know," Leah said without thinking.

Steve picked up on the comment. "Leah, you aren't thinking of me, are you afraid of me?"

"Steve, I'm sorry," Leah cried. "Of course I wasn't talking about you. You're one of the few people I totally trust. I read about those three girls in the paper. They've been on my mind lately. It's hard to believe someone could kill so easily."

"Yes, things like that happen too often," Steve replied.

Leah was quiet as they walked toward the primate habitat. Did Steve believe her explanation? Should she confide in him? It surprised her to realize that she did trust him. Before long they were laughing over the antics of the monkeys, and the incident was forgotten. Steve bought candy apples, and they continue strolling through the zoo.

"Have you worked up an appetite?" Steve asked. "Are you ready for dinner?"

Leah laughed, "I am!"

"Let's get out of here." Steve took her hand and led her toward the zoo's entrance.

Soon they were pulling into the parking lot of a quaint Italian restaurant. As they entered, an older woman greeted Steve. "Steven, it is good to see you. It has been much too long since you have been to see us," she said, giving him a big hug.

Returning the older woman's hug, Steve told her, "Mama Sophia, it's good to see you. I have missed seeing you and Papa."

"Come in." Mama escorted them to a corner table. "Who is the beautiful lady?"

"This is Leah," Steve answered.

"Leah, it is a pleasure to meet you," Mama Sophia said.

"Mama Sophia's son, Dom, and I went to school together," Steve told Leah, and then turned to Mama Sophia. "Leah and I met through a mutual friend. I told her I was bringing her here for the greatest Italian food in California."

Mama reached up and patted Steve on the cheek. "You are such a good boy, you sit. I will tell Papa you are here."

"You're going to love this," Steve told Leah as he pulled out a chair for her.

In a few minutes an older man comes barreling out of the kitchen. In one hand he carried a bottle of wine, and in the other he had four wine glasses.

"Steven!" he said in a booming voice. "It has been way too long. Mama said you had brought your lady, so we shall have wine," he announced. He set the glasses on the table and gave Steve a big bear hug.

"Papa, I want you to meet Leah," Steve said making the introduction. "Can you and Mama sit down with us for a while?"

"But of course. We will have a glass of the grape, then Mama and I will go prepare your favorite dishes," he answered before expertly popping the cork on the bottle of wine.

"You don't have to do that, Papa. Leah and I can order from the menu." Steve said.

"Nonsense," Papa said as he poured the wine. "Salute," he said, raising his glass. "To old and new friends."

They all drank to his toast. After visiting for a few minutes, Mama and Papa excused themselves and went back to the kitchen. Mama returned with salads and an antipasto plate that she placed on the table. "Enjoy," she told them and went back to the kitchen.

"I really hope you're hungry; it looks like they're pulling out all the stops." Steve laughed. They talked while they ate their salads and sampled the appetizers. Soon, the main course arrived. Presented family style, it included spaghetti with large meatballs, lasagna, and a golden brown calzone with marinara on top. In the middle of the table they placed a large bread basket filled with crusty garlic bread.

"Eat, enjoy," Mama said. "For dessert we have Steven's favorite, tiramisu."

"There's enough food here for a family of eight! Do they expect us to eat all of this?" Leah asked after Mama went back to the kitchen.

"When we leave, we'll be loaded down with takeout boxes," Steve answered and then laughed. "They're trying to stamp out world hunger."

"I can believe it," Leah said, and then all got quiet while they enjoyed the fantastic food.

After Steve and Leah had stuffed themselves, Mama and Papa returned. Papa was carrying a tray with coffee and four slices of tiramisu.

"We give up," Steve laughed. "There is no way we have room for dessert."

"Mama will pack it up for you to take home," Papa told them.

When Mama came back, Leah told them how much she had enjoyed everything. "The garlic bread was out of this world! Where do I vote? I agree with Steve, this is the best food in California."

They shared a cup of coffee with Papa and Mama, and when they left they were indeed loaded down with bags full of food containers.

In the car on the way home, Leah told Steve, "it was a perfect day, and I liked meeting Mama and Papa."

When they reached the apartment, Steve started collecting the bags.

"You aren't going to leave all of this with me, are

you?" Leah asked.

"I am, but I hope that you will invite me to share it with you." Steve never got tired of spending time with Leah.

"Will you have lunch with me tomorrow?" Leah didn't want the night to end.

"It would be an honor."

They went upstairs and Steve helped Leah put all the food away. Turning to leave, he took her face gently between his hands before leaning in and giving her a tender, first kiss. She moved closer and slipped her arms around his waist, but a minute later Steve felt her grow tense and then she suddenly backed away.

"It's alright," Steve told her in a quiet voice. "I can tell someone has hurt you, and I'm prepared to be patient. Good night, I will see you tomorrow." He turned and let himself out of the apartment.

Leah went to the door and quietly turned the dead-bolt before going down the hall to get ready for bed. She slipped between the sheets, and lay there recalling the wonderful day. *Steve has the most alluring blue eyes. I remember that first day we met. His eyes were like magnets; they just pulled me in. That's never happened to me before. The unexpected shock of it was why I've been so standoffish. No, it wasn't just that, I was determined not to get involved. To Serve and Protect, there's a certain power behind that badge. Maybe that's why I'm drawn to him. He's everything I want, all in one very nice package.*

When sleep came, she had a smile on her lips.

CHAPTER TEN

It had been a few weeks since Joe's big meeting and it was exciting to see the changes in the bar. He hired Barbara's mother for the day shift and Sue was pleasant, with a sunny smile. They had two new girls on the evening shift. Both were college students trying to finish their last year of school. Emily was short and bubbly, always laughing and joking, while Sally was tall and skinny except for a pair of magnificent breasts. This led Emily to suggest that Joe change the name of the bar to one belonging to a popular chain out of Florida.

"Sorry Emily," Joe laughed and told her, "I think that name is already taken."

Business was booming so the extra people were coming in handy. Hiring the three ladies had been a good decision and Joe was thinking about two more in the near future. It was nice to be able to give both Leah and Barb better hours. Ted didn't seem to care, but that could change someday. If he ever found someone, he would want more time to spend with that special person. With the two extra girls, Joe could be more flexible. *Maybe someday I might take a day or two off,* he thought. *I could leave Leah in charge. She's learning the ropes and doing a good job. How long has it been since I've gone deep sea fishing?*

Joe also watched Steve and Leah as they grew closer. Leah was going to let Steve take her hiking in King's Canyon National Park. She had never been hiking, but Steve loved it and she was willing to give it a try. She asked Joe for Monday off, which gave her a three-day weekend.

Leah felt like the week was crawling by. She was looking forward to her trip, and Steve had taken her shopping for new boots. She was to wear them for a few hours each day. Steve told her that if she broke them in properly, they wouldn't hurt her feet. He had insisted she get them roomy enough for a pair of nice, soft socks. According to him, it was important to have a good pair of boots and to break them in before you went hiking.

Finally, it was Friday night and Steve came in to have a late dinner. He had gotten in the habit of coming at odd hours so that Leah would be free to join him. It was Ted's night off, and Leah signaled for Joe to give her a break. Steve looked up and smiled as she sat down next to him.

"Are you all packed?" he asked. "It's going to be early for you, but I thought we could leave around 6 o'clock. I'll bring a blanket and pillow so you can sleep in the car. I'd like to get out of the city before the traffic gets bad."

"I'm already packed, and with extra socks as instructed." Leah still didn't understand all the special attention to boots and socks.

"I can still remember basic training," Joe groaned. "New boots and they rubbed blisters on my blisters. The only thing more sore was my shoulders from carrying that heavy backpack."

Steve laughed. "Been there, done that. We went shopping a couple of weeks ago. It gave Leah time to break in her boots. I'll carry our pack."

"Now wait a minute," Leah cut into their conversation. "I'm a big girl, and if I'm going to do this I'll carry my own pack. Don't treat me like a baby."

"I wouldn't think of it," Steve said with a smile. "This first time, we'll take short hikes and give you a chance to see if you like the sport. For day trips, you carry a light pack. A first aid kit, some protein bars and a few bottles of water don't weigh much. Since I'm used to hiking and often carry a pack large enough for an overnighter, this one will seem like nothing."

Steve wanted to see how Leah handled the great outdoors. Some women were open to hiking but didn't want to spend the night in a sleeping bag on the ground. Steve ate dinner and then wished everyone a good night. He leaned in and kissed Leah. "I'll see you in the morning."

The bar got busy after Steve left and Leah didn't have much time to think. Soon, it was 12 o'clock and Joe joined her behind the bar.

"Why don't you go ahead and call it a night. I can handle things until closing," Joe told her. "Get a few hours' sleep before Steve picks you up."

"Thank you, I think I will. I'm so excited Joe, I love the mountains." Leah told him. "I bought a camera and hope to get some pictures. Steve said King's Canyon is really beautiful."

"I have heard that. Have a good time, girl." Joe hoped Leah enjoyed her weekend. Hiking wasn't everyone's idea of fun, but it rated high on Steve's list. It would be wonderful if Leah liked it as well.

It didn't seem like Leah's head had touched the pillow when the alarm rang in her ear. She crawled out of bed and dashed for the bathroom. Brushing her teeth, she threw her toothpaste and toothbrush into the suitcase. She ran a brush through her hair, put on a little mascara and lip gloss, and slammed the lid on her suitcase just as she heard a knock. Opening the door, she found Steve with a takeout bag in his hand.

"Good morning," he smiled. "I come bearing coffee and bagels."

"Great! Since you want to get an early start, could we eat them in the car? Are you suppŏsed to eat and drive?" Leah asked.

"Since there isn't much traffic, maybe it will be safe," Steve said with a chuckle. "I wouldn't want to set a bad example."

"Setting a good example is a big responsibility," Leah laughed. "Let me get my bag and we'll hit the road."

"You take this," Steve handed her the takeout bag. "I'll get your suitcase."

Once they were on I-5 and headed in the right direction, Leah opened the bag and handed Steve a large coffee container. "Do you want cream cheese on your bagel?"

"If they have strawberry," Steve answered.

"That's my favorite too," Leah dug around in the bag. "These are still warm."

Leah fixed them both a large bagel layered with strawberry cream cheese. She put a stack of napkins within easy reach of Steve and settled down to enjoy her breakfast. There wasn't much conversation until they finished.

"The pillow and blanket are in the back seat," Steve pointed out. "Do you want me to stop and let you crawl in?"

"No, I think I'll put the seat back and stay right where I am." Leah couldn't hold back a yawn.

Steve noticed she was asleep in a matter of seconds. How could life be more perfect? Three days in the mountains and the woman he loved beside him.

Three hours later, Leah began to stir. "Where are we?"

"We're just a little north of Bakersfield. We should be inside the park in another three hours. Are you ready for a rest stop?" Steve thought that he wouldn't mind a break. "That bagel didn't last long. Do you feel like a late breakfast?"

"That sounds good to me," Leah said, stretching. "First stop, the ladies' room."

They pulled into a truck stop and Leah looked around, almost expecting to see Ed and the guys. How would she explain that?

A half hour later they had eaten breakfast and were back in the car.

They entered the park from Highway 198. Not far from the entrance was Buckeye Campground and Paradise Creek Trail. It was in the foothills area and the hike would be one of the easier ones.

Steve asked, "Do you want to get out and stretch your legs? There's a trail here; I think it is about three miles. Why don't we give it a try?" Steve reached into the back and pulled out a small backpack. "Here, spray your clothes with this insect repellent and make sure to get your boots and pant legs."

Steve had taken this trail before so he didn't wait for a guide. After they left the parking lot, they saw a raven soar through the clear blue sky. They had a breathtaking view of the mountains and Leah stopped to take some pictures. They saw Indian drawings on the rock formations, and Steve stopped to point out a western fence lizard sunning himself. "This is the Middle Fork of the Kaweah River," He told her as they came upon a small waterfall with a large pool at its base.

"Want to go swimming?" Steve asked with a smile.

"No way," Leah laughed. "I have a feeling that pool is cold as ice."

"You're right, it's cold all year around." They hiked on and Steve pointed to a high rock rising in the distance, topped by a layer of mist. "That's Moro Rock."

Everywhere Leah looked, the scenery was breathtaking. Steve pointed out Castle Rock for Leah to photograph, and they were now high enough to view the cascade of water that formed along the Middle Fork of the Kaweah River. All too soon they were back at the campground.

"I can't believe how beautiful that was!" Leah was amazed at the views. "I can see why you love hiking these mountains."

"You haven't seen anything yet," Steve told her. "How are the legs; are your feet hurting?"

"My feet feel great, quit fussing." Leah laughed. She placed her camera back into its case. "I hope I got some good pictures."

They checked each other's clothes for crawly critters and then got back in the car. "I reserved two rooms for us at the John Muir Lodge. It's nothing fancy, but the view is fantastic," Steve explained, "I hope you like it."

Leah quickly looked out the window and Steve saw her turn her head away. "Is something wrong? Come on, you can tell me."

Leah thought, *how do I explain?* She was quiet for a minute. "I'm embarrassed, I was kind of hoping, I thought..." She couldn't go on.

"What were you hoping? Leah, what's wrong?" Steve asked.

"When you invited me for a weekend, I thought we had reached a point where we only needed one room. There, I've said it and now I'm totally embarrassed." Leah's face was red and she didn't want to look at Steve.

Steve reached out and gently turned Leah's face toward him. "Leah, I have dreamed of us being together since the first moment I saw you. You had trouble accepting us as a couple at first, and I didn't want to rush you."

"Please, you aren't rushing me. I want to be with you." Leah was embarrassed. She had practically thrown herself at the man.

"Maybe I shouldn't say this but, I have fallen in love with you." Steve leaned over and placed a tender kiss on Leah's lips.

"Steve, I care a great deal for you. I thought I was in love once and this is so much more. Maybe I do need for you to be patient just a little longer. I'm afraid." Leah knew she loved Steve. She just wasn't sure she could say the words. *Will I always be tied to the past?*

Steve pulled out of the parking lot. "Take your time," he told her. "Good things are worth waiting for."

When they got to the lodge, Steve changed the reservations. He got a larger room with a king-size bed and tipped the bellboy, asking him to take their bags up.

Steve turned to Leah. “How would you like to get something to eat?” Leah was still looking a little shy. “I'm hungry after all that walking,” he added.

They entered the lodge’s restaurant where they were seated at a corner table. The waiter handed them their menus and they both decided on the trout. Leah was still quiet.

“Not having second thoughts?” Steve asked as he took her hand.

“I can’t believe I just came out and asked you to share a room with me.” Leah felt like a brazen hussy.

“Thank God you did,” Steve laughed. “I don’t know how much longer I could have lasted.”

They ate their meal and went up to their room, hand in hand.

Seeing the suite, Leah was clearly pleased with the rustic décor. It had a lovely view out of the sliding glass door. “It’s perfect,” she said.

Looking at Steve, Leah said, “I’m not a school girl anymore. I know I've been giving mixed signals, but I never liked being pushed.”

“I haven’t tried to force you, have I?” Steve slipped his arms around her.

“No. That’s my point. I’d been resisting until we decided to make this trip. It goes against my nature, throwing myself at someone. You're a hard man to resist,” she admitted. “It seems like I’m the one pushing you!”

Steve was glad she had finally come to terms with them being together. His patience was wearing thin, but he wanted her to be comfortable with their first night together. He reached out and took both her hands. “You are so beautiful.” His voice was soft as a caress. "Leah, the first time our eyes met, I wanted you. To be honest it scared me. I have never wanted anyone else like this." Drawing a deep breath, he kissed her tenderly. "I realized that you weren't ready for what I had in mind yet." He smiled into her eyes. "So you see, it's not just you. Even Joe knew we had feelings for one another. He kept advising me to give you time. Keeping my hands off you was killing me."

He knew weeks ago that he would never be the same. He had told himself in the beginning, *I'll get over her once we sleep together.* The thing was, they hadn't made love, but that was what it would be. He knew he wanted her in his life, not for a week, or a month, but forever.

Going for the practical, Steve asked. "Would you like to have the bathroom first?"

"Go take your shower," Leah answered with a smile, adding, "I'm glad you told me how you felt. It makes me feel less like I propositioned you."

"Feel free to proposition me anytime you like. I'll be out in a few," Steve said, grabbing his shaving bag and a clean pair of jeans before heading for the bathroom.

After his turn in the bathroom, Steve laid on the bed, waiting. When Leah emerged, he felt a knot catch in his throat. She was wearing a provocative negligee in a beautiful turquoise color. She quickly turned out the light but not before he saw her breast peeking out above the neckline. Steve could see the outline of large breasts and shapely hips through the shear fabric of the gown. He shifted, uncomfortable with the effect she had on him, and then swallowed past the hard lump in his throat. He wanted this woman, but he knew she'd had a bad experience which was why he wanted this to be perfect.

Leah gave Steve a shy smile. She wanted him more than her next breath, but she was suddenly feeling nervous.

Steve watched her move toward the bed. It seemed to take a lifetime for her to reach him. He lifted the sheet as she slid onto the mattress and into his waiting arms. He draped the sheet over her, then leaned in and softly kissed her. She nipped at his bottom lip and the next kiss was deep and hungry, one that stirred her all the way to her toes. She wanted him now, but Steve had waited too long to let her rush him. He planted kisses along her jaw and down her neck.

"I need you," Leah whispered, "now!" It had been too long and Leah knew what she wanted. Steve was holding back, determined not to be rushed.

He reached down and pulled the gown from her lush body. "You are driving me crazy." He said as he ran his hand down her beautiful form.

Steve wanted to make it good for both of them and he wouldn't be hurried. He rained kisses down her face, only to come back to make love to her perfect mouth. Their lips locked in another passionate kiss and he reached out for her, his fingers touched the spot at the center of her core. Instantly Leah squirmed, arching her body toward him as she reacted to his touch. This part was exactly like the dreams she had of them together. The way he felt as she ran her hands over his body, his muscles so hard and his body so hot. This time however, it was real; he was here beside her.

It was then that Steve slid his muscular body atop

hers. She was wet and ready for him. He slipped into her welcoming body, finding a gentle rhythm that pleased them both. There were no words to describe how right this felt. Leah's head was spinning and they both eagerly rush toward that faraway place.

"Come with me," Steve whispered as he increased the tempo.

Leah clung to him and Steve took her over the highest mountain. Finally they relaxed, wrapped tightly in each other's arms and waiting for their hearts to stop racing.

Steve kissed Leah tenderly. "Are you alright?"

Leah smiled. "I'm wonderful, and you are perfect!"

"I love you," Steve whispered as they both fell asleep.

Leah woke early. The sun was shining and casting a soft glow through the closed curtain. She turned to find Steve was already awake.

"Good morning," his lips found hers in a soft kiss.

"Did I dream last night?" Leah moved closer. "It seems this man with magnificent blue eyes made love to me. It was beyond incredible."

"They say you get better with practice," Steve smiled and kissed her passionately. It was a long time before they left their room.

Later that morning found Steve and Leah eating breakfast in the lodge's restaurant. Steve planned to drive them up Highway 180, known as the King's Canyon Scenic Byway. It was approximately a three hour drive. He didn't want to push Leah; too much hiking in these mountains and she would be sore. That would mean it wouldn't be an enjoyable experience, and Steve wanted her to enjoy hiking with him. He ordered them a boxed lunch before they left the restaurant.

As they drove up highway 180, the scenery got progressively more breathtaking with the views of King's Canyon. At Yucca Point you could almost see straight down to the Middle Fork and South Fork of King's River. Just past Yucca Point, the road was carved out of sheer rock. They stopped along the way, but didn't leave the car until they reached Grizzly Falls. A short walk up the trail led them to a sparkling water fall. Steve sat on a large rock and watched as Leah took picture after picture of the impressive falls. She totally enchanted him and he couldn't keep his eyes off of her.

At Don Cecil View, they took a three quarter mile hike up a trail to look across the canyon at Monarch Divide. Steve couldn't help but laugh because the camera never left Leah's hands. It was a good thing it was digital, because in her hands a roll of film wouldn't last very long.

Back in the car, Steve decided to stop at Roaring River Falls. Leah seemed to like waterfalls, and you could practically feel the power as the water rushed through a narrow granite chute that formed this one. Leah was fascinated by the raw beauty of the area.

When they reached Roads End, they found a pleasant area that offered excellent views of high granite walls and access to Muir Rock. Steve took the lunch out of the trunk and found a nice sunny spot to spread their blanket. As they sat and enjoyed the food, Leah was trying to figure out how to preview the pictures she had taken. Steve helped her and they scrolled through all the pictures from the last two days. She had a natural talent, and had captured some wonderful scenes.

"Where do we go from here?" Leah asked.

"Let's go back down 180. I want to show you Hume Lake." Mist Falls was relatively close to where they were having lunch, but it was a five hour hike and Steve didn't think Leah was up for that. The hike around Hume Lake was an easy two and a half mile trail. They'd had a good day and that should be a perfect ending.

Hume Lake was beautiful, with beaches formed by a historic, multiple arched dam. It took a little over two hours to hike around the lake and Steve could tell Leah was tired. Not only was she not used to hiking, but she also wasn't used to the high altitude. They drove back to the lodge with both thinking that it had been a beautiful day.

Steve stopped in front of the lodge. "I want to find a gas station. Why don't you fill up the whirlpool tub and have a nice long soak. You aren't used to hiking and you may have sore muscles tomorrow."

"That sounds like a great idea. See you later," Leah said.

Leah went into the lodge and up to their room. In the bathroom, she started running hot water into the tub. While it filled, she retrieved the throw away phone she had bought in San Diego. The lodge was on the west side of the park, so Leah hoped she could get a signal; she needed to talk to Jess. Turning on the phone and watching it light up, she said to herself, "Thank God, it's working." She locked the door and dialed Jess before turning on the jets and climbing into the tub. She might as well enjoy a good soak while she talked to her friend.

Back in Oklahoma, Jess answered the phone, "Hello?"

It took Leah a minute to find her voice. "Jess, it's so good to hear your voice."

"Carrie, is that you?" Jess whispered. "I can't believe it's you, I've been so worried. Tell me, are you alright?"

"I'm fine, I need to talk to you," Leah explained, "Jennifer, the real Jennifer, is dead. It was a hit-and-run accident in Mexico City. Sometimes I think it was just that, an accident, and sometimes I wonder if it had anything to do with Jeff. I'd feel so guilty if I sent that girl to her death."

"It's not your fault. If Jeff was responsible then he's the one who should feel guilty. If it was an accident, then it was God's plan. Where are you?" Jess asked.

"Right this minute I'm in King's Canyon National Park, but I'll be gone tomorrow. I'm not ready to tell you where I'm living. When I feel safe, I'll call again. I need you to call my parents and let them know I'm alright. They must be worried sick," Leah explained.

"I hope you don't think I betrayed you, but your mother called," Jess explained. "I told her I'd come visit her. I told her everything, Carrie. I couldn't just leave her to worry; she was driving herself crazy."

"It's alright, Jess. You did what you thought was best." Leah didn't know what else to say. "Could you call her back and tell her I'm fine?"

"Why don't you call her? I know she would like to hear your voice. After all, you're calling me." Jess questioned.

"Because I still don't think it's safe. If I talk to her, I'm afraid I might say more than I should." Leah needed to hang up; Steve would be here any minute. "Please Jess, call them for me. Tell them I'm safe and that I love them. Tell them I'll call when I can. I've got to go, I love you Jess." Leah pressed the disconnect button and turned off the phone with tears streaming down her face.

"Leah," Steve called through the door a few minutes later. "The door is locked. I hope you haven't gone to sleep in the tub."

"I'm awake. I'll be out in a few minutes." Leah told Steve.

He was so wonderful; Leah wished she could tell him everything. She washed the tears from her face and climbed out of the tub.

CHAPTER ELEVEN

They left the next morning around 9 o'clock. Steve wanted to show Leah the San Gabriel Mountains and she had been sleeping when they drove through the area early Saturday morning. They took their time on the way home, making several stops along the way, and pulled into the bar parking lot about dinner time.

"I'm hungry," Leah told Steve. "Let's get something to eat before we unload the car."

"That sounds good to me," Steve replied. "In case I haven't mentioned it, I had a wonderful time."

"Me too," Leah said. "I liked hiking, and the mountains were beautiful."

They were holding hands as they entered the bar. Joe noticed them and smiled; they looked relaxed and happy.

"Well, look who's here. Did you have a good trip?" Joe didn't really need to ask.

Frank popped his head out the kitchen door. "What do you kids want for dinner?"

"I want one of your special cheeseburgers and onion rings," Leah told Frank.

"Make that two," Steve said.

"That's two Hawaiian cheeseburgers with fried onion rings, coming right up."

Leah got glasses of iced tea for them and carried the drinks to the end of the bar. They spent the next hour eating and telling Joe about their trip.

"I can't wait to show you the pictures I took," Leah told Joe. "I can't believe how beautiful the mountains were, and the waterfalls were breathtaking."

After they ate, Steve and Leah excused themselves.

"We need to unload the car. See you tomorrow," Steve said.

They got her things from the Steve's car and as they climbed the stairs, Leah thought about how much their relationship had changed in one weekend. Things were different now, they had grown closer over the last three days. Leah opened the door to the apartment and Steve dropped Leah's suitcase just inside the door. Then Leah stepped into his arms and Steve kissed her tenderly. Leah knew she had learned how to make Steve's blood boil and she didn't hesitate. She nipped at his lower lip and got the desired reaction. Steve kissed her, long and passionately.

Leah laughed, running down the hallway dropping clothes as she went. When Steve caught her in the bedroom, they were both naked from the waist up. Leah smiled as she slid her slacks down her long legs, taking her panties with them. She turned to pull down the bedspread and Steve took a playful nip of her backside. She fell onto the bed with Steve's body pressing her into the mattress. He held her face down on the bed as he pressed kisses to the base of her spine. Leah twisted, trying to turn over on her back.

"This isn't fair," she giggled. "I can't touch you."

Steve was laughing as he turned her over and rained kisses over her face. Before long, they were both lost.

Later that night Steve nuzzled Leah's neck. "I need to go," he told her.

"Do you have to?" Leah snuggled closer. "I like having you in my bed."

"This is the real world, Kitten. I don't have a suit

for work tomorrow, and would you want Joe and the gang to know I spent the night?" Steve answered.

"Joe's been matchmaking for months, and I don't think you sleeping over would shock anyone. Set the alarm so you can go home and shower." Leah snuggled closer, wrapping her arms around his waist.

Steve reached for his phone to set the alarm. He was right where he wanted to be.

Joe noticed Steve's car was still in the parking lot when they closed the bar and he couldn't be happier. He hoped it worked out for the two of them. Everyone deserved someone like his Mary.

When Leah came to work, she brought her pictures from the trip. The girl was a natural with a camera, and by the time she had passed the photos around the bar, half the people who saw them were talking about a trip to King's Canyon. California wasn't all congested highways; there was a lot of rugged and beautiful country, and Leah had managed to capture it. She was already talking about a second trip to Yosemite. It would be a full day's drive since it was farther north than King' Canyon.

"How did you like hiking?" Joe asked. "Did you get blisters?"

"No, I think Steve watched me to make sure I didn't," Leah laughed. "He loves the sport so much and he wanted me to like it as well. I like to hike and I enjoyed the waterfalls and the mountain scenery. What do you do for fun, Joe?"

"I used to like to deep sea fish. You know, I can't remember the last time I went fishing," Joe told Leah.

Leah had come in early to show off her pictures so Sue was just leaving. She heard the comment Joe made about deep sea fishing and replied, "I used to like going, there's nothing like being out on the ocean. One time I caught a tuna so big, I couldn't reel him in." Sue was laughing as she recalled catching the fish. "They had me strapped in that seat and the rod strapped to me. That fish just about pulled me apart before I finally admitted I needed help."

They all laughed thinking about 90 pound Sue trying to land a fish bigger than she was.

"The catching might be fun, but what you do when you catch it sounds gross." Leah wrinkled up her nose at the thought of cleaning a fish. "I like my fish better after Frank has cooked it."

"There's nothing like the thrill of pulling a fish out of the water. Those saltwater fish give you a good fight. You can work it for an hour, fighting until you get it on board." Joe explained. "Isn't that right, Sue?"

"You don't have to sell me on the sport." Sue laughed, "I love it, and I love being out on the water. It is so peaceful."

Joe liked matchmaking, Leah thought. *Wonder how he'd like it if I turned the tables on him. Great big Joe and little petite Sue, wouldn't they make a cute couple? I'll talk to Barb, see what she thinks of the plan. Joe is in a rut and it would be good for him.*

"Well, I have work to do," Leah said "If anyone needs me, I'll be upstairs checking on the laundry."

* * *

It was a Friday and Leah had the day off so she got up and lounged around, catching up on her reading. After noon, she cleaned the kitchen and ran the dust mop over the floors. She had told Steve to come for dinner and planned to fix a roast with all the trimmings. She put a chocolate cake in the oven before starting the roast. When the phone rang she rushed to answer, thinking it might be Steve.

"Hi Babe," Steve said. There was something in his voice, he sounded a little down.

"You sound tired. Is everything alright?" Leah tried not to ask too many questions; there were things Steve couldn't talk about.

"Something happened today, and I believe Joe should know about it. Would you mind if we invite him up for coffee?" Steve asked.

"Not at all, I'd like that. I'm going to cook a large roast; why don't I invite him to dinner?"

Steve was quick to say, "This is your day off and that's a lot of extra work."

"Nonsense," Leah said. "It's no trouble to add a few extra vegetables. A roast is simple to fix."

"I'm glad, you make a fantastic roast. My mouth is watering just thinking about it. Would you mind calling Joe?" Steve asked.

"Not in the slightest. I'll call him the minute you hang up." Leah said. "Is there anything else, something you need to talk about?"

"No, I'll tell you tonight. Got to go." Steve couldn't believe it, he was a lucky man. He had a fabulous lady who was beautiful inside and out, and she could cook.

Leah immediately called Joe. "Steve and I want to invite you to dinner tonight."

Joe was happy to get an invitation, but they were a new couple. "Have you ever heard the saying, 'two is company and three's a crowd'? "

"Yes," Leah answered. "What's your point?"

"Well, are you sure you want a chaperone?"

"No," Leah told him. "I have no desire for a chaperone, but I would love to have a friend come to dinner. Something's happened and Steve wants to talk to you. He sounded tired and, I don't know, maybe sad. Anyway, come to dinner, please."

"You got it, girl," Joe replied. "What time shall I be there?"

"Steve usually gets here around 6 o'clock." Leah told Joe. "Come on up anytime and you can keep me company."

It was 5:30 when Leah heard a knock at the door, and she had just finished the salad. She could tell it was Joe. He always tapped lightly on the door.

"Hi, I'm glad you came early; you can open the wine." Leah had never gotten the hang of opening a bottle of wine. She wasn't a wine connoisseur so a lot of the bottles she bought had twist-off tops.

Joe shook his head and laughed. "I can't figure it out. Why would I hire a bartender who can't get the cork out of a bottle of wine?"

"First, when you hired me I was a waitress, not a bartender," Leah answered with a grin. "And second, with a little help from a friend, why should it be a problem?"

Leah led Joe into the kitchen where she showed him the wine and corkscrew. While he was opening the bottle, she started a pot of coffee.

"Leah, you don't have to make coffee for me," Joe told her.

"I like making coffee for you, and sometimes Steve has a cup," Leah said as she led Joe into the living room. "He pops in the bar all the time to unwind, but you know he doesn't drink all that much. He likes the food and the company."

"I can't tell you how glad I am that you and that boy have gotten together," Joe told her. "You were spending all of your time alone or working. Now you have a life."

"Sounds like someone else I know," Leah said. "You do the same thing, my friend."

"It's different with me; I've lived my life," Joe answered.

"You make it sound like you're an old man and at death's door. You are not that old, Joe. Is it because you still miss Mary?" Leah asked.

"I will always miss Mary. She was the love of my life," Joe answered. "She wasn't my first love, but she was my true love, my soulmate as they say."

"I understand," Leah told him. "Sometimes we think we're in love, then something happens and we realize we don't really know what love is. I'm beginning to think I've found someone who will teach me about true love."

Approaching her apartment, Steve decided to knock. He could care less what anyone else thought, but Leah might be embarrassed. He would keep the key she gave him for another time.

"You didn't have to knock, that's why I gave you a key." Leah smiled after she opened the door and stepped close for a kiss. "Joe's here, come join us. I need a minute to fix the gravy and get the food on the table. I have both wine and coffee, what do you want to drink? It's fun having my two favorite men to dinner."

Steve had a long day. "I could do with a glass of

wine," he answered and turned to greet Joe, "Why don't you move to the dining room table and we can talk while I help Leah finish dinner."

Leah was standing at the stove making the gravy. Steve enjoyed helping her in the kitchen. He got Joe another cup of coffee and then filled two wine glasses, taking one to Leah. By the time Steve had carried the food to the table, Leah was finished. She handed the gravy bowl to Steve and turned to retrieve the salad from the refrigerator.

"Leah, this smells wonderful," Joe remarked. "You and Steve working in the kitchen reminded me; I used to help Mary get a meal on the table. She was a good cook, used to make the best fried chicken."

Leah made a mental note to invite Joe for fried chicken some night. Her chicken might not be as good as Mary's, but she would enjoy fixing it for Joe. *Maybe I'll invite Sue as well*, she thought. When they finished dinner, Leah asked if they wanted their cake and coffee in the living room.

"If it is alright with you, I'd like to stay where I am. I enjoy sitting around the table talking. It reminds me of home," Joe said. He had enjoyed the meal, and although Steve looked relaxed, Joe could tell he had something on his mind.

Steve got up and helped Leah clear the table. When they returned, Leah was carrying a chocolate cake and Steve had a tray with cups, plates, and the coffee pot.

"Alright, out with it. What has got you all tied up in knots?" Joe asked Steve.

Leah cut the cake and started to excuse herself, until she heard Steve say, "Stay Leah, this concerns you too."

She saw the look on his face and sat back down.

"This isn't the best after dinner conversation, but there's no good time to tell you this. They found a dead woman this afternoon and I am not sure why they called me to the scene, since I'm a homicide detective. The coroner will probably rule it death by natural causes, although I personally would call it a suicide," Steve had trouble going on. "This job isn't pretty. I've seen a lot, but it's different when you know the person. I'm sorry Joe, it was Aline. It looked like she had died while sitting in her recliner. We found empty mouthwash bottles all around her chair. If I was guessing, I would say she hit rock bottom and was trying to get a buzz from the alcohol content of the mouthwash. God, it was sad. To think someone would throw their life away like that... I didn't want you to read about it in the newspaper."

Joe dropped his head into his hands. "I should have done something. I could have tried to get her into a program. I knew where she was headed. I was just so angry because she was stealing from me."

"There was nothing you could do." Steve knew Joe was hurting. "You can't help someone who doesn't want help. When you caught her stealing, all she was interested in was that next drink. She wouldn't have excepted help."

"I didn't know Aline all that well. Does she have family?" Leah asked.

"They haven't found anyone, yet," Steve answered.

"Let me know if no one comes forward to claim the body. I wasn't able to help her in life, but I can see that she gets a proper burial," Joe said.

They had their cake and coffee, but the evening

was ending on a sad note. After Joe left, Steve and Leah curled up on the couch to watch the 10 o'clock news.

"I know what you do is hard, I guess I didn't realize how hard until tonight," Leah confessed.

"Yes, you see death, and when someone takes that life I work to see that the killer pays. A dead person can't speak for themselves; they need someone who will see they get justice. It's all I ever wanted to do, to see that justice was served." Steve was quiet for a minute. "Can you handle it, Leah? Loving a cop isn't easy."

"I can handle it," Leah whispered. "I love you, Steve."

Steve smiled and pulled her close. She had finally said the three words he had waited so long to hear.

CHAPTER TWELVE

In Nashville, Jeff's organization was thriving. He'd gotten rid of all his problems in one night. Well, not quite one night. It took a little time to hunt Carrie down and eliminate that problem. Who would have figured she'd run all the way to Mexico City? That's where his mob connections had paid off. He didn't have to get his hands dirty. The odd thing was, he still missed her. Carrie was special. *You can't afford to be sentimental,* Jeff told himself. Still, he couldn't help being proud of her. She was smart and had gotten to Mexico before getting caught. She was so beautiful, she had been his angel.

Carl Higgins knocked on his door. Carl had been Jeff's shadow since grade school. He was a little on the stupid side, but totally loyal. Carl had proved his devotion more than once. Jeff needed someone like him to take care of things, and Carl always did whatever Jeff wanted him to do.

Jeff looked up as Carl entered. "What's up?" Jeff didn't invite Carl to sit down. He needed his muscle, not his friendship.

"I need to take some time off," Carl stated as he shifted from foot to foot, "There's been an emergency," he said. "I have to take my mother to California."

Jeff didn't like watching Carl fidget. "Maybe you had better sit down and tell me about this emergency."

Carl dropped into a chair. He'd known his boss since second grade and Jeff had always made him nervous. "My baby brother, Jerry? You remember, I told you he joined the Navy. He was aboard ship and a boiler blew up. He got burned pretty badly. They don't know if he's going to make it or not. They sent him to Bob Wilson Naval Hospital in San Diego. Mother wants me to take her to California."

"I remember sitting at your mother's table after school drinking milk and eating her chocolate chip cookies." Lucy was one of the few people that Jeff was truly fond of. "You're my right-hand man and I depend on you. When will you be back?"

Carl liked that Jeff relied on him. "I'm not sure. They say he's really bad."

Carl wasn't looking forward to this trip. His brother, Mr. Clean as Carl thought of him, had gotten himself into this by joining the Navy. Jerry didn't care for Carl's connection to Jeff and had constantly nagged their mother about Carl's money being dirty.

Jeff leaned his chair back. "Keep in touch and let me know how things are going."

Carl got up and left. In his mind they were friends, but Jeff made him uneasy. He never knew when the man might explode. *That book about Dr. Jekyll and Mr. Hyde fits Jeff to a tee*, Carl thought, and then grinned at the idea. Carl's dad had gotten shot during a bank robbery but Carl was smart, no bank jobs for him. He had hooked up with Jeff, who was the smartest man he knew.

Carl collected his mother and drove to the airport. There were no direct flights so Carl and Lucy arrived in San Diego at 3:25 p.m. after gaining two hours by flying west. They hurried through baggage claim, got a cab, and rushed to the hospital.

When they arrived, they went up to the information desk where they learned Jerry was on the fifth floor. Lucy's eyes were full of hope when she walked up to the nurse's station and asked about her son.

Jerry was in Intensive Care. It was on the same floor, but at the far end. The nurse told them, "You'll have to be cleared by the doctor, and you can only see him for about fifteen minutes. The staff is trying to stabilize him so that he can be flown to the burn unit in San Antonio, Texas. That's the best place for him," she assured Lucy.

They went to the waiting room, but Carl couldn't sit so he paced the floor. Minutes seemed like hours as the two waited for word of Jerry.

Finally, the doctor saw them. "His vital signs are better, it's going to take time, but I think he's going to be alright. He's stable, and if he stays that way we will fly him to Texas sometime tomorrow afternoon. Currently he's heavily sedated, but you can see him for a few minutes. I'll make arrangements for you to accompany him to Texas. I'll be back in the morning to check on him."

Walking into the Intensive Care wing, they located Jerry's unit and found him wrapped up like a mummy. Lucy was all teary eyed and weeping and Carl couldn't take seeing their mother cry. A nurse entered the room. Seeing Lucy crying, she went up and tried to comfort her, "Don't worry, he's stable and getting the best care we can give him."

"Thank you, sweetie," Lucy sniffed and dabbed the tears from her eyes.

The nurse walked over to add a pain medication to Jerry's drip and then left. Lucy stepped up to his bed and leaned in to kiss Jerry's bandaged cheek. "We're here, Jerry. You're going to be alright."

Seeing his brother badly burned, Carl could barely stay in the room with Jerry. There was an odor of burned flesh. Carl was desperate to have another cigarette and he needed a break. “Mom, we should go get settled into a hotel room.”

“No, this chair is plenty good enough for me,” she replied.

“They told us we can only stay fifteen minutes, Mom. He doesn’t even know we're here.” Carl tried to explain.

“I don’t care about that,” Lucy said. “If they won’t let me stay in his room, then I'll stay in the waiting room. I've got my knitting and I’m not leaving. I want to be here if Jerry needs me.”

Carl saw that their mother was determined to remain at the hospital. “Alright, I need a smoke break and I can’t do that on hospital grounds. I’ll be back in a little while.”

At the Ocean Beach Bar and Grill, it was Leah’s night off. She made her way downstairs around 7 o’clock to get something to eat. She and Steve had spent a wonderful day together before he was suddenly called in to work. That hadn’t happened a lot, but she knew he could be called in unexpectedly. She was prepared for times like this; it was just how his job worked. She went up to the order window and spent a minute chatting with Frank before deciding what she wanted to eat. Leaning against the wall, she waited for her plate. Tonight she was planning to take her dinner back to her apartment since there was a program on television that she wanted to watch. She was standing in the shadows when she saw a man walk in. She couldn’t believe her eyes, it was Carl

Higgins. *What's he doing here? Jeff's shadow is the last person I expected to see. How did he find me?* Stunned by the sight of him, she watched him choose a bar stool and sit down. She then heard his deep, cold voice as he ordered a shot of whiskey. *It's definitely Carl, Leah thought. What are the odds that he would just show up here? He doesn't appear to be looking for anyone. It's like he just came in for a drink.*

Frank was putting the garnish on her plate when he looked up and saw Leah's face. He recognized a look of sheer terror when he saw it. He was just about to say something when she bolted and ran out the back door.

Frank left the kitchen and strolled up to Joe, who was sitting at the end of the bar. His eyes searched the room, looking for an unfamiliar face. Frank had never seen Carl before, but he was the only stranger in the room. The cook whispered to Joe, "Come with me. I need to talk to you in private."

Joe got up and followed Frank into the office and then closed the door, turning to Frank with a questioning look on his face.

"A man came into the bar," Frank explained. "When Leah saw him, she turned as white as a sheet and ran out the back door. Someone needs to go check on our girl."

Joe's eyes widened with surprise and then anger gripped him. "You keep an eye on that man and I'll go find Leah."

"I'll watch him like a hawk," Frank replied.

Joe hurried out the back door and up the stairs.

Frank returned to the kitchen and peered out of the service window. From there, he had a perfect view of the bar. He didn't take his eyes off Carl as the man threw a shot of whiskey down his throat and then motioned for Ted to pour another.

Joe rushed down the hall to Leah's apartment. He knocked, but she didn't answer the door. He was worried so he used his key. Unlocking the door, he darted inside and locked the door behind him. He heard her in the bedroom opening and closing drawers. "What in the hell are you doing?" he barked at her as he entered the bedroom.

"Joe, you don't know me. I'm not the person you think I am. I'm sorry for deceiving you but I've got to get out of here. If I stay, I'm going to bring all kinds of trouble right to your doorstep!" Leah said as she threw things into a suitcase.

"What the hell are you talking about?" Joe reached out taking hold of her arm. "You're not going anywhere! No matter what you've gotten yourself into, I'm here for you. Now tell me, who is that man downstairs?"

"His name is Carl Higgins," she answered but that's all she was willing to say.

Joe saw the defiance in her eyes. "Leah, I want you to tell me what's going on." Joe took her shoulders in his strong hands, making Leah look at him.

Leah was shaking so hard she could barely stand. Her worst nightmare had just come true. "You don't need to know, Joe. What you don't know can't hurt you," she snapped as she turned, pulling out of his arms. With shaking hands, she zipped her suitcase.

Joe reached out again to pull Leah into his arms.

Determined to leave, Leah jerked away from Joe's embrace. She pulled her suitcase off the bed and proceeded to go around him. "I have to go!" she yelled.

"I don't give a damn what you think you have to do!" Joe shouted as he grabbed her arm, holding her in place. "Don't you sell me short, little girl. I can take care of myself. Now explain to me why you think you've got to leave!"

Leah wanted to confide in Joe. She thought the world of him, but she wasn't ready to divulge anything that might jeopardize his life. "You don't need to know," she said again. Tears, so close to the surface, began to fall down her cheeks. "Please Joe, you've got to let me go."

Joe held her with one hand and took the suitcase away from her with the other. "I don't understand why you think leaving is the answer. You aren't going anywhere, and you are going to tell me what the hell is going on! Now start talking," he demanded.

They had been screaming at one another, but suddenly Leah heard the music downstairs over her pounding heart. She didn't really want to go. She'd been happy here. Joe's voice finally registered over the fear coursing through her veins. Her determination crumbled and she wilted back onto the bed before burying her face in her hands and starting to sob.

Leah was strong and tears were the last thing Joe expected. Bewildered, he wondered what could make her act this way. He put the suitcase down next to the bed and sat down beside her. Wrapping his strong arms around her shoulders, he pulled her into his embrace and began rocking her like a child. Trying to comfort her, he said, "Nothing can be all that bad. Just tell me what's going on and somehow we'll make it right."

What he said was the same thing Jess had said to her all those months ago. Joe had finally reached her. As briefly as she could, Leah told him what had happened. "Joe, I'm the only witness to a murder. I ran to keep from ending up the same way."

Downstairs Frank watched Carl pick up his loose change. He set down his empty glass, left a tip and walked out. Frank left the kitchen carrying a pitcher of water and followed Carl to the front door. Walking to the planter next to the door, Frank began watering the plants. He nonchalantly looked out the glass and saw Carl hail a cab.

Once inside the cab, Carl pulled out his cell phone and made a call to Nashville. "I just saw someone that looks just like Carrie. Her hair is different, so I'm not one hundred percent sure. She didn't see me, so if it was Carrie we won't have to worry that she'll rabbit. The thing is Jeff; I can't deal with her right now. They're transferring my brother to a burn unit in Texas tomorrow morning. I have to take my mother to San Antonio. I'll get her settled in that hospital and then come back. I just need an extra day or two. Don't worry; I'll personally check this out. If it's Carrie, I'll make sure that it's done right this time."

On the other end of the phone, Jeff thought about what Carl had just told him. He didn't believe it was Carrie. "I can tell you right now, it's not her. She's been taken care of. They say everyone has a look-a-like and you probably saw Carrie's. You're right though, it needs to be checked out. Go do what you need to. Take care of your family and then go back, just to make sure. Tell Lucy I'm thinking of her."

"Will do," Carl replied and hung up.

At the same time that Frank was watching Carl leave, he saw Steve coming in. He waited for him to get inside the front door and then whispered, "There's something going on with Leah. Joe's up in her apartment trying to make some sense out of what happened. You should go up. Let Joe know that the man has left. You passed his cab on the way in."

Panicked, Steve rushed through the bar and made his way up the back stairs.

In Leah's apartment, Joe was relieved to finally understand. "Steve and I can take care of this. We'll keep you safe.

"No! I don't want Steve getting involved. It's bad enough that you know. Jeff's a killer and I won't let him hurt Steve. Jeff killed that man without a second thought!" She was shaking and needed to make Joe understand.

"You need to get a grip on reality. Steve is a professional, a police detective. He's trained to deal with situations like this. I told you not to sell me short, well don't sell Steve short either. He will know what to do, and in case you haven't noticed, the man is crazy in love with you. We need him, Leah. He can help us trap this Jeff and put him in prison where he belongs. When he's locked away, then you'll be safe. You can build a life and not have to run, always afraid and watching over your shoulder."

Leah made up her mind. With these two strong men, she would face Jeff. She looked at Joe, "Call Steve."

Reaching her apartment, Steve found her door locked so he used his key. Joe and Leah heard the door squeak as it opened and they got quiet.

Terrified, Leah whispered, "Joe, I pray that isn't Carl."

"You stay here. I'll go see who it is." Joe got up and quietly left the bedroom.

Steve closed the door and turned the deadbolt. "Leah, Joe, where are you?" he called.

Coming down the hall, Joe was relieved to hear Steve's voice. He turned back to the bedroom door and told Leah, "It's alright honey, it's Steve. You're safe, now."

Seeing them both come out of her bedroom, Steve asked, "What in the hell is going on? Frank said something about a man. He's worried about Leah."

Leah had never heard Steve cuss, was she going to lose this remarkable man? It was something she didn't even want to think about. *Dear God, please don't let him come to hate me,* she prayed.

The moment Steve saw Leah he reached for her, pulling her into his warm embrace. As he slipped his arms around her, he realized she had been crying and rubbed her shoulders, trying to comfort her. Looking over her shoulder at Joe, he said, "Frank says to tell you that man downstairs is gone. He caught a cab and left just as I was arriving."

"I'm glad," Joe answered. "It gives us time to talk."

"Come over here Kitten and tell me what is going on." Steve settled Leah on the sofa and handed her his handkerchief before sitting down beside her.

Leah was afraid of what the two men would think. "I do have something to tell you. I hope you and Joe don't hate me when you know the whole story. There's so much about me that you don't know."

"There's nothing in the world that could make us hate you," Steve softly said and touched Leah's cheek where her tears lay. He took his handkerchief, still clutched tightly in her hand, and wiped the tears running down her face before telling her, "I love you, and nothing can change that. Now tell us what's wrong."

There was no way out now. Leah knew she had to tell Steve and Joe the entire story. She just prayed they would understand! She hadn't exactly lied; she just hadn't told the truth. *Lying by omission, isn't that what they call it? She* thought. This time, she went into more detail. "It started out in Nashville with me thinking I was in love with Jefferson Randall. He's very rich and powerful, but I had no idea what he was really like. One night, I went to a party with friends while he had to work. Someone made a comment about Jeff's wife. I said, 'surely you mean his ex-wife', and the woman got all flustered. They all tried to cover it up, but the damage had been done and I shockingly realized I was engaged to a married man. I knew Jeff would be in his office. I was hurt and angry so I decided to confront him." Leah wiped more tears off her cheeks and then continued.

"Jeff owns Randall Construction and they build large office complexes all over the country. As I said before, he's very rich and he has powerful friends. I'd gone with him to the Governor's mansion and to dinner with the Mayor."

Leah stopped to grab a box of tissue from the coffee table and blow her nose. "I knew his office was on the top floor of a large office building because I had been there before. When I got off the elevator I heard loud voices, but because I was upset I didn't pay any attention. I walked in..." By this time Leah was trembling. "I walked in and saw Jeff's associates standing around a man who was tied to a chair. He looked awful. Someone had beaten him and blood streaked his face. It all happened so quickly. Jeff took a gun out of his desk drawer and shot that man in cold blood. I saw a red circle, a hole I later realized, appear on his forehead and then he slumped in the chair. I screamed, and the next thing I knew I was running for the elevator."

Steve held her tenderly, "You don't have to go on."

"Yes I do," Leah said. "You need to know everything."

"Wait just a minute," Joe said before getting up and going into the kitchen. He poured them all a glass of wine, and for the first time in a long time he was wishing he had something stronger. It killed him to see Leah in so much pain.

He came back and handed them each a glass before he sat back down.

Leah took a sip of the wine and continued her story. "I don't know how, but I knew the man was dead. I ran from the room, and as I was leaving I heard Jeff tell his men to leave me alone, that he knew where to find 'the bitch'. If he thought I was going to go back to my apartment to wait for him, then he was in for a big surprise. I went home and dumped clothes, identification, everything I thought I would need into a suitcase. I kept expecting Jeff to appear; I didn't want him to catch me. I loaded up the car and drove to Memphis, where I bought a ticket to Mexico City. I had hoped that it would throw Jeff off my trail.

Now this is the part I really regret. I promise, I didn't know she would die. I thought Jeff's men would find her, realize it wasn't me and leave her alone." Leah started sobbing again.

Joe couldn't stand seeing her so upset, "Stop Leah, you don't need to finish it tonight."

"I think she does," Steve answered. If someone was dead they needed to know who it was. "Go ahead, tell us everything."

Leah couldn't look Steve in the eye. She was terrified that he was going to hate her. "After leaving Nashville, I called an old friend who lives in Oklahoma. I asked her to come get me. I ditched my car in the Memphis airport parking lot and caught a shuttle to the Peabody Hotel. I didn't want to rent a room in my name since I was afraid Jeff would find out, so I walked across the street to a bar. That's where I met this young woman, her name was Jennifer Anderson. She was playing pool and complaining about never getting to go anywhere. She looked enough like me to be my sister, so I took that ticket to Mexico City out of my purse and offered her my passport, credit card and driver's license. She jumped at the chance for a free trip." Leah looked up with pain in her eyes. "She never made it home! I found out later she'd been run down by a hit and run driver in Mexico City. I think it was Jeff's doing. I have no way of knowing that for sure, but I feel responsible for her death. The saddest part about it is, I secretly hoped he thought it was me so he would forget about me and I could be free." Leah got quiet for a moment.

Steve knew she needed to tell it all. "How did you end up in San Diego?"

"My friend from Oklahoma picked me up the next morning at a Memphis park and took me home with her. I met her husband and his Uncle Ed. Ed drives a truck, and he brought me to California. I used Jen's name up to that point. I forged some papers and got a dead girl's birth certificate in Sacramento. Leah Scott died before she was fourteen and had no family left alive. I had an uncle, Richard Adams, who was in the Navy. He knew Joe and had been to this bar. He told me lots of stories about San Diego and his friendship with Joe. He said Joe was the most trustworthy person he ever knew. I needed someone like that, and so here I am. That's it. I'm sorry that I lied to both of you."

Leah took a deep breath. She was mentally and physically exhausted, but at the same time she felt like a heavy weight had lifted from her chest. It was a relief to finally tell the truth.

"Damn," Joe said. "I knew you reminded me of someone. Richard is a very good friend. Mary and I were sorry to see him go home to Texas."

"Do you both hate me?" Leah quietly asked.

Steve still hadn't said anything. "Of course I don't hate you, but I am having a hard time taking all this in. Can you tell me what happened tonight to set all this in motion?"

"That man I saw in the bar was Carl Higgins, Jeff's right-hand man. He was there the night Jeff killed that guy. I was standing in the hallway downstairs waiting for Frank to fix my dinner and I saw him come in. I was in the shadows so I'm pretty sure that Carl didn't see me, but I certainly saw him. I was going to run and Joe stopped me. Now I realize I'm tired of running. I want to stop Jeff and find some way to make sure he pays for all he's done. When he's in prison, I hope I can make it up to you and Joe. I didn't want to lie, but I didn't see any other way. I had hoped I could stay hidden. You don't know how powerful Jeff is. He has contacts in almost every city, and more money than God. He owns everyone in Nashville. I know I'm going to have a lot to answer for when this is over. Please, will you help me?"

Steve pulled Leah into his arms. "We're going to make this right," he told her. "The first thing I'm going to do is go back to the office and run a background check on Jefferson Randall. I'll see if I can find out where that cab dropped Carl as well. You stay put and keep the door locked. Give me a chance to see what I can find out." He looked down at his watch. "It's almost nine o'clock. It will take me at least a couple of hours. I'll be back as soon as I have something to report."

Steve kissed Leah lightly on the forehead, got up, and went toward the door. Reaching out for the door knob, he looked back at them. "Take care of our girl, Joe. I'll be back as quick as I can."

Joe locked the door behind Steve. He then turned to Leah and asked, "You got any of the hard stuff up here? I think you and I need a double, then maybe you can get a little sleep."

"I have a bottle of Tennessee whiskey under the kitchen sink; that's what Steve prefers," Leah answered. "But there's no way I can sleep."

No wonder I couldn't find it, Joe thought as he retrieved the bottle and got two glasses out of the cabinet. He poured them both a generous portion. "Here, drink this. I'll keep watch and you try to get some rest."

Leah took a drink and felt the strong whiskey burn down her throat. "I'm going to go back to my bedroom and lay down on the bed," she told him, and took the glass with her. She curled up, not expecting to rest. Something about the whiskey and Joe's presence in the living room relaxed her however and she dozed off.

On his way to the police station, Steve was trying to make some sense out of all he had heard. He couldn't help but wonder who he could trust. *Does Randall really have connections all over the country? Sounds reasonable, most mobsters do, but I would like to think that San Diego is different.*

Arriving at his office, Steve sat down at his desk computer and started the background check on Jefferson Randall. He also ran a check on his known associates and Carl Higgins in particular. While the computer searched, he contacted the cab company to see where they dropped Carl. *That doesn't add up, why the Navy hospital?* He was just getting started. He went back to his computer to see if the search was done and found it had just finished. Maybe Randall did have connections. Going over the background check, he wasn't seeing much. The phone rang, and wondering who knew he was in the office this late, Steve reached for it.

"Steve Burke, I'm surprised you're in your office at this time of the night."

Steve's friend, John Bell, had graduated from high school at the same time and they had both been interested in law enforcement. John had caught the attention of the FBI during college, and Steve had eventually returned to San Diego. He hadn't talked to John in months however and he was caught off guard hearing his voice on the phone. Right off, it hit Steve as peculiar.

"How are you doing, John? I wasn't expecting to hear from you this late."

"Steve, if you weren't such a good friend, I would beat around the bush trying to find out why you're interested in Jefferson Randall." John Bell had been with the FBI for five years and he usually played his cards close to the vest. "Your background check sent up all kinds of red flags, my friend. May I ask what's going on?"

"I have a personal reason for wanting to know about Randall." John wasn't the only one who could play his cards close to the vest. "Why would a simple background check be of interest to the FBI?"

"We need to talk, but I don't want to do it over the phone. Stay where you are and I'll come to you." John was putting his jacket on as he hung up the phone.

Steve had a feeling John knew something and it might help him find out about Randall. He wanted to help Leah, and he wasn't getting anywhere with his search. It suddenly occurred to him that he didn't even know her real name. *What if Leah's not the person I believe her to be? No, that can't be true. I know her! She just got mixed up with the wrong person. There's no way my Leah is guilty of anything bad. She simply doesn't have a mean or dishonest bone in her body. I'm not that bad a judge of character.*

Fifteen minutes later, John was walking through Steve's office door.

John's husky build filled the doorway. He nodded

his head in greeting and then closed the door behind him with a click before addressing Steve. "You said personal reasons, so I don't think I'm going to get anything out of you until I come clean. This conversation doesn't go outside of these four walls, agreed?"

Steve leaned back in his chair and lifted both his eyebrows. "Alright, this is between you and me. At this point, it goes no further. If we decide we can help each other, we'll renegotiate later," Steve answered while trying to cover all the bases.

John dragged up a chair and sat down across from Steve's desk. "We've been investigating Jefferson Randall for over a year now. Drugs, laundering money, racketeering, you name it. We had a mole in his organization but he turned up dead. Someone beat the shit out of him and then put a bullet right in the middle of his forehead. I want this bastard and I want him bad. Now it's your turn," he said.

Steve let his chair fall forward and put his elbows on the desk top. "Well now, I believe I can help you with that John. I may have a witness to the murder. She happens to be the woman I intend to marry, so I want to see her protected. I'm sure she didn't know what the bastard was doing, but she stumbled onto the murder. She's broken a few minor laws trying to get away from Randall before he could kill her. She might be open to putting Randall's sorry ass behind bars, if you can work it out so that she isn't charged with anything illegal." Steve could tell by John's eyes that he wanted to make a deal.

Testing to see if Steve really had her, he called his bluff. "What kind of laws did Carrie Adams break?"

John knew Carrie had disappeared and he hoped Steve had somehow found her. "It is Carrie we are talking about, isn't it?"

What a way to find out Leah's real name, Steve thought. He still wasn't giving anything away. "My witness exchanged identifications with a young woman in Memphis. Then in California she took a dead girl's name off a headstone and somehow managed to get a birth certificate and identification in that name. Last month, she learned that the young woman from Memphis was dead. They said it was a hit and run, but my witness suspects its Randall's doing. Maybe she could help you pin that hit and run on Randall."

John took out his phone and made a call. "This is Special Agent Johnson Bell. We have someone who might be willing to step forward and name Jefferson Randall as the man who killed our agent. When she ran, she changed her identity twice. She's committed no crimes, other than identity theft. If we give her immunity on those charges, she's willing to testify."

John's ear was pressed to the phone as he listened to the voice on the other end of the line. "Yes sir, San Diego Police Detective Steve Burke vouches for the witness."

John ended the call and looked back at Steve. "We have a deal."

"Let me run this by my witness first. Knowing how much she wants to see Randall behind bars, I believe we can work together." Steve stood up, reached out and shook John's hand. "She ran because she was afraid for her life, now she's tired of running. She wants Randall to pay, and she wants to feel safe. Carl Higgins may have seen her earlier tonight. So we don't have a lot of time."

John didn't like the idea that Carl might be on her trail. Carl was mean as a snake. "When can we meet her?"

"I'll call you in the morning. In the meantime, see if you can find out why Carl's hanging around the Naval Hospital." Steve thought that he might as well let the FBI earn their pay.

John left while Steve put his jacket on. He needed to get home to Leah. They weren't out of the woods yet, but it looked like they were going to get a break. Steve hoped that Leah was getting some rest.

By the time Steve reached the bar, it was almost midnight. Frank must have been watching, because when he got out of the car the cook emerged from the back door.

Steve asked, "Has that guy been back?"

"No, but I've been watching for Joe." Frank replied. "I thought he would've come and told me something by now. Where is he and what in the heck is going on?"

"I asked Joe to stay with Leah while I went back to the station." Steve realized that he was between a rock and a hard place. How much should he tell Frank?

Suddenly, the problem was solved; Joe appeared at the head of the stairs. As he came down he said, "Leah dozed off for a little while. We saw you pull up so I decided to come down. I thought you two might need a moment alone so you can tell her what you found out," Joe said.

"No, I'll only want to tell the story once. Let's go back in," he said.

"Am I invited?" Frank asked, curious.

"Come on up you old coot," Joe told Frank. "Leah said she's through keeping secrets, at least from her second family." Joe knew that Leah's statement would make Frank feel better. She had become close to all of them.

"How long did she sleep?" Steve asked Joe as they climbed the stairs.

"Not long," Joe confessed. "I gave her a glass of your whiskey. She laid down in the bedroom and tried to rest. Maybe she thought I would stretch out on the couch."

Leah was watching out the drawn shade and saw them coming.

"Frank, come in," Leah said when she opened the door. "I'm sorry for all the commotion I've caused tonight. That man, Carl, he's a ghost from my past. I can't go into everything just now, but I witnessed a murder and some bad people are trying to find me. Hopefully, Steve is going to help me out of the jam I've gotten myself into. Please, I'll explain it all later. In the meantime, can you keep an eye out for Carl and if he shows up, let us know?"

"You bet, girl. We take care of our own." Frank was quick to add, "I'm going to go. I just wanted to see for myself that you're alright." He let himself out and went back downstairs.

"He'll be curious, but he won't gossip," Joe assured them. "What did you find out at the station?"

Steve was tired, but he knew none of them would get any rest until he made his report. "The background check didn't tell me much, but before I had a chance to worry about it the FBI was calling my office. It seems that information request set off warning bells in their office, but we got lucky. My friend John is the one who called, and they sent him to question me. He wants Randall in the worst way. They believe the man in the chair was their plant, and an FBI agent. John described him as being roughed up and shot the same way Leah did."

Leah couldn't forget about Jennifer. "What if they learn I sent Jen to her death?"

"John will need you to tell him about that so they can connect the dots. If it turns out Jeff had that young woman killed and they can prove it, that's another nail in his coffin. The only crime you've committed is identity theft. I know John like a book. They'll give you immunity if you testify in court and help them get Randall. Do that, and all the charges will disappear."

Steve grinned and took Leah by the hand. "You help them and you're home free. You can do anything you want after that, even go home if that's what you'd like to do."

"I'll be happy to help the FBI. Then I would love to go see my parents and my friends," Leah told the men. "After that, I want to come home to San Diego. That is, if you two can forgive me?"

"As far as I can see, girl," Joe told her, "You got yourself in some mighty hot water and need friends to help you out, but I don't see anything to forgive."

"I agree," Steve said "It takes a clever person to elude someone like Randall. I've got to call John in the morning and let him know what you've decided. He'll set up a meeting with the FBI tomorrow afternoon, if that's alright. For right now, I'd say we should get to bed and try to get a good night's sleep."

"Sounds good to me," Leah said. "What about

Carl?"

Steve laughed. "I have the FBI on Carl's tail. They know where he is, and should he leave, John will call. We'll probably find out what he's doing in San Diego at the meeting tomorrow afternoon."

Joe headed for the door. "I'm going to go check on the bar, close up and then go home. Let me know how everything turns out with the FBI. It's all going to work out, Leah. I told you Steve and I would take care of things. Call if you need me, Steve."

"I'll call," Steve answered and watched Joe close the door. He locked it behind the other man and then led Leah to the bedroom.

Once they settled in bed, Steve told Leah, "I know your real name now. For the time being, I think you would be safer using Leah. Like you said before, Randall's no fool. He can buy his way out of this if it's not handled just right. That's where John is going to come in handy. He can offer you more than just immunity. He's capable of putting you into a witness protection program."

"I don't think anyone other than Jeff would try hurting me. Once he's behind bars, I should be able to live my life anywhere I want."

"That's not exactly true. There are a lot of gangsters who run their empires from inside prison walls. Unless we get one of his associates to flip, you're the only witness who can testify against him. He'll want to deal with you before he goes to trial. He's going to want you dead, Leah."

"So, you're saying that I should go into that program to keep me safe until we go to court?" Leah didn't want to run and in her mind that program would be like running.

"That's exactly what I'm telling you. I love you, and I want to keep you safe." Steve couldn't help worrying about her.

Leah thought about it for a moment. "I'd rather be a pawn and lure him out here to California."

"Do you know how dangerous that is?" Steve asked her, "There's no way I will allow it."

"I hate to burst your bubble, Mr. Detective, but there's no way you can stop me!"

There's that attitude, Steve thought. "Alright, we'll wait until tomorrow and see how John wants to play it, then decide what to do."

They were tired. Steve pulled Leah into his arms and as they nestled together he thought. *We can do anything as long as we're together.*

CHAPTER THIRTEEN

The sound of the alarm woke the two of them. When Leah had gone to bed she wasn't sure she could sleep, but when Steve had pulled her so lovingly into his arms, she had promptly nodded off. The next thing she knew the alarm was buzzing in her ear.

"Where are we going to meet the FBI?" Leah asked as she got out of bed.

Steve had gotten up earlier and called John to set up a meeting. Wanting Leah to sleep as long as possible, he had lay back down beside her and eventually had fallen back to sleep himself.

"They don't want to draw attention to you by bring you downtown," Steve explained. "I hope it is alright; I invited them here."

"That's fine." It was anything but fine since Leah was starting to get nervous. "I'll make a big pot of coffee. Would you go downstairs and see if Louie has something to snack on? He sometimes makes cinnamon rolls and saves some for me."

Steve took Leah into his arms. "It's going to be alright, Baby. We'll get through this. Always remember, I love you."

Leah held Steve tight. "I love you so much. I pray you'll still love me when all of this is over." A thought suddenly occurred to Leah. "Could this affect your career?"

Steve's voice took on a teasing quality. "My helping the FBI will probably earn me a gold star." In a more serious tone he added, "If you're worried about it having a negative effect, then don't. Nothing you did will affect my job, or my love for you." Steve held Leah tightly for a few moments. "Am I going to have to get used to calling you Carrie?"

"You mean when this is over?" Leah was quiet for a second. "I've been so worried, that was the last thing on my mind. You know I kind of like Leah."

"I believe that you will be better off if you use that name, at least until this is over. You don't want to draw any attention. You said it yourself, Randall is no fool.

Steve jumped into the shower while Leah made coffee. As she turned the coffee maker on, she heard a quiet tap on the door. It was Joe waiting in the hallway with a plate of cinnamon rolls.

"I knocked lightly in case you were asleep," Joe said as he stepped into the room. "Louie made fresh cinnamon rolls this morning."

"We're meeting with the FBI here." Leah said as she took the plate from Joe. "I had asked Steve to see if Louie had something to serve them. In fact, I was just talking about Louie's cinnamon rolls and you show up with a plate."

"Louie knows you like them. He heard about last night and he's been worried about you." Joe turned to leave. "I won't keep you."

"Joe," Leah said. "You've done so much, and I hate to ask…"

Joe turned at her words. "You're special to me, girl, I've told you before, you can ask me anything."

She set the plate down on the snack bar. "Stay? You know the whole story, and I want to know what you think of anything the FBI comes up with."

"I'm sure Steve is more than capable of protecting your interest, but if you want me, I'll stay." Joe walked over and pulled Leah into his arms. She looked so small and fragile this morning. He decided to ask her about her uncle, not because he didn't remember, but because he wanted to get her mind off her troubles. "How did you say you were related to Richard?"

Leah stepped away and walked around to the kitchen side of the bar to set the rolls, plates and cups on a tray.

"He's my dad's brother," Leah smiled. "He and dad have had their differences. Uncle Richard is a tease and my dad is more serious, but I adore them both. He told me about you and your Navy days, and about you buying this bar. He said you had hired a Navy cook to help you. Richard was real proud of you for helping out your buddy. I assume that was Frank."

Steve came into the room wearing fresh jeans and a tee shirt.

"Joe came up and brought fresh cinnamon rolls. He and Louie must have read my mind," Leah told Steve. "I've asked him to stay."

"Whatever makes you comfortable." Steve leaned in and gave Leah a quick kiss. "I don't know what kind of plan they'll come up with, and I want to make sure that you stay safe."

"I'm safe, here with you and Joe. I'm going to take a shower," she said and went back to her bedroom.

The two men sat drinking coffee as they waited for her, and then there she was, as pretty as a picture in a soft blue dress. She barely got a sip of her coffee before they heard a knock on the door.

"It's show time," Steve said, and then pulled a gun out of the back of his jeans. "Leah, go to the bedroom until I'm sure everything's alright." After she was out of the room, he checked the door before opening it to two FBI agents.

John came in and shook Steve's hand. "Steve, I would like you to meet Special Agent Samuel Ellis. Sam, this is one of San Diego's finest, Detective Steven Burke."

The men shook hands before Steve turned to introduce Joe to the two agents. "Let me get Leah," he said.

Leah had heard the conversation and walked into the room. The agents immediately recognized her from her picture even though her hair was shorter and was still brown from her trip to the Sallisaw beauty shop.

"Good morning, gentlemen." Leah reached out to shake hands.

Sam Ellis took her hand in a firm grip. "Carrie Adams, I presume."

How would he know me? Leah thought as she shook hands with him and then the other agent.

Steve invited the men to sit down while Leah brought the tray from the kitchen and placed it on the coffee table. "Help yourself to refreshments, gentlemen." Leah told them. "About the name, can we stick with Leah for now, and would you mind telling me how you know about me?"

"We had an FBI agent in Jefferson Randall's operation. He was a mole and deep under cover, or so we thought. You disappeared the same night he did. We couldn't bug the building; Randall was too smart for that, but we had a camera on the outside and saw you enter the building that night. When you left approximately ten minutes later, you were in a big hurry and looked extremely upset. We also saw them carry a roll of carpet out of the building; it turned out to be our guy," Sam said and then prompted her, "We've been looking for you ever since. Do you want to tell us what happened?"

"I came into the office in time to see Jeff shoot that man. I panicked and ran, and I guess Jeff thought I was stupid. I heard him make a comment, to leave the bitch alone and that he knew where to find me. I was around long enough to know that Jeff's very powerful and I was afraid to trust anyone in Nashville, so I ran for my life. I've had enough running though, and have realized that I won't be safe until Jeff is put away. What can I do to help you?" Leah addressed her question to Sam adding, "One other thing, Jeff's right-hand man was in the bar last night. I don't think he saw me and if he did, I hope he didn't recognize me. Did you find out why Carl Higgins is in San Diego?"

John answered Leah's questions. "Steve traced Carl's cab to the Navy Hospital. We were able to find out that Carl's half-brother was burned in a boiler explosion on board a Navy ship. He's pretty bad, and Carl brought their mother out to be with him. They're shipping him out on a plane to the burn unit in San Antonio, and Carl and his mother are on the passenger list. In fact, they should be leaving about now. We have someone keeping an eye on him so we'll know when he leaves Texas."

Sam took a recording device out of his briefcase and turned to Leah, "I want you to tell me everything. Start at the beginning, and leave nothing out." He turned on the device and spoke, giving the date, time and the name of everyone in the room. "Start by giving your real name," Sam stated.

Leah took a deep breath, "The name I was born with was Carrie Ann Adams." She said and then went back through the whole story. She told of her love for Jeff and when that had started to fall apart. Then she told about the horror of seeing the man she thought she loved kill someone. She told how she'd run, and of meeting Jennifer. When she told them of her friend Jessica and how Jess and Bob introduced her to Bob's Uncle Ed a smile played around her lips. "Please don't blame them. They were just helping a friend."

"Go on," Sam encouraged her.

"By that time, I was using Jennifer's name," Leah continued. "I rode across the country with Ed, until he had a problem with his truck. He stopped in a little town in California. I ended up in an old cemetery; killing time while he got the truck fixed. That's when I saw a marker for Leah Scott, buried close by was her mother and father." She told them everything she had done to get a fake ID in Leah's name. "I came to San Diego and got a job at the bar downstairs. That was where I met Joe and Steve. I saw Carl the other night and I was ready to run, but Joe talked me out of it, and that's was where you came in."

"Where did you get the money to run?" Sam wanted to be sure he knew all the facts.

"I had some extra money in my bank account. I took everything except a few dollars. Then Jess and Bob loaned me some money. I did feel guilty about the plane ticket; I put it on my credit card. I owe the card company some money, but I was afraid to make the payment," Leah said and looked at Sam. "I was raised to be honest. When this is over I will pay my credit card bill."

Sam stared at Leah for a moment. "You've told me everything, just like it happened?"

Leah raised her right hand, "All that I have said is the truth, so help me God."

Sam pushed stop and put the recorder back in his briefcase. "I'll have this transcribed and bring it back in the morning for you to sign. We're keeping an eye on Carl, but we don't know what he may or may not have seen. I want to be prepared for anything. We're going to bug this apartment from top to bottom. Joe, don't you need to hire an extra busboy? I'll want to put an agent in the bar. He'll work Leah's hours."

"I'll do anything to help Leah," Joe assured Sam.

"One more thing," Sam looked at Leah. "I want to implant a high tech tracking device under your skin. We can turn it off and on by remote control. If it's not turned on, no one can detect it. I don't want to take a chance on Randall getting to you. Witnesses have a way of disappearing, and I want to know where you are at all times."

"I told you, I would do anything to help you and if that means a tracking device, then so be it," Leah said. "I just want this to be over."

"I have one thing to say." Steve was determined to protect Leah. "The agreement stating that Leah will not be prosecuted and that all charges will be dropped; have it with you tomorrow. Leah does not sign anything without that agreement," Steve firmly stated.

"What are you, her lawyer?" Sam replied.

"No," Steve answered. "I'm the man who loves her, and I know enough about the law to see that she's protected."

"None of this would have happened if she had

stayed put." Sam was not backing down. "You know none of the crimes she committed will get her jail time."

"If she hadn't run, she might not be alive to testify for you." Steve was beginning to get angry. "She could be in a court of law for years clearing this up and you know it. One phone call and the FBI can take care of it. Have the agreement tomorrow or don't come back. I'm not without connections and believe me, I can handle this."

Steve showed the FBI agents to the door and slammed it behind them.

"Why does this cop want to have a pissing contest with the FBI?" Sam asked as he turned to John.

"Well it's like this," John told him. "His dad is Chief of Police, and you've heard of our esteemed US Senator from California? I believe Steve was named after his Uncle Steven, and if I am not mistaken there is a judge or two in the family tree. Hell Sam, you were going to agree not to prosecute that girl all along. Why are you dragging your feet?"

"Beats me," Sam shrugged.

The two men walked out into the sunny, California day and made their way down the stairs to the back parking lot.

Upstairs, Leah went to Steve and put her arms around him. "I do believe that the man I love has a little bit of a temper. I've never seen that side of you before."

Steve grinned, "I try not to let it show. You get more flies with honey and all that crap. Joe, will you stay with Leah? I need to go downtown for a little while." Steve had some time off coming and he'd decided to take it. He'd also decided to have a talk with his father since he would be in the neighborhood.

"No one has to babysit me," Leah popped back. "I'm scheduled to work tonight, and you heard the FBI; Carl's in Texas."

"Alright," Steve knew when to pick his battles. Leah had a point, no need to keep her locked in this apartment. "I'll be home before you get off work."

"We'll keep an eye on her," Joe said. He was no dummy and saw the determined look on Leah's face. "See you downstairs, Leah."

Steve and Joe walked out the door together and they heard Leah bolt the door behind them. When they reach the outside door, Joe made sure that it was locked as well.

"She's locked up tight and I'll keep an eye out," Joe said. Then he turned and waved at Steve over his shoulder before heading toward the back door of the bar.

"I'll just be a couple of hours, three at the most," Steve called. "Thanks Joe, for everything." He was glad Joe was there. Leah should be alright, but there was no need to take chances.

A few hours later, Leah came down and worked her shift. Steve was back before she took her dinner break. They ordered their dinner and Leah got them both a glass of tea. Joe was sitting with them at the bar when Steve told Leah, "I'm taking a few days off. I want to be with you."

"I'd like to have you here in the morning," Leah said. "After I sign those papers you can go to work."

Leah didn't mention the FBI, not in the bar where they could be heard. Steve waited for Leah's shift to be over and they climbed the stairs together.

They were up and waiting the next morning when the two FBI agents knocked on the door. There was a young woman with them, and Sam introduced her as Lisa. She was the technician who would insert the tracking device.

"Isn't that going a little overboard?" Leah asked.

"People who can testify against Jefferson Randall have a tendency to come up missing," Sam explained. "We're not going to let that happen to you. Your testimony will be the clincher; we have him this time."

Sam presented Steve with some papers while Leah and Lisa went into the bedroom.

"I'm going to deaden the skin and make a shallow incision just above your waist. I'll slip this device just under the skin, then glue the skin together. If someone should notice, it will look like the cat scratched you," Lisa explained to Leah.

When the women come out of the bedroom, Lisa went to the bar and opened a computer. A minute later, she looked at Sam, "I turned it on and checked the signal, then turned it off. Everything checks out, so I'll see you back at the office."

When Sam returned from showing Lisa out, he looked at Steve. "Do those papers work for you?"

"These work for us," Steve answered. "What's next?"

Sam motioned for them to sit down. "Carl is on the move, he caught a plane bound for San Diego. I think we need to move Leah to a safe house."

"No way," Leah said. "I've been thinking, I know I may be fooling myself but I believe Jeff really cared for me. I could lure him to California. Maybe I could trick him into telling me about Jennifer. If he had someone kill her I need to know."

Leah spent the next hour telling them about her plan to trap Jeff. Mid way though, Steve began to pace. When she had finished, she turned to Steve and said, "What do you think?"

"I think that's the worst idea I have ever heard." Steve couldn't believe she was so willing to risk her own life. What he had heard put knots in his stomach. "Randall kills people Leah, you know that. I can't believe you want to do this, and I am not going to let you get yourself killed."

Leah walked over to Steve and put her hands on his face, making him look into her eyes. "Remember when you told me why you wanted to become a cop? You said that when someone takes a life; you stand up for the person that's dead. You said you see that justice is served. I have to do this Steve. If Jeff killed Jennifer then I need to know, and I have to stand up for her. I have to see that Jeff is punished, please say you understand."

Leah turned to John and Sam, "What about you, do you think it will work?"

"I think it might." John said. "You're a civilian though. You could be hurt."

"I agree, but I think we can keep the danger to a minimum." Sam said as he placed a phone call. "I want someone out here to bug an apartment. I need to be able to hear a person breathe, and I want it ASAP." Sam disconnected the phone call. "I had thought of bugging the apartment to see if we could get more information, but I gave up that idea when I thought we would put Leah in a safe house. We'll give you a chance, Leah. I hope you're a good actress."

"Me too," Leah replied in a soft tone of voice. "One more thing; Jeff had his own plane and he was a qualified pilot. He can be in and out of California with no one the wiser."

"He certainly knows where to bury the bodies in Tennessee," Sam noted.

That surprised Leah. She instantly realized that Jeff had killed more than one person. "Whatever you have to do, don't let him put me on that plane. I would rather die here than be at his mercy."

"Don't worry, we won't," Sam said. After that everyone got quiet for a minute.

"We don't have much time and we need to get things rolling." Sam knew there was a room across the hall and he didn't like the idea of being parked outside in a van. "Could we set up in that area next door where we can be close? We'll need a place for the electronic monitors, and it would be nice if we had access to a bathroom."

Leah spoke up, "Joe uses that space for storage. There's a laundry room and a bathroom, plus an old table and some chairs. I do inventory in there and that hallway door always stays locked."

"We would have all the comforts of home," John laughed.

"I could bring up a coffee pot and maybe a microwave," Leah said.

"No coffee pot or microwave. We never eat on the job," John told them. "Nothing gives you away like the smell of food in what is supposed to be an empty space."

"The back part of storage area should work." Leah told them, "It's away from the hall and there's plenty of room."

"Good, we'll get everything set up," John said as he got up to go downstairs and meet with the electronics team. He would show them where to put the monitors.

Before John walked out the door, Sam told him, "When you're through, have them ditch the van. I don't want anyone to see anything out of the ordinary." He turned to Leah. "It's your call, what do you want us to do?"

"I'm going to work and I hope Carl comes back in." Leah was nervous but she knew she could do this. She knew Jeff and his ego better than anyone, and she knew he would come to San Diego. This had to work; she needed to lure him in. "It's a good plan and I know I can make it work. Since Carl is on his way to San Diego, he must have seen me."

"Alright, we'll move in next door and get everything ready," Sam said, and then went to talk to his team.

Leah got ready for work while Steve started packing up all of his things. He had moved some clothes into Leah's apartment over the last few months, and if she was supposed to be lonely for Randall, she wouldn't be entertaining another man. He didn't like the idea, but he had to let her try. When Leah was ready to go downstairs he kissed her goodbye.

Leah gave him a hug. "Thank you for trusting me."

"It's not a matter of trust. I love you and I don't mind telling you that I'm scared to death." Steve put himself on the line every day, but it was hard to see Leah do the same thing.

"I love you too," Leah replied and walked out the door.

Downstairs everything looked the same except that there was a new busboy. It was amazing, he didn't look like FBI. His hair was a little shaggy, and he was wearing jeans with a small rip in one knee. Joe made sure that he wore an apron to cover it up, but it showed when he walked. Under normal circumstances he would not have met Joe's dress code. They told the employee's nothing, afraid that someone might give something away.

Leah was trying to appear normal but she had butterflies in her stomach. Joe passed her a note around 9 o'clock. It said that Carl's plane had landed at the airport and he had caught a cab headed in her direction. It was going to happen. *Please God, help me do this right*, Leah prayed.

A short time later, Carl walked in and went to a corner table where he could observe the bar area. Leah saw him and signaled to Barb. "I know that guy," Leah explained when Barb approached her. "I'll get his table."

"Sure thing," Barb told her with a smile. "I hope Steve isn't the jealous type."

"Hi, Carl," Leah said, approaching the table. "What are you doing in California?" She glanced at the other chair, "Do you mind if I sit down? I have a break coming up."

Carl couldn't figure it out. Carrie was acting as if nothing had happened. "Sure go ahead and join me." Carl thought, *two can play this game*. "My brother was burned in an accident. I brought our mother out to see him. What are you doing here?"

"I made a terrible mistake when I ran from Jeff." Leah wished she could cry on demand. "I still love him. I'm lonely and I want to come home. Would you talk to him for me, see if he can forgive me? Maybe he would come get me."

"I don't know, Carrie." Carl wasn't sure what to do. "I guess I could try."

"Tell him I'll do anything if he'll forgive me." Leah decided to cool it a little. Carl may not be as stupid as she thought. "I live in a little apartment over the bar. This is my phone number. Ask him to call me, please." Leah took out her order pad and wrote her phone number on the back of a ticket. As she passed the number to Carl, she told him, "I better get back to work. What would you like?"

Carl placed his order and waited for his drink. He wished he could have told her to bring the whole bottle, but he had a phone call to make. When Leah brought him his shot of bourbon, he swallowed it in one gulp and left a fifty on the table. It was the smallest bill he had, but he didn't wait for the change. *Let Carrie have it, I can get it later, off her dead body.*

Outside, Carl walked down the street to the end of the block and made a phone call to Nashville and waited for Jeff to answer. "It's her. She walked up to me bold as brass and acted like nothing had happened. She went on and on about making a terrible mistake. She says she loves you and wants to come home."

"What kind of game is the bitch playing?" Jeff wondered out loud. "Why isn't she dead? That's what I paid for!" He could feel his blood pressure rising.

"I don't know, boss. It was a shock for me too." Carl didn't want Jeff angry with him. "I'm down the street from the bar where she works. She said she lives in an apartment above the joint. She gave me her phone number so you could call her. Carrie was always crazy about you, boss. Maybe she is lonesome and sorry she ran."

Jeff was quiet, thinking. *If Carrie is begging for forgiveness, maybe I should fly to California and see her one last time. I can't let her live.* "I'm curious to know how she managed to get away," he told Carl without giving away everything he was thinking. "Keep an eye on her. I'm on my way."

Carl walked around to the back of the bar. Seeing the back door, he noticed the stairs leading to the second floor. He was only one person; he couldn't watch the back and the front. He decided to take a chance and found a place where he could hide and watch the back of the bar. At 2:15 in the morning he saw all the employees leaving, all except for Carrie. He observed her climb the stairs and unlock the outside door. Everything she had told him checked out. Carl wished he had taken the time to rent a car. Sitting in a car was a lot more comfortable than being out in the open. He settled down on the hard ground to wait for Jeff's arrival.

When Leah got upstairs, the men were waiting for her with the storage door propped open. Steve came out in the hall and pulled her into his arms. "You did great," he told her. "Carl made a phone call to Jeff and then hunkered down in the dark to watch the back of the bar. Joe's security cameras are really coming in handy. John wired them into the monitors and we can watch every move Carl makes."

"Jefferson Randall took off from a private airport

in Nashville. His flight plan listed the destination as San Diego." Sam told Leah. "He's on your hook and all you have to do is reel him in. We'll be right next door listening."

"This is going to be a long night," Leah told the men. "Would you guys like coffee and sandwiches before you go back to the storeroom?"

John was the first to say, "My stomach is growling. I didn't know if I was going to last much longer. It's not like we can go out with Carl hiding in the bushes."

Leah laughed, "Come on over and I'll start a pot of coffee."

"Make sure you close the curtains. We'll stay back so we don't cast shadows for Carl to see." Sam instructed.

Leah had bought a large ham and it was still in the refrigerator. In a matter of minutes, she had a big platter of sandwiches sitting on the table. She put out cheese for those who wanted it, and a large bag of chips. She also left all the lights off except for the one over the kitchen sink so no shadows could be seen from outside. After everyone finished their meal, Leah ushered them out of the apartment.

"I don't like leaving you alone," Steve told Leah on his way out. "We have no way of knowing exactly what time Randall will get here."

"I thought Sam's men were watching the airport?"

"They are, but what if they miss him? It could happen, so be careful."

"We have got to play this out Steve, we can't back out now," Leah said and gave him a pleading look. "Please, you said you would let me do this. You'll be next door and you can hear everything." She gave him a quick kiss and pushed him out the door.

Leah locked the door behind him. She wanted to clean up; the last thing she needed were signs of a big meal, left out for all to see. *Will Jeff get here before noon?* She wondered. Leah had no way of knowing how long it would take to fly from Nashville. She remembered flying with Jeff before. They could have head winds and all kinds of things that affected their flying time. Leah tidied up the kitchen and then finally showered and went to bed. She thought that sleep would be impossible, but at least she could rest.

Leah awoke to the feeling of someone caressing her cheek. She thought of Steve and smiled, but when she opened her eyes she saw Jeff Randall sitting on her bed.

"Jeff!" she screamed, only to realize she had a role to play. "You scared me half to death! Is it really you?"

"It's me alright," he answered.

"I've missed you so much." She smiled at the snake.

"I've missed you too, Carrie," Jeff smiled that same sweet smile he always gave her. "I would love to join you in that bed, but I think we need to talk first."

The last thing Leah wanted was to sleep with this man, especially with the FBI and Steve listening to everything. She hadn't thought of that, and didn't know if she could stand it if Jeff tried to touch her in that way. She needed to get them out of the bedroom. She got up and grabbed for her robe, putting it on as she lead Jeff down the hallway to the living room.

"Make yourself comfortable and I'll put on some coffee." Leah put her arms around Jeff, hugging him close. "Thank you, for coming to California. I'm sorry I ran. Can you ever forgive me?" She smiled and snuggled close. "I was shocked when I saw you kill that man. I was so scared that I didn't know what I was doing. I've never seen anyone shot before. Who was that man Jeff?"

"No one you knew," he answered.

Leah wanted to keep Jeff talking, "But why did you shoot him?"

"Would it make a difference if I said I enjoyed it?" Jeff asked her.

Jeff set down on the sofa and pulled Leah down beside him. "Forget about the man, and the coffee. I've got to know, how did you get away?"

"I had a little money saved. I'd planned to buy you a diamond ring for Christmas. After what I saw, I was so afraid. I thought I would get away and go to Mexico until I figured out what to do. I met this girl who looked like me. She was complaining about not ever getting to go anyplace, so I traded my identification for hers and sent her to Mexico while I came to San Diego. Please Jeff, say you forgive me? Leah was looking into Jeff's eyes, eyes that had turned cold and hard as ice.

"They sent me your identification, I thought you were dead," Jeff told her.

It was then that Leah knew, Jeff had ordered Jennifer killed. Leah was puzzled, "The newspaper said there was no identification found on the body. How did you get my ID?"

Jeff smiled that cold smile of his, the one Leah had rarely seen. "Because my angel, I thought Mexico was the perfect place for you to die. You've caused me a lot of trouble, Carrie," he said and took hold of her wrist. "Now, we're going to walk out that door and get in my car. When we reach the airport we're going to get on my plane, but you aren't going to Nashville. You're getting out somewhere over the desert. After that fall, and some time with the scavengers, your body will never be found. It is a pity; you made such a pretty trophy on my arm. I might have even loved you, once. You were my special angel.

Jeff pulled Leah off the sofa and shoved her toward the door. It was then she noticed Carl in the shadows; sitting in her favorite chair. *When I get out of this, I'm going to burn that chair,* she told herself.

"Get the door," Jeff told Carl. "Let's get her out of here. I want us to be gone before the rest of San Diego wakes up. I don't want anyone to see us leave."

Carl was first out the door; Jeff followed, pushing Leah ahead of him. It all happened in seconds; Carl reached the outside door just as Leah threw herself at the storage room door. Carl heard Leah hit and turned around, making a grab for her. The door opened and Steve pulled her into the room, out of harm's way. The two FBI agents side stepped Leah and advanced though the door, guns drawn. Jeff and Carl were both shocked by the sight; they were looking down the wrong end of two gun barrels. They froze when they saw the black vests with FBI written in large letters across the front.

"Both of you turn around and put your hands on the wall," Sam told them. Soon they were in handcuffs.

"What in the hell is going on?" Jeff demanded. "You're making a mistake."

"Jefferson Randall you are under arrest for the

murder of FBI Agent William Spencer and Miss Jennifer Anderson." *They had him*, Sam thought. "That's just for starters, because I'm sure we'll have several more charges to add to the list before this is over." Sam read Jeff and Carl their rights and then turned to his team as they came up the staircase. "Get this garbage out of the lady's hallway."

Leah was standing in Steve's arms shaking, but there is a big smile on her face. "We did it!" she squealed.

"You did it." John told her. "I thought Sam and I were going to have to sit on Steve when Randall broke into your apartment. We were afraid that you were asleep and would forget about your role, but you played it perfectly. It's over."

"Not quite over," Sam told them. "There will be a trial, but with the way Leah handled herself I have no doubt this lady will get through it with flying colors. The prosecuting attorney is going to love her. I'm going to start on getting your name cleared. You'll have the name 'Carrie' back before you know it."

"Can you do me a favor?" Leah asked.

"I don't know, let's hear it," Sam was inclined to do almost anything Leah wanted. He was happy they were going to bring Jefferson Randall and his organization down.

"The name I was born with is Carrie Ann Adams." Leah couldn't forget Jennifer, and she wanted to remain Leah. "When you get my name back, could you change it to Leah Jennifer Carrie Adams? I want to spend the rest of my life remembering the two women who, in their own way, helped me through this mess. Jen didn't have any family and Leah died before her life even started, and I'd like to honor them by taking their names. Can you make it legal?"

"I don't know why not," Sam answered. "I'll see if I can make it happen."

Steve was smiling as he teased, "You were afraid I wouldn't remember what to call you."

Leah put her arms around Steve's neck and kissed him. "Let's go make a pot of coffee. I'm sure Joe will show up once the FBI has left."

CHAPTER FOURTEEN

Jeff was in jail, and Leah could breathe easier than she had in months. Bail had been denied him; the fact that he had a pilot's license and unlimited funds made him a flight risk.

Leah had a tearful phone call to her parents. It was hard to make them understand that she wasn't free to come home. "I have to be available in case the FBI needs me, and they're worried someone might come after me. I'm better off in California under a different name," she told them. Her parents immediately made plans to come to California.

Leah's next call was to Jess.

Jess answered the phone in Oklahoma. "Hello?"

"It's over," Leah said. "Jeff's in jail."

"Thank God!" Jess replied. "Start at when you left with Ed and tell me everything, Carrie."

Leah gave her the short version of everything that had happened. "I'm going to have to be available until the trial. Then I'll be free to live my life again. I've met a wonderful man. Steve is a police detective and you're going to love him, Jess."

"When can I see you?" Jess couldn't truly believe the nightmare was over until she saw Carrie for herself.

Leah laughed; it was wonderful to not have secrets. She gave Jess her address and phone number. "Mom and Dad can't wait to come out; they'll be here next week. You and Bob are welcome any time you want to come. I work at a bar and have an apartment upstairs. Joe, the owner of the bar, is a friend of my Uncle Richard's and didn't know that until recently. Then there's Steve; I didn't know what love was until

I met Steve. Oh, and one more thing, everyone here knows me as Leah. This name thing is going to be difficult for a while. The FBI will straighten it all out in exchange for me giving evidence against Jeff in court. What he did, it was worse than anything we could imagine."

Leah and Jess spent another twenty minutes on the phone. Jess was coming in two weeks. She would give the Adams a chance to visit their daughter before she took her turn.

Leah got off the phone and turned to Steve. He couldn't help but hear Leah's end of the conversation.

"So I'm wonderful, am I?" Steve asked with a grin.

"The most wonderful man in the whole, wide world." Leah couldn't stop smiling. Her life was suddenly perfect. She knew the trial would be difficult, but she'd get through it and Steve would help. She couldn't have done it without him.

Steve pulled Leah into his arms, brushed away the hair that fell across her forehead. "I've known for a while now that you're the only woman for me," he softly said. "I love you Leah."

"I love you too, Steve. I've known it for a long time, but I was afraid to admit it. My life was such a mess."

"There's no reason for you to ever be afraid again. This has shown us that together we can handle anything." Steve stepped back and dropped down on one knee, smiling. "Leah, will you marry me?"

His asking her to marry him after all they have been through was perfect. He could have ended up despising her and she could have lost him forever. "Yes," she whispered. Suddenly something occurred to her, "What will your parents think? When all of this comes out, you know the papers will have a field day."

"I think they will admire you," Steve said, standing up. "It took courage to do what you did, and they will be the first to see that. The day you marry me will be the happiest day of my life. Can we set the date?"

Leah wanted to marry Steve right that minute if it was possible, but she couldn't do that to him. "We'll be married as soon as this mess is over. Can you be patient just a little longer?"

"It will be hard, but you're worth waiting for," Steve replied. "I want us to have dinner with my family tomorrow night."

"I don't know if I can face your family." Leah was afraid they wouldn't approve. "What will we tell them?"

Steve knew he had to go easy. "Honey, my dad knows it all. I went to see him that night the FBI pissed me off and he understood why you ran. If I know my dad, he's already discussed it with mom. They don't keep secrets from one another, and I hope we'll be the same way. They're going to love you, for no other reason than because I love you."

Leah was off work the next day and she reluctantly agreed to meet Steve's family. When the time came, she was a bundle of nerves. She tried on everything she owned before selecting what to wear. She finally settled on a simple black dress with a soft blue lacy Jacket. A pair of black, strappy high heels completed the outfit. By the time Steve got to the apartment, Leah was about ready to jump out of her skin.

"Come on, it's time to go," Steve said and laughed. "I want to get this over with so you can relax. They really are nice people!"

"Just wait, you're going to be meeting my family next week," Leah told him. "Are you going to be cool, calm and collected?"

"Terrified, I'm afraid they are going to try to talk you into returning to Texas." That was what Steve would want to do; lock her up to keep her safe, and never let anyone hurt her again.

They arrived at Steve parents' home just before sunset. Like most of the houses in southern California it was beautiful, a tan stucco with a red tile roof, and it showed the Spanish influence. They rang the bell and when Steve's father answered the door, Leah knew exactly what Steve would look like in another twenty five years.

"Come in," the older man welcomed them just as a beautiful blonde woman entered from what appeared to be the living room. At a distance, she didn't look old enough to be Steve's mother.

"Steven, we're so glad to see you," she said and gave her son a hug.

Steve made the introductions. "Mom, Dad, I would like you to meet Leah Scott. Leah these are my parents, John and Rita Burke."

Just then, a younger man came barreling through the front door. "Sorry I'm running late." The young man said before stopping in his tracks and eyeing Leah. "Boy big brother, how did you get so lucky?"

"Leah," Mrs. Burke said. "Please, won't you forgive our youngest child's manners?"

"Youngest children are always brats," Steve said with a fond look on his face. "Darrin, I'd like you to meet the woman I intend to make your sister, just as soon as I can talk her into tying the knot."

"It is a pleasure to meet you, Leah." Darrin cuts his eyes in Steve's direction. "Are you sure you want to marry this old guy? I, on the other hand, am much younger and much better looking."

"You two behave," Mrs. Burke scolded. "It is a good thing Tammy is away at school. It gives Leah a chance to get used to the family in small doses."

"Come into the living room and we'll have a drink." Mr. Burke beckoned and led them into an elegant living room.

"Leah, what will you have? I have a nice Cabernet, which Rita prefers, or I can make you a cocktail," Mr. Burke offered.

"I would love a glass of wine," Leah said.

"Son," Mr. Burke asked. "What will you have?"

"I'll have a martini, shaken, not stirred," Darrin laughingly answering his father.

"You will have a coke, James Bond, since you aren't twenty one," Mr. Burke told him.

"Darrin came along a little later in life," Mrs. Burke explained with a laugh. "God gave us Darrin to keep us on our toes. He's a challenge, and one day I hope he's blessed with a son just like him. Tammy is two years younger than Steve. She worked in the Crime Scene Investigation Department until recently, but decided last year that she wanted to go back to school and add to her degree."

"If I get out of school, I'm never going back," Darrin told the group. "Sorry, I can't stick around!" He leaned in and kissed his mother. "I won't be late."

"See that you're not," his dad warned.

Mr. Burke passed them each a glass of wine. "Leah, we're aware of the situation you've found yourself in. It's like the elephant in the room, hard to ignore. I wanted to tell you that we admire you for coming forward to testify against Randall."

"Mr. Burke," Leah said. "I don't mind telling you that the thing I am having the hardest time with..." Leah paused, finding it hard to continue. "I feel responsible for Jennifer Anderson's death. I sent her to Mexico City with my identification."

"First of all, we're John and Rita. From what my son tells us, he plans to make you his bride as soon as this mess is cleared up and that makes us family." John Burke said before continuing, "I have never been one to question what life sends my way. I feel that, in the grand scheme of things, our life is destined to be what it is. If I was going to question what happened to you I would wonder; if you had stayed in Nashville would you be dead? Jennifer Anderson might still be alive, but what if she was destined to die at that time? Maybe she would have been killed in Memphis, instead of Mexico. One thing we do know; if allowed to go free, Randall would have killed again. When someone got in his way they would have been eliminated. You stopped him. To me, that's what we should remember."

Leah was quiet for a minute. "I don't know if you said that just to make me feel better, but it does. Thank you." Leah turned to Rita. "Your husband is almost as wonderful as your son."

"I agree, they're both pretty fantastic," Rita said and went on to point out. "Let's not make a habit of telling them though, it might go to their heads. Thank you son, for bring me such a lovely new daughter."

Just then, an older woman entered the room. She

reminded Leah of Alice from the Brady Bunch reruns.

"Dinner is ready," she announced.

"Hazel, come meet Leah." Steve made the introductions. "Mother is an artist and has a studio over the garage where she works. Hazel takes care of the house. Wait until you taste her enchilada casserole."

"No enchilada casserole tonight. Your folks have been so excited to meet your Leah that your mom ordered prime rib," Hazel told Steve. "I hope everyone is hungry."

The meal passed with everyone enjoying the prime rib. Leah was happy that Steve's family seemed to like her. They didn't stay late; Steve and John both had to be at work the next day. Leaving his parent's home, Steve teased her as he escorted Leah to the car. "See, they weren't so bad. Now all I have to do is charm your parents, like you have mine."

"Mom and Dad are going to love you," Leah replied, and had no doubt about it. "You're right about them wanting to take me home. I love them Steve, but my home is in San Diego now. Once they see what a fine man you are and that you make me happy, they'll come around. Texas isn't that far away, and they can visit anytime they want."

When they arrived at Leah's apartment, Leah turned to Steve. "You can stay, can't you?"

"I want to," Steve told her as they climbed the stairs. "That night when I was clearing all my things from your apartment, I realized that I never want us to be separated again."

* * *

The next week went by quickly. The deeper the FBI dug, the more they found on Jefferson Randall and his empire. Leah dreaded having to testify. So far they have managed to keep her out of the papers, but when the trial started that would change. The crazy thing about the name change was that it was working to her advantage. Each time they referred to her, it was always as Carrie Adams, while she was living quietly in San Diego as Leah Scott. The governor of Tennessee was having a hard time explaining his friendship with Jefferson Randall. The newspapers were hounding him constantly, and just before an election year. If Jeff hadn't been unmasked, he would have put the governor back in office. The way things looked now, the man was out of politics for good. The mayor of Nashville was trying to keep his friendship with Jeff quiet. According to His Honor, the Mayor, it was all business. Mr. Randall was the head of a multimillion dollar construction company whose headquarters were in Nashville; of course the Mayor would know him.

The FBI called Leah on a sunny California day; the trial was set. She had six months to get ready for her life to be turned upside down. Leah wanted Jeff to pay for all he had done, and she was ready to stand up in court to make sure that justice was served.

CHAPTER FIFTEEN

Leah and Steve were having their first argument. Steve had always been such a sweetheart and now he was being impossible in Leah's opinion. He refused to let her out of his sight and wanted to let the FBI put her in protective custody. He was afraid Jeff's men would come after her.

"Steve we can't go on like this, it's tearing us apart." Leah was cooking them breakfast. "I have Joe and Frank around during the day, and you're here at night. I'm never alone." She placed a plate on the bar, in front of Steve. "Be reasonable, I don't want to hide out for six months. Please understand, I'm through running."

"Leah, listen to me. One bullet and you won't be alive to testify against Jeff." Steve had to make her see reason.

"It's not just my testimony; they have tons of evidence against Jeff. What purpose would it serve to kill me?" Leah asked.

"With you out of the picture, Jeff's lawyers would have an easier time casting doubt on the other evidence." Steve was about to run out of patience. "When you factor in that you personally helped put the cuffs on Jeff, he isn't very happy with you right now. It would be better to have you in a safe house. "Steve ran his hands through his hair; she was driving him nuts. "Alright, I'll take a six month leave of absence from the Police Department so I can protect you."

"Are you crazy?" Leah's voice raised an octave. "Not just no, hell no! That is the stupidest thing I've ever heard. We're talking about your career and I won't let you ruin it."

Joe was coming up the stairs to the store room and could hear loud voices from Leah's apartment. He thought to himself, *I didn't get Steve and Leah together to have this trial tear them apart.* He knocked on the apartment door and when Steve answered, Joe could feel the tension in the room.

"May I ask what's going on? I can hear you from outside." Joe looked at the two of them. He'd never seen them like this.

"Someone is being unreasonable," Leah said.

"I agree, Leah is being unreasonable." Steve turned to Joe. "She's not safe, Joe."

"He's talking about taking a six month leave of absence so he can protect me. Talk to him Joe, tell him what that could do to his career." Tears ran down Leah's checks. "I can't stand this. I feel like I'm caught in the middle."

Steve pulled Leah into his arms, "it's okay baby, we'll work this out."

Joe walked into the kitchen and poured himself a cup of coffee, then sat down at the end of the bar and addressed the couple.

"Leah you want to stay in San Diego and Steve doesn't think you will be safe. Have I got that part straight?" Joe took a sip of his coffee as they both nodded. "Maybe we could find a compromise if we looked hard enough. Frank and I both have experience with firearms. Maybe we could check out one of the local firing ranges and brush up on our skills. What if Leah took a course in self-defense? If she had one of us with her at all times and someone came looking, we wouldn't make it easy for them.

Maybe Steve's dad would be willing to run a squad by more often." Joe turned to Steve. "You could talk to him. He might have some other suggestions. You know the FBI beefed up my security system, added all the extra cameras."

"Joe," Steve addressed the older man. "I don't want to offend you but I don't think you're trained to protect Leah."

"Well now Steve, that's where you would be wrong." Joe calmly sipped his coffee. "When I first went into the Navy I was a Seal, and I'm extremely qualified. I was injured on a mission and couldn't dive anymore so the Navy transferred me out of the seals unit. I finished my service as an M.P. Now Frank was just a crusty old Navy cook, and his skills don't match mine or yours, but you will find that not much gets past him. Remember how he zeroed in on Carl that first night? We're as capable as anyone they would assign to a safe house, maybe more so."

"Let's say I'm buying this; I don't want Leah messing with guns. She's a civilian and it isn't safe." Steve was giving it some thought since he didn't want to be separated from Leah.

"Wait a minute, buster!" You could see the steam rising from Leah.

Joe smiled to himself. *This was going to be fun.*

"I grew up in the country. My Dad and brother had guns around and I was taught to use them safely. I'll admit that I haven't had a gun in my hand in some years, but I can take care of myself. And, because my brother thought he was going to grow up to be Chuck Norris, I've had a few lessons in self-defense. I know we need a plan, but as Joe says, don't count me out." Leah was angry but she had at least had her say. "All of you, quit thinking you have to protect me."

Steve smiled, "I stand corrected. I'll schedule us some gym time and we'll spend some time on the shooting range to brush up on our skills. I still don't like this, but I see I'm outnumbered. I can see Jeff letting down his guard and coming here. He didn't think Leah was any danger to him, and now he knows she's not alone and helpless. If he has the connections we think he does, he will try to eliminate her."

"Why would he do that? The FBI has him, even if I don't testify against him." Leah asked.

"Revenge," Steve stated. "Leah, you successfully got away and that had to be really hard on his ego. Then you helped the FBI to close the net on him and his operation. I imagine he would like nothing better than to see you dead. He'd probably like the pleasure of doing it himself, but that's no longer possible. He hired a hit man once, he can do it again. Just because he's in jail doesn't mean he can't hire a hit."

"Alright," Joe said. "I think we all have the picture, and we have six months to plan. The first thing I want to do is add to my security system with extra cameras and sensors. Maybe the FBI will help with that, offer some suggestions. A lot of what they added before required a person to monitor the cameras. We need more sensors, something that trips an alarm."

Steve wasn't completely happy as the next weeks settled into a routine. The four of them spent several days a week in the gym and three at a local shooting range. They found that Leah had a natural ability to hit the target she aimed at. She settled in with her weapon of choice in a .22 caliber semiautomatic pistol with magnum rounds. Steve would have preferred that she used something larger. A .38 caliber with hollow point ammo would have made him feel better but, with Leah's slim wrist, she preferred the smaller caliber weapon. Since she could hit the smallest target at 10 feet and 15 yards, Steve gave in gracefully. They gradually changed their schedule to one day a week at the range and increased their time at the gym. Leah's small body definitely put her at a disadvantage in hand to hand combat, so Steve taught her to fight dirty and it was getting to a point where he was afraid to make her angry. What she didn't have in size, she made up for in cunning. The girl definite had spunk.

As the first month passed and they were well into the second, Steve felt like they were as prepared as possible. Joe was good, and his skills came back with very little work. Frank was skilled with a gun, but the man was getting older and didn't move as fast as a younger man. He had a sharp mind though and always seemed to know where Leah was at any given time. With the beefed up security, they had Leah covered, or so they thought.

It happened at the end of the fourth month. Jeff had either given them time to get sloppy, or he'd had trouble finding a man he wanted for the job. Life in jail had made running his empire more complicated.

Leah stopped by the kitchen to tell Frank she was going upstairs to do inventory. She grabbed a glass of iced tea and left through the back door. Frank was keeping an eye on her through the security cameras as he was preparing an order for two steak dinners.

The skin on the back of Leah's neck told her that something wasn't right as she headed up the back stairs. She put her hand on the gun she carried in a shoulder holster under her jacket, and turned to check behind her just as a hand wrapped around her from behind. He had to be tall, because a single step up on the stairs didn't give her an advantage when she tried to kick backwards. Leah had just opened her mouth to scream when she felt the needle enter her arm. Whatever was in the syringe instantly made her feel dizzy. The scream died in her throat as she went limp in the man's arms.

"Come on," the tall man yelled to his partner waiting below. "Let's get her out of here before someone comes along. She may be little, but she weighs a ton."

The second man took Leah's feet as the two started down the stairs. Suddenly, the back door opened with a bang as Frank and Joe erupted into the alley, guns drawn. The second man dropped Leah's feet and turned with a gun in his hand. Frank didn't hesitate, he knew they were hurting Leah. His shot hit the man in the chest, and the kidnapper toppled down the staircase. The tall man turned, pulling Leah in front of him.

"Drop your guns," the man demanded. "I'll kill her right here."

What could they do? He had his gun pointed at Leah. Then Joe noticed movement behind a car parked in the alley.

"Don't hurt her," Joe said trying to buy time. "Where are you taking her?"

"Where they will never find her, she'll never be able to testify against anyone again. Now drop your guns, turn around and go back in the restaurant." The tall man instructed.

Steve grabbed the man's hand holding the gun

through the railing and turned the gun away from Leah before slamming the gunman's wrist on the guard rail. The gunman let go of Leah and she slowly fell, landing on the stairs. The man was strong and it appeared that he and Steve were an even match as they fought for control of the gun. Joe and Frank surged forward as the man broke free and aimed the gun in Steve's direction. Joe fired his gun, and the man dropped where he stood. As he fell, his gun went off and a hole appeared in Leah's right shoulder.

Steve ran up the stairs and took Leah in his arms. "Leah," he called to her.

Joe ran across the parking lot and leaned down to check the tall man. He was still alive, but barely. "Call the police and an ambulance, Frank."

Steve was still cradling Leah in his arms trying to get her to respond.

"What did you do to her?" Joe shook the tall man.

"Drugs, is the bitch dead?" The tall man groaned as he answered Joe.

"You better hope she isn't dead or I'll put another bullet right between your eyes." Joe said. "Why drug her if you were just going to kill her anyway?"

The tall man's breathing was shallow and blood was pouring from the wound. He laughed, "Whoever wanted her dead didn't want it to be easy. I had orders to make sure she was never found." Then the tall man drew one last breath and was gone.

Frank came back outside. "Help is on the way!"

Joe went up the stairs, skirting Steve with Leah in his arms, and picked up the syringe the man had dropped. "Maybe this will help the doctors identify the drug they used." He said, as he came back down the stairs. They could hear the sirens in the distance.

Two black and whites, an unmarked SUV and an ambulance all arrived at once. Leah still hadn't stirred, and Steve sat holding her tenderly with his handkerchief pressed to the wound.

"Dear God," Steve prayed as he released her to the medics. "Please don't let her die."

Steve held Leah's hand as the ambulance rushed them through the streets to the hospital. He had never been a very religious man but he prayed that God would not take this woman from him. He loved her more than he had thought possible, and they had just begun their life together. He couldn't bear to lose her.

At the hospital, the doctors soon determined that the bullet in Leah's shoulder was not serious and she was unconscious because of the drug that had been given to her. They treated the gunshot wound and waited for the drug to wear off.

Leah was coming around and it felt like a ball of fire had settled in her right shoulder. She moaned, wondering where she was. Noticing the antiseptic smell, she opened her eyes to see stark hospital walls. Then she remembered the tall man and cried out.

"It's alright," Steve said as he gently stroked Leah's hand. "You're in the hospital and everything is going to be okay."

Leah turned her head to see Steve leaning over her, a worried expression on his face.

"That man, what happened?" Leah's mouth felt like it had cotton in it. With her mouth so dry, she could barely speak.

"He's never going to hurt you again." Steve explained as Leah drifted back to sleep.

When Leah woke the second time it was to see Steve asleep in a chair beside her bed. Her shoulder hurt, and she moaned when she tried to move.

Steve immediately opened his eyes. "Hi, Kitten," he said. "How are you feeling?"

"I've felt better. What happened to my shoulder?" Leah asked.

"Just a little hole, you were hit by a stray bullet. You gave us quiet a scare." Steve stood to give her a tender kiss. "Just relax and I'll tell you what we know. The police can't wait for you to be well enough to fill in the blanks."

Steve told her what had happened after she had been drugged. "Your safe, just relax."

"I heard something behind me and was reaching for my gun when he grabbed me. He was so tall, and he had his arms wrapped around me from behind. I was getting ready to kick out when he stuck a syringe in my arm. After that everything got fuzzy and I went blank. I never realized a drug could work that fast." A shiver went up Leah's spine.

"No one can hurt you here," Steve assured her.

Steve pushed the call button to let them know Leah was awake. Within a few minutes a doctor and nurse were in Leah's room.

"How are you feeling?" the doctor inquired. He checked Leah's shoulder while the nurse checked her pulse and blood pressure.

"My head hurts and my shoulder burns like crazy when I move it. All in all, I've felt better." Leah answered.

"We can give you something for pain. We were holding off, letting the other drug work its way out of your system. All you need now is some time. I'll be back to see you in the morning." The doctor shook hands with Steve and quietly left the room.

The nurse straightened Leah's bedding and added notes to her chart. "I'll be back with a shot for the pain," she told them. "You really should go home and get some sleep," she added, addressing Steve with a smile.

"I go home when this lady goes home." Steve's voice left no room for argument.

"Then why don't I have them send in a cot?" The nurse said as she quietly closed the door.

"I would rather slip in next to you," Steve told Leah. "I don't think you need anyone bumping you in the night though, or I might give it a try."

Housekeeping was in next with a cot for Steve.

The nurse came back with a pain shot for Leah. After she left, Leah slipped into a sound sleep. Steve sat by her bed for a while before he laid down on the cot. When he awoke, it was morning and Agent John Bell was pushing open Leah's door.

John walked into the room with a frown on his face. "How is she doing?" He inquired.

"About as well as you would expect for someone who's been drugged and shot," Steve answered as he shook his friend's hand.

"I'm sorry about that. Is she up to talking to me?" John inquired.

"I think so, but you aren't going to get much from her. The creep drugged her and she doesn't remember much." Steve explained.

Leah woke up when she heard voices. She greeted Agent Bell with a good morning and then explained. "I'm sorry John but I didn't see anything. I had a creepy feeling that something wasn't right and as I turned, he attacked me from behind and shoved that needle in my arm. After I felt the sting of the drug, well everything just went fuzzy. I didn't know anything after that. I didn't even know he shot me."

"I'm glad you're going to be alright." John said before turning to Steve. "We'll give her some time to recover, but I think we need to transfer her to a secure location and prepare her for trial. Randall's attorney is going to attempt to shake her, make her give conflicting information. He'll try to make her look like an unreliable witness."

"I thought you had enough evidence to convict him, even without my testimony." Leah had been told they had him, no room to escape.

"We have a tight case, but you're going to add the final touches. We haven't been able to get anyone in his organization to flip. The murder charges will be hearsay without your testimony." John told Leah.

"You have that tape you made in my apartment, where he confessed." Leah was getting upset.

"Look baby, they need your testimony to present the tape into evidence. What you know will just pull the noose a little tighter. We have him, don't get upset." Steve assured her.

The nurse came in to take Leah's vitals. "You guys give us a few minutes."

John turned to Leah. "I'm going to leave and come back later. Stay calm and get well. Everything is going to be alright, I promise."

"If you're going to put me in a safe house could you remove this tracking device? It's started to itch like crazy and the area seems to be red. I think I may have developed an allergy to it." Leah told them.

Steve was instantly on alert. "Why didn't you say something before?'

"I thought that as long as I needed it, I could put up with the discomfort," Leah answered. "If I'm going to a safe house, it might as well come out."

"I'll get a tech over here to remove the tracker," John told them. "Leah is right, we have her covered now. There's no use in her being uncomfortable."

"I'm going to walk John out. There's someone on your door. You're safe." Steve explained to Leah before the two men stepped outside.

It was two days before Leah got out of the hospital. The FBI moved into the restaurant's storage room for a second time, and they were adding a security detail to Leah. No one thought Randall would make another try this soon, but they weren't taking chances with Leah's safety. She would be given a few days, and when the stitches came out, she would be transferred to a cabin in the mountains of east Tennessee. There, they would prepare her for the trial. Steve would be going with her; he hadn't left her side since the shooting.

CHAPTER SIXTEEN

The doctor had checked Leah that morning and removed her stitches. She was good to go, and the U.S. Marshals had her on a plane for Asheville, North Carolina. They would transfer her to a helicopter from there, and fly her to a remote cabin in the mountains of east Tennessee. She was going back to the place she had once thought of as home and there was nothing more beautiful than those mountains. Maybe there, she could get her strength back and she would prepare herself to make sure Jeff paid for everything he had done. God help her, in spite of the brave front she put on, she was still afraid.

Steve sat across from Leah studying the maps that John had provided for him. He looked up and smiled. "You okay, babe?"

Leah smiled back at him; this man was the world to her. How did she get so lucky? "What's going on with the maps?"

"I wanted to see the layout of the area. You've been in the hospital and haven't been able to exercise. I thought we might take a few leisurely hikes and build your strength back. It's a shame to waste all these beautiful mountains." Steve leaned over and pointed to an area on the map. "See? This is where we're going. There are a lot of places to hike out there."

"That's why you had me bring my jeans and boots." Leah looked at the map Steve was holding." I'm glad you understand that map. It doesn't look like the ones I'm used to."

"This one shows all the elevations and gives you a view of the terrain. There aren't that many roads in this part of the state, but there are a lot of trails if you know where to look." Steve wanted to trust the marshals, but they had messed up in the past. He had gotten a map like the Navy used for recon and if they had to run, as a former Seal, he knew how to get lost in those mountains. He didn't like that Leah was weak from the blood she had lost. It had been superficial, but the gunshot wound had still slowed her down. "How are you holding up?"

"Quit worrying, I'm fine. You could have stayed in San Diego. I know your dad won't fire you, but the press may have a field day." Leah shook her head, "I don't want to cause your family any trouble."

"Leah, I'm not leaving your side until all of this is over. Soon, we'll be back in San Diego and I'll make it up to my department, and my dad." Steve pointed to a place on the map. "This looks like an old logging road. It's probably all grown up, but you can see the outline. See how much bigger this growth is?"

"Can I tell you a secret?" Leah smiled. "I can't tell a darn thing from that funny looking map."

"We should be landing soon." Steve wouldn't rest easy until Leah had testified and all this was behind them. He folded the map and put it in a safe place.

The plane landed in Asheville and taxied to a waiting helicopter. In less than fifteen minutes they had transferred Steve, Leah and their luggage. On board, they were introduced to two of the U.S. Marshals who would be staying with them at the cabin.

Leah was tired and ready for this trip to end. "How much longer?"

The older of the two marshals spoke up. "I know

this must be tiring for you. We'll be there in a little over an hour. We left Turner back at the cabin. He likes to think of himself as a master chef, so hopefully he'll have something for you to eat when we get there. It's going to be a little cramped, but you'll be safe."

It had been a long day, Leah realized. "I just want this to be over. I want to testify and get my life back."

An hour later, they landed in front of a two-storied log cabin. Passengers and luggage were unloaded, and the helicopter gracefully lifted up and flew north. Soon, the quiet of the forest closed in around the cabin. It was a beautiful spot.

Jake, the senior marshal, showed them inside. It was a good size, with huge living and dining areas across the front of the building. A large staircase led to the upper three bedrooms. There was a forth bedroom on the main floor, but it had already been decided that one of the marshals would use that one. They wanted Leah upstairs where she would be less accessible.

Steve checked out the upstairs and chose a bedroom over the kitchen for Leah and him. There was a porch under one of the windows, and in an emergency they could climb out the window and down the porch roof. Steve prayed there would be no need for an escape route. One week, and they would move Leah to Nashville. Soon this would all be over.

The days settled into a routine. Turner was indeed a master chef and seemed to enjoy the KP duty. Leah liked to cook, but her mind was on other things and she was afraid she might poison them. There were four marshals in all, and they were convinced they had the mountain all to themselves. There were motion detectors and security cameras around the perimeter, plus they had cameras high in the trees monitoring for any activity in the area. Steve hoped they were right, but he had this itchy feeling. Someway, somehow, Jeff would make one last try. Because Randall knew this would be his last chance, Steve was positive that he would call out the big guns.

Since the marshals were so sure that the area was secure, they allowed Steve and Leah to go for short hikes around the cabin. Steve set up a small day pack for their trips. Inside he stashed more than a couple bottles of water and energy bars, he also had his maps, first aid kit and an extra gun. He made sure Leah was almost always dressed in boots and jeans in case they needed to leave on a moment's notice.

Four days before they were to go to Nashville, it happened. Steve and Leah awoke a little after 2 o'clock in the morning from a sound sleep by the echo of automatic weapon fire coming from the front of the cabin. Immediately, Steve noticed the smell of smoke.

"Hurry, get dressed!" he told Leah. "Boots, jeans and jacket; its cold in the mountains after dark."

Steve and Leah quickly pulled on their clothes. Steve handed Leah a shoulder holster with a gun already tucked into it, and grabbed his gun and the day pack. Smoke was starting to rise from the bottom floor, and the marshals were firing from the upstairs windows. It sounded like there was a small army outside.

Jake knocked on the door before entering. "Good, you're dressed, we have to get out of here!"

"A couple of you go out the window and across the porch. Put down a cover for us and I'll take Leah out," Steve said. He needed the marshals' help if he was going to get Leah to safety.

Jake signaled Turner and Turner went first, distracting the men trying to smoke them out. Steve pulled Leah out of the window and pushed her down low. Jake was lying on the porch roof firing, while Turner had climbed down and moved behind a small shed, close to the back door. The third man was still upstairs, firing from a window. They hadn't heard from the fourth marshal downstairs. With the cabin on fire, Steve hoped he had gotten out the back. Steve pulled Leah from the roof, but instead of finding a hiding place, he pulled her toward a stand of trees at the back of the house. Most of the gunfire was coming from the front of the cabin. The goons had been too busy keeping the front door and the garage covered to think about the back of the house. Steve didn't slow down until he had Leah several yards back in the woods. He stopped and pulled her into his arms.

"Are you alright?" he whispered.

Leah nodded her head yes. "A little out of breath is all. Are you okay?

Steve could still hear the gunfire. "I'm fine. Let's get out of here, it isn't safe."

Steve led the way through the forest. He had found a faint trail while they had been hiking, and he hoped they were on it. He had a flashlight in his pack but it wasn't safe to use it. The light might give their position away.

There was a full moon high in the sky, but on the forest floor you couldn't see much. They finally came to an animal trail Steve remembered, and he pointed them north toward an abandoned fire watch tower. It was old and wouldn't be of much use to them, but it was far away from the cabin and there was a clearing not far from it. Steve knew it was a place where a helicopter could land. He still had friends he could call from his days in the Navy, and one had a charter helicopter service out of Chattanooga. Pulling a satellite phone out of his pack, he soon had his friend on the line. Yes he would pick Steve up, and no one would follow him. He would make sure of that.

Steve couldn't depend on the U.S. Marshals Service. From here on out, he and his old Seal buddies would keep Leah safe. Randall was going down, and his lady was going to make sure of that. Steve just had to make sure nothing happened to Leah before then.

It took them almost two hours to hike to the clearing. Steve had to slow down; they had been on the run since 2 a.m. and it had been hard on Leah. She didn't complain, but just concentrated on putting one foot in front of the other. When they walked into the clearing, there sat a helicopter with a camouflage net thrown across the rotors. Sitting on a rock was a man dressed in greasy coveralls.

"Hello Steve, it's good to see you! What have you got yourself into?" The man asked.

"I can't tell you how good it is to see you, man!" Steve turned to Leah. "Leah, I want you to meet Ralph Williams, 'Billy' to his friends. I can't tell you the times he has had my back side. We were in BUDs training together and then later assigned to the same unit for a while. Billy, I want you to meet Leah."

Billy turned and extended a hand to Leah. "It is a pleasure to meet Steve's lady."

Billy looked older and harder than Steve, but there was a twinkle in his eye as they shook hands.

"How did you know I'm Steve's lady? Leah asked and smiled as she shook his hand.

"My friend here was always the serious type. He didn't play the same games most of the guys did. He has that look in his eye now, a 'don't mess with my lady' look!" Billy laughed and started pulling the net from the rotors. "Let's get out of here. You can explain while we're in the air. I feel like a sitting duck for some reason."

The helicopter was lifting off, heading southwest, when Steve started talking to Billy over the headset mike. He had soon given Billy a short version of what had happened. When they landed in Chattanooga, two men walk out of a nearby hanger and greeted Steve like old friends. Both had that same look, like long ago they had worn a very special uniform and laid their lives on the line for their country. Steve introduced them to Leah and then they walked into the office of Billy's Charter Service. Steve planned to pick up a half dozen throw away phones. He would let the marshals know Leah was safe and arrange to have her talk to the prosecuting attorney, but now it was his turn to protect her. He and his friends would guard her back until she testified. Four days from today, he would deliver her to the Federal Court House in Nashville. Thank God they had removed that tracking device; it could have gotten them all killed.

Billy had a cabin on the Cumberland River, not far from Nashville. They would spend the next few days there, where no one would know where to find them. They picked up food and headed out in a dilapidated old panel truck. It looked ancient, but the engine ran like a thoroughbred.

When they walked in the door of the fishing cabin, Leah had to hold her nose to keep from gagging. Billy was a bachelor and this was a fishing cabin, which said it all. It sure wasn't the style that the Marshals Service had offered, but Steve didn't trust them. With all the failed attempts on her life, the way he felt was understandable. Leah sent one of the men back to the nearest discount store. She wanted cleaning supplies and since she didn't have anything else to do, she might as well clean.

The cabin was still crude, but at least it smelled better. The cots had clean sheets, and dinner was cooking in the oven. The men had given Leah orders not to be seen outside. Their cover was that the men were on a fishing trip, no women allowed. At least there was a small bathroom with a shower. A lady could stand anything for a few days as long as she had a shower. At least, that's what Leah told herself.

The Marshals Service kicked up a stink when Steve contacted them, but he wouldn't budge and he wouldn't bring Leah in until the court date. The marshals had messed up. No one knew how, but Randall had a pipeline into the marshals' office. Steve agreed to make Leah available for a meeting with the prosecuting attorney, but only with an elaborate plan in place. Billy would pick the attorneys up at a motel and fly them to a neutral place where they could talk to Leah. In the meantime, Steve would make sure they weren't followed. As soon as their meeting ended, they would take Leah back to the cabin and the attorneys would be flown back to their motel.

Steve was determined; no one would know where to find Leah. The marshals had lost two men when Randall's thugs had trapped them at the cabin and they wouldn't get another chance.

Leah was to testify at 1 p.m. the next day and Steve wasn't going to let down his guard now. He had the guys acquire some uniforms from the cleaning service the courthouse used. The company cleaned the courthouse at night, so Steve and Leah entered the back entrance just after eight o'clock dressed as the janitorial service. He had a floor plan for the building and they would use an empty office until the cleaning crew left. His guys had managed to get them keys to all the doors. When the coast was clear they would find a place close to the courtroom to spend the night, and then he would time it where Leah would appear just before she was supposed to testify. He had alerted the Marshals Service so that they would make sure the corridors and the court room was safe. Surely they could manage this one thing.

The next day, Carrie/Leah dressed in a slim gray suit walked into the court room with a young man in a dark suit beside her. Most would have thought the striking couple to be lawyers, but Jefferson Randall knew differently. He drew in a loud breath. He had once thought she looked like an angel, his angel. If she was an angel now, it was an avenging angel. She should be dead; instead it was him who was the dead man. The mob wouldn't let him live after she testified, he knew too much and the powers that be would kill him. He wondered if he could strike a deal and work something out with the Feds. He didn't understand how he could have let a mere woman bring down his empire.

CHAPTER SEVENTEEN

Six months had gone by and Leah had gotten through the long, tiring trial. She had stood firm in keeping the name; it was the one she had used to make her life in San Diego. Even Jess had started calling her Leah. She had seen Ed again, and since he had called her girl most of the time anyway, Leah worked for him. Her parents continued to call her Carrie and that was fine.

The moment Arnold and Alice Adams met the Burkes, they became the best of friends. Rita had shown Alice around San Diego and they had planned Leah and Steve's wedding together, right down to the last napkin. They would probably have planned the honeymoon as well, but Steve wasn't disclosing any information. Steve and Leah wanted a small wedding, so they were only going to have one attendant each. Joe was Steve's best man, and Jess was serving as Leah's matron of honor. Joe had closed the bar to the public and hosted the rehearsal dinner. Since the wedding would be private, everyone they knew was invited to the big party being held after the rehearsal dinner. Joe was so proud that you would have thought he was the father of the bride.

Leah and Steve were upstairs getting ready. "This is going to be so much fun. Every one we know will drop in after dinner." Leah was so happy she could burst. "We aren't having the traditional wedding, so you aren't getting a bachelor party. No naked lady jumping out of a cake!" Leah giggled.

"You are the only lady I want, and I fully intend to see you naked later tonight." Steve announced.

"Oh no, I'm going to leave the party before midnight." Leah was going to spend the night with Jess. "It is bad luck to see the bride on your wedding day. I'll see you at the church my love, tomorrow at 1 o'clock."

"We've had enough bad luck to last a lifetime. I have us scheduled for happily ever after." Steve couldn't imagine anything except happiness, as long as he has Leah.

Downstairs, Frank was clucking around in the kitchen like a mother hen. He had insisted on preparing the food for both the rehearsal dinner and the party to follow. They had hired servers so Frank could join them at dinner.

They walked into the bar to see all of the special people in their lives. Champagne was passed around and Joe raised his glass, "To the bride and groom; May they always be as happy as they are this minute."

No one could look at Steve and Leah and not see how thrilled they were. Their faces were glowing and their eyes sparkled. Never had two people looked more joyful. Everyone raised their glasses and drank to the happy couple.

Dinner was a lively affair. Joe was setting next to Leah's Uncle Richard catching up on their lives, and Uncle Ed and Frank were fast becoming friends. The parents were on cloud nine since their children had found one another. Alice and Rita were already planning for grandchildren, but they haven't informed Steve and Leah of their plans.

"We thought we had lost her," Alice told Rita. "Steve is perfect for her, I've never seen her so radiant."

"Steve was always so serious," Rita confided in

Alice but Leah makes him laugh. And look at them, you can't tell me they won't make beautiful babies together."

"Absolutely, gorgeous," Alice agreed.

Dinner ended and the party began. Friends started coming in, and there were drinks and dancing. Barb and her husband arrived, and Leah introduced them to Jess and Bob. They planned on staying an hour or two before going home to relieve Sue who had babysitting duty.

Uncle Ed had been talking to Maggie, and soon she was pulling him out on the dance floor.

"Who knew Ed could dance like that?" Jess commented to Bob. "He's full of surprises."

The hit of the night was when the guys turned up. Tommie Toes, Bee Catcher, Bronc Buster, Jake Brake; Leah didn't know them by any other name. The night got really lively when Bee Catcher, turned out his real name was Bill, took a shine to Sally. Bill taught Sally the Texas Two Step, and boy could those two dance.

At 11:30 p.m. Leah was getting ready to leave. She went over to the table where Ed, Frank, and some of the boys were swapping stories. She looked at 'the guys', as she had referred to them when she rode with Ed. "I'm so glad you could come," she told them.

"We've found loads that come close to San Diego. You'll see us from time to time, girl," Ed explained. "We missed you and we're glad everything worked out."

"I do hope you'll all come back soon," Leah said with tears in her eyes.

"Don't you go bawling," Ed told her. "We've

found you again and now that we know Frank and Joe, we'll be back before you know it."

Leah gave them all a hug and then went to find Steve. "One last dance, then Cinderella is leaving the ball," she told him. "Don't you dare get drunk and miss our wedding."

"Don't worry," Steve hugged her tight. "Nothing is going to keep me from that chapel. This is the last night we spend apart. I plan for us to grow old and gray together."

Leah said her goodbyes after dancing with her fiancée, and then she and Jess quietly slipped out the back door.

"I remember when I married Bob," Jess said, a dreamy look in her eyes. "My mom told me she would lock me in my room if she had to. I was not to see Bob before the wedding. It's silly, but I think that made it special, to walk down the aisle and see him waiting for me."

They went to the hotel, where Jess and Bob had a two bedroom suite. Leah would occupy the second bedroom for the night. The girls chatted until Bob came in at around two in the morning.

"Boy am I tired," Bob complained. "This old cowboy is used to turning in early. I'll see you ladies in the morning," He said as he headed for the bedroom.

"I had better let you go to bed with your husband," Leah told Jess. "Jess, why have you and Bob never had children?"

"It just hasn't happened," Jess confessed. "We've talked about getting it checked out. We'd like children. What about you and Steve?"

"We'd like to have children too. Our life was such

a mess until now though." Leah was thoughtful for a minute and then suddenly she was at a loss for words.

"What's wrong?" Seeing the look on Leah's face, Jess was worried. "Leah, talk to me; what's wrong?"

Leah looked up with wonder in her eyes. "Jess, I can't remember when I had my last period. Everything was such a mess, and then the trial was over and we were planning the wedding. A baby... It's a good thing that we're getting married," she giggled.

"There's a pharmacy on the corner," Jess said. "Let's go get a home pregnancy test."

Both women jumped up and ran for the door. They were back in twenty minutes with two kits. After all, they want to be sure. Leah went into the bathroom and used both kits. They waited the required time and there lying on the counter were the results: two positives. The first thing Leah thought of was how much she wanted to see Steve.

"OH no, you're not!" Jess was adamant. "You are not to see Steve before the wedding. Boy, do you have a wedding present for him," she said, laughing

"Please Jess, I want to see him. Just think we are going to have a child," Leah cried.

"I'll lock you in the bathroom," Jess threatened. "You cannot slip out and see Steve. Oh Leah, how I envy you this baby."

Leah finally decided that if Jess wouldn't let her see Steve tonight, then she would tell him the minute they were alone.

The wedding was to be in a small chapel close to the Burkes' home. Both mothers were at the hotel by 11 o'clock to help Leah with her wedding gown.

"They are driving me crazy," Leah whispered to

Jess. "Steve and I may have to move to Oklahoma, just to get away from the dynamic duo."

Jess giggled, she knew Leah loved both mothers. "They're a little too much, aren't they? They're having so much fun."

Then they started in on what beautiful children Leah and Steve were destined to have and Leah lost it, dissolving into gales of laughter. Both mothers looked at her in shock.

"It's just nerves," Jess explained. "We'll order her some tea. She'll be alright." She ushered both mothers into the setting room while Leah managed to get herself under control.

"If only they knew," she said, trying not to laugh.

"Quiet," Jess told her. "You can't let them know before you tell Steve. He'll never forgive you."

That thought instantly settled Leah's nerves.

A limo was waiting outside to take them to the church. Once there, the mothers got out first and entered the church. It's only five minutes before Leah burst from the limo.

"I can't wait another minute," Leah told Jess.

"Okay" Jess laughed. "I hope they're ready for the bride."

Jess helped adjust Leah's dress and they entered the chapel. Jess paused at the door and the music swelled. Leah's father was waiting to walk her down the aisle, and when the music changed to the bridal march he and Leah entered the sanctuary.

Steve turned to see the most beautiful creature ever, walking down the aisle toward him. When Leah and her father reached the front, her father placed her hand into Steve's and seated himself beside Alice. Steve smiled and placed Leah's hand on his arm as they turned to face the minister.

"Dearly Beloved, We are gathered in the Presence of God and these witnesses to unite this couple in the bonds of Holy Matrimony," the minister intoned.

Neither Leah nor Steve remembered the rest of the ceremony. They must have said all the right things, because soon the minister was pronouncing them husband and wife.

'You may kiss your Bride' were the most wonderful words Steve had ever heard.

Steve pulled Leah into his arms for the first kiss as husband and wife. They turned and started down the aisle.

The party and ceremony behind them, they were off to a hide-a-way Steve had chosen for their wedding night and they had a flight to Hawaii in the morning. The next week would be just for them, family and friends could take care of themselves.

Steve and Leah quickly walked down the aisle of the chapel and to the waiting limo. Steve tucked Leah into the seat and ran around to the other side. As he got in beside her, the crowd caught up and rice rained down on the newlyweds' limousine.

In the limo, Steve kissed Leah tenderly. "Well Mrs. Burke, I hope the wedding was everything you wanted. This is the only wedding you are going to have because I will never let you go," he said teasingly.

"Mr. Burke," Leah laughed. "There is one thing that I've been missing lately. It seems with everything going on, I can't remember the last time I had my period. I hope you want children sooner, rather than later." Leah said with a smile brighter than the sun.

"Hooyah!" Steve yelled loud enough to startle the driver. "How can life get any more perfect?" he asked before kissing Leah passionately. "What a wonderful beginning to our beautiful new life."

The End

Linda Laughlin spent her early childhood in Eastern Oklahoma and most of her adult life in the historical town of Fort Smith, Arkansas. Her first career consisted of raising two fantastic children, and her second was in banking. She is hoping for a third career as a writer, and 'Run For Your Life' is her first novel. She hopes you've enjoyed reading it as much as she enjoyed writing it! To contact Linda, you can find her email address at her website: www.LindaLaughlin.com, or visit her on Facebook.

Made in the USA
Charleston, SC
30 August 2016